LOGOS

Nicholas Nikita

PUBLISHINGS

© 2024

Logos

Nicholas Nikita

Published by Fearache Publishings.

Reg. Number. EE 39186

Datasure Certificate of Anteriority No 8826

Print distribution in the US and Canada via Ingram Book Group, a subsidiary of Ingram Industries.

Library of Congress Control Number: 2024905131

Hardcover ISBN: 978-9963-7467-7-4

Paperback ISBN: 978-9963-7467-6-7

Digital ISBN: 978-9963-7467-8-1

Printed in the United States

First Edition

www.nicholasnikita.com

"If I have seen further than others,

it is by standing upon the shoulders of giants."

- Sir Isaac Newton

LOGOS

I

GENESIS

The boy leans his back against the cave's wall and shakes his head in denial. Refusing to let go of her hand. Ragged edges of rock as thorns to his skin. Cracks on the roof allow a strong moon to spill enough light inside for sweat to shine over figures that form in shades of black and darker black like the shadows of shadows. One slap alone would have been enough to start the boy crying. A single scream enough to turn his every fine memory rotten. Yet mother keeps screaming and writhing in his arms and twice in a breath's moment father leans over from between her legs and slaps the tears out of his eyes. Red blooded eyes struggling to make out shapes in the dark. Itching from the sweat and the filth running down his forehead. Shush ama, father says to him and tosses a stick to his side and imitates biting the stick and then points at mother and he's quick about it for the boy blinks just once and father's hands are back in the dark between her legs. A warm breeze skins the cave's floor and blends mother's growing pains with dust and the stench of rotten remains. Oun apa, says the boy. He won't let go of her. A drained voice. Weak and thin as a whisper. Father leans over with the threat of another slap and the boy covers his face to protect himself. A trail of blood on his sore cheek from the last two slaps. He wipes the blood away with the back of his hand and gasps. No wound on his face. Not the one bleeding. Ama?

Alfa e sy, she once told the boy and pointed straight at him when he inquired about her belly growing. Was the same day she first taught him how to make straps out of the skin of fallen trees. Beta e to, she said soon after and caressed her belly. The second one of what? Of me? Alfa sy omio beta to, she finished by bringing both her hands together. And am I not enough for you mother, the boy then wondered in silence, for the few words he knew were not enough to adorn his thoughts with order and clarity. Days passed all the same as her belly got bigger and bigger with the boy by her side learning the way of the stone. How to grind and sharpen them. How to force some life and usage out of all that lies dead and useless around them. Didn't take long for him to notice. Death is common. Life is scarce. Every tree still standing mourns the fall of countless others. Father leaves at dawn and heads downhill and into distant barren fields of dirt stained with a wrinkled piss colored crust even fierce winds fail to unsettle. He never takes him on the hunt. Ever. Sometimes he comes back with prey before dusk. Old beasts with craggy horns on their heads and flat teeth. Barely any meat on their bones and death in their still eyes. Most often he comes back with nothing. And no words or gestures of mother can bring him comfort. Only the next dawn can. The same dawn the boy so yearns for now. Didn't take much to notice. Didn't need any words to learn this either. All that matters in the world is the light. Making it to the next day. Alive.

Father takes another nervous glance towards the cave's mouth. A cluster of rocks and branches and thornbushes is blocking the way inside. Took father the entire day to gather and stack all this mess. A barrier strong enough to keep most things out. Weak enough not to trap themselves in. Father peers through the gaps between the branches at every hint of movement coming from outside. Even the trembling of sticks and leaves trying to upset the wind's flow sends him reaching for his spear. The boy clutching on mother's hand harder as her cries plunge into brief moments of deep groans.

Mother screams as if to rip her own throat apart and shakes off the boy's hand before snatching it right back. She slides her fingers between his fingers and sinks her rough half broken nails in his palm. The boy moans and picks up a small stone from the ground and tries to slide it in her hand but she tosses it aside. She picks up the stick herself and bites on it hard and forces the boy's hands over her mouth. She looks to him with weary eyes and nods a sign of approval. He has to shut her up right now. He pushes his hand against her lips just as father wants and she pushes her hand over his. Her nails rip through his flesh looking for bone. Teeth grind against wood and blood and spit comes rushing between his fingers. She lifts her head up and back and screams pure violence out of her and keeps moaning and twisting and pushing out one heavy gasp after another and no matter how hard the boy tries to ease her pain it keeps coming back hungrier and thirstier as her agony finds new heights beyond the cave's roof bursting out of the cracks and into the silent nothing of nowhere they call home. Distant howls outside. Brief. Fading. The young night warning him. Unlike any other. Her darkness may last forever.

A rock tumbles from the barrier.

Shhh. Father moves a finger over his lips as if he could hear the boy's thoughts. He raises the other hand at them. Palm out. His stare lands at the cave's mouth and stays there. Hand won't come down. The boy's eyes suck all the moonlight in. He tries to swallow spit but has none. Breaths are as stones crammed down his throat. Every movement is a threat. Every minor sound demands attention. The rules of the night are clear. The back of father's hand has taught him well. The night doesn't belong to them. The darkness favors only the fast and the strong. For the slow to last until dawn any habit that has kept them alive thus far should remain unchanged. Silence at night must never be broken. And it has. Nothing would have changed if I had been enough. Because of me, everything has. This thought the boy inflicts upon himself as he swallows his sobs at the sight of father as still as the darkness around him. Mother taps his hand urging him to push it harder against her mouth. To force her silent. The moment the boy does so a burden grows in his chest for he can no longer feel the air of her breaths on his fingers. Mother is holding her breath. So he holds his own. A rare moment of calm. Pretentious. Dishonest. Waiting on father to react. To do something. Howls slash through the silence. Raging. Persistent. They start low. Distant but gradually getting louder. Closer. Desperate for air his next gasp is a long and trembling one. Hands are shaking.

Mother tries to calm him down by caressing his forefinger with her thumb.

The howls soon become the frantic laughter of many wishing him dead. The rulers of the night. Mocking him. He lowers his head and sinks his face from the nose down into mother's rough hair and hides his neck in a shrug. Eyes dashing wide left and right as if something vile comes. As if something is lurking in the cave right now. Breathing down his neck. But he just can't see it. Sharp claws scatter the dirt outside. Rocks fall and smash onto each other. Twigs snap amongst the dead bushes. The boy's breathing quickens. Shadows of furry bodies spill inside through the gaps. Long sniffs clear the scents of the hunt from dust. Father taps mother's knees and speaks words full of worry

the boy has yet to learn their meaning and mother pushes harder than ever before. She screams so loud the cave sends echoes of her pain bursting through its dark bowels. A long gasp and she loosens her grip on his hand. The tension trapped in her body for so long becomes air the moment father pulls the second one from between her legs. The crying starts. Loud. Constant. Father does nothing to silence it. Inevitable. Mother's gasps turn to sobs. Father grabs the boy's arm and drags him to his side and rips the bonds between mother and infant from its belly like dry grass pulled from the ground. Mother reaches out with knees buckling and arms shaking and takes the second one in her arms and lays it in a pelt with leashes. The boy rushes to help her find her feet as she struggles to get up. Father grabs his spear and stands facing the cave's mouth and instructs them to stand back. The boy rushes to hug him. The top of his head barely reaching father's waist. Father shoves the boy back to his mother and makes it clear with a strike of the bottom of his spear to the ground. They are out of time. Shadows come dashing forward. Fighting each other. One trying to beat the other on who enters first but none faster than the moon rushing ahead to shed its light on the cave's floor. The boy's eyes halt wide open. Hazy shadows with shivering jaws and frothing mouths maddened by hunger are tearing the barrier apart. Wild beasts the likes of which father never brings back from the hunt. The ones who carry the stars in their eyes.
Te ama?
Expressions of fear and confusion clash on the boy's face as mother ties the pelt's leashes together around the side of his neck and under his arm and straps the second one to his chest. He's no longer just a boy. He's the eldest now. She lifts them both up on one of the tall rocks reaching out from the walls and directs the eldest's gaze over their heads at a crack on the roof where most of the light comes pouring through. It forms an upward slanted tunnel. Narrow yet

wide enough for a child to pass through. The eldest shakes his head in denial. The second one is crying so loud even the earless could hear it. Mother tries to climb up the rock but slides off. She falls on her knees groaning and holding her belly. Beasts creep over the rocks scraping away all that stands in their path. One wails when it meets the sharp edge of a branch with its eye but keeps ripping through everything and gushing its blood on the rocks. It doesn't stop. Slow and ominous steps take it out of the moonlight. The stars in its eyes retreat into a void of dark intentions. More rocks tumble behind it. Shadows gather and toss aside broken branches as they make their way inside. Mother moans and struggles and finally manages to lift herself onto the rock alongside him. She hugs him tight but can't make him still. Father rushes forward waving his spear across the cave's short width thrusting its sharp edge at the beasts and for a moment a faint smile sneaks out of the eldest's broken lips for it seems father can hold them back but a blink of an eye later and a shadow leaps through the air with the speed to outpace a dashing gaze and takes father down. The eldest looks away. His smile hangs dead. Father squeals.

Apa, the eldest shouts and tries to climb down the rock but mother pushes him back up. She brings her hand over his head and spreads her fingers over his eyes to stop him from looking but he still has ears. Father cries like mother cries. The eldest pisses himself. Father never cries. Is this how death sounds like? All the horrors of mind and body come together in one resonance. Shines of panic dawn in his eyes when he opens them wide for a brief moment as if trying to see the entire world in a single stare through the narrow slit between her fingers and once he catches a glimpse of the shadows converging over father he makes them shut. He stands motionless as a leafless branch in her arms and surrenders to a muddle of howls and sloppy sounds of things that turn and grind and slide and twist and laugh and rip and tear flesh and darkness to shreds. Mother lifts the boy on her shoulder and then higher up by grabbing him by the waist. He remains still. She shouts for him to climb up through the hole in the roof. He tries to reach out. Can't feel his arms. Father stops screaming. The eldest sees himself hollowing out. Breaking down. Shrinking into a speck of dust in the air. Cracked. With no will of his own. Forced to dwell wherever the wind decides. The screechy sound of long claws sliding off the rock snaps the eldest out of his numbness. A beast drenched in blood leaps on the rock but slips on blood and piss and falls over. Mother supports his weight by his lower legs as he reaches out and pulls himself between the treacherous rocks that form the crack. Once he steadies himself and gets a foothold on the rocks she lets go of him. He looks down from his side and sees mother looking up. Standing still. No fight left in her. Shadows gathering all around her.

Ama elthe, he says and tries to lower his hand as much as he can so she can reach it. She doesn't even try. She shakes her head and gestures for him to keep climbing. He can't hold himself steady any longer. No more strength in his legs. He rests upright with his back against the cold stone and looks up at the steep tunnel that leads to the stars. A distance about four or five times his size. The tunnel carries a horrid smell. Unfamiliar to him. The wind's whistle is skinning the dry grass above. He spits to rid himself of the taste of dry dirt falling in his mouth. The tunnel is so tight the warmth of his breath comes bouncing off the rocks back to his face. Mother's screams come surging from below. A rush of dread fills his chest with heartache. Her misery pours straight through him as the howls smother the sound of her voice.

Ama.

He calls for her many times. He learns the limits of his voice for the first time. One reply he gets. The overlapping sounds of mouths ripping meat and tongues licking bones.

His heavy breathing takes turns with spitting vomit. He tries to look down but the tunnel is too dark. Blackened stones all around. The newborn won't stop crying. His tears and vomit are dripping all over it. A sudden weight comes crashing down his whole body. A sorrow so heavy no other burden can match. The numbness returns. Lines and shapes dissolve around him. Thoughts drowning in mud. The tunnel breaking down. Closing in around him. He weeps. He weeps the howls below no more. He weeps his eyes dry shut. He weeps his throat barren begging the night for a cut. To slice him from ear to ear. Then the silence comes in. Absolute. Unnatural. Either he has gone deaf or the world has gone mute. Little it matters. He makes peace with the dark. Only the dark and the silence matter. A dying heart in a dead and silent world. Still beating. Beating. Beating.

Elthe.

Ama? His eyes open straight to a wide state. Lost. Unsure of how or where or what has happened. Mother's voice. Calling him. Her whispers as creatures with no head and no tail dashing back and forth between his ears. He looks up. Everything rests in a blur. Black rocks fade into lighter shades of grey. He squints at the bright light shining over him. Pure white. Nothing else in the world so spotless. Vibrant. It must be him. The one who shines above all. Aeos, father calls him. Days don't exist without him. When Aeos sleeps the land drowns in darkness and begs of his return and when he wakes up the land suffers under his rule for he's a cruel parent who favors none. Not even the fast and the strong. Elthe, says a firm voice. Father's voice. Asking for him. He climbs with bleeding knees and pushes himself through a void of light so fierce it makes him wonder whether Aeos has fallen from the sky and landed right above him. Warmth crawls on his face. He reaches out and feels strength overwhelming. Father's hand dragging him up. The moment he crawls out of the hole the light flees as if running away from him. His eyes are fast to adjust to the morning haze.

Ama? Apa? Oda. He looks around. No answer. He keeps crying out for them. The rustling of the grass from the wind beating against the hillside is the only response to his cries. Sparse grass. Dry and yellow. A stunted tree nearby with leaves pale and falling. Alive still somehow and rising over a barren land of stone and dirt and not much else. He finds Aeos high in the sky where he should be. Breathing down the covenant of heat insufferable upon the thirsty and the unwashed. He must have come down and taken mother and father, the eldest reckons. They must be up there by his side. I will find a way, mother. There must be a way up there. Wait for me, father, I will meet you in the light. He sits on his knees and wipes his sore eyes. Covered in dirt all over and a type of water black as night and thick as blood. He gathers some in his palm and takes a whiff at it. The cause of the horrid smell back in the tunnel has made his careless mane slimy and heavy and his head aching under the light of Aeos. The newborn is crying no more. In a moment of panic the eldest realizes he doesn't remember how long it has been since the crying stopped. Could have been a few moments or a whole night ago. He lifts it out of the pelt and sighs and wipes the sweat running down his face once he feels it breathing and trembling in his hands. It's covered all over with patches of dry blood. A wound around the hollowed area of its belly. The one apa and ama have in common. Harsh but bleeding no more. Between its legs lies hidden what the eldest has in common with apa. Another boy like him. And no longer just a newborn but the youngest of two. The eldest wipes the blood from the youngest's cheeks with the little spit he has left. Unsure of his place in the world. Is he a brother now? A father? A mother?

I'm everything to you now.

He heads downhill. Passing over dry bushes and logs and snags for no other reason than down is easier than up. Fallen trunks of trees lay naked like corpses. Few trees still stand scattered like moles on the world's skin. He roams through arid lands with no real sense of direction. Anywhere far from the cave will do. The youngest always strapped to his chest. Either making too much noise or none at all. Blisters eager to burst across his back. Every now and then he takes a glance at Aeos. The one above all punishes the fools who wander out in the open for too long. He makes his way down the hillside and leaves behind a morning of grief made even worse by his ignorance. Endless fields of thornbushes and pale grass extend ahead. An orphaned land begging strangers for care. He finds shelter under a cluster of dying trees. Two trees still standing tall but barely. Many fallen trunks at their feet wait for them to yield. He looks to see if they carry any food on their leafless branches. Some sporadic shade is all he finds. He picks up a rock from the ground and carves a hole in the trunk of one of the trees. Looking for its blood. Mother gathers it whenever they run out of water while father is still away. A sort of food and water in one. Deep brown like man's skin and thick like mud. He finds none. Aeos has drained this tree of its life. He checks the other one too. All bled out.

Aeos reaches his highest point. The eldest's eyes are itchy and dry and the more he wipes them the worse they get. His cracked lips have swollen. Only thing thirstier than him is the ground he walks on. All hope is buried deep in the waterless soil where the crawlers fill their bellies with rot from the bodies of the slow and the careless. The acrid taste of vomit in his mouth worsens his thirst. His stomach hurts and flutters and the youngest won't stop crying.

He is probably as hungry as I am, the eldest reckons. Or as thirsty as I am. Or maybe he longs for mother and father, as I do.

He turns some rocks over in search of tiny crawlers. Mother usually finds them under the heavier ones. He turns over one lying under the shade of a large thornbush and finds a handful of them. The slender and squiggly kind. They leave the taste of dirt in his mouth while he chews them. They are soft and easy to kill. He saves the last few for the youngest even though he's hungry still. He takes the youngest out of his whiffy pelt and opens his tiny mouth with his fingers. He first tries to feed him a crawler but then halts and raises an eyebrow. The youngest has no teeth. Where are his teeth? It baffles him for a moment. He has no memory of himself with no teeth. He remembers some of them falling at some point. Then gradually growing back out again. His teeth have been strong and fully grown since before mother grew a belly. The youngest has none. He's not sure if he should let him swallow the crawlers alive. He has never swallowed anything not dead before. Food is always either dead already or killed while chewing. Takes him a long time to decide. He chews the crawlers hard and makes a mash of them in his mouth and spits it out in his palm instead of swallowing it. Just as he's about to feed the mash to his brother he wonders whether the fact the youngest has no teeth is a sign he shouldn't eat anything yet. Maybe he's only supposed to drink things for now. He stirs his finger in the mash to gather the smell and the moisture and lets his brother suck on the edge of his finger. He starts walking and the youngest keeps sucking his finger even though there's nothing there for him to eat. It keeps him calm it seems. And quiet.

The plains stretch as far as eyes can see and the blurry shimmer of heat hides the line where the sky rests on the ground. Right there at the edge of the world a mountain stands looming over most. But not all. Aeos is the highest. The eldest heads towards another tree barely visible a long way further down a field of long grass half his height with edges rough as sharpened stones and as dry as the ground beneath it. He turns every rock hiding under its shade and finds nothing. No blood in its trunk either. He keeps walking towards the mountain for no other reason. There's nothing else to follow.

He squints his eyes at Aeos while dragging his feet through the dirt thinking he might see mother and father resting in the light if he looks hard enough. He can't stare at them for long. Aeos forbids it. The one above all isn't caring like mother. Heat is the tongue of Aeos slithering along with the eldest's every move. Relishing every drop of his sweat like a father refusing to help his son find his steps. Mocking him every time he falls on his ass. Father beats him sometimes but he's never happy about it. Father just as bright as Aeos to his eyes. Mother is too. Brighter even. Probably came down and took them away because he was jealous, or maybe because up there is where they truly belong. Yes. He caresses the youngest's lips. We belong up there, you and me. By their side.

Stagger through empty fields long enough and the mind will find tracks where there are none and make vast silent lands seem dense and clamorous. Aeos is on a path of descent but still shines strong over the eldest. Heat has claimed most of the strength in his legs. He keeps the youngest calm. Now and then letting him suck on his finger. Small beasts the size of a foot and tails long as his forearm are lurking in the dead bushes around him. He tries to catch one and gets a glimpse of fur as it dashes through one of the many nostrils of the land. A hole the size of a fist in the gasping soil. He shoves his hand in but finds nothing. The beast is long gone. He keeps moving.

The erratic sounds of small beasts scurrying through the bushes soon become an annoyance. One failed attempt to catch one leads to many. Annoyance grows into obsession. Hunger into rage. He finds another hole in the dirt. This time he digs till his fingers bleed and pounds the ground with his fists till his arms go numb. The youngest is crying louder than ever by the time the cloud of dust around him settles. He lies on his back with his arms trembling and stays there for a long while. Eyes shut. The shivers of a new life on his chest. All he has left of mother and father.
He gets an eerie sense of someone watching him. He raises his head above the grass and catches with the corner of his eye a beast standing not too far away. Peering at him with guarded eyes. Like the ones father brings from the hunt. Its horns are long and curve backward and add an extra head to its actual height while its figure rises firmly over the bushes. He gets to his feet with newfound hope. Their eyes meet. The beast raises both ears at the sound of the youngest. Ears long and curvy like leaves. The eldest moves a few steps closer with caution. Feet barely unsettling the dirt for the slightest noise might scare it away. The youngest remains calm for now but not silent. Still making all sorts of awkward sounds the eldest can do without. He lays the pelt with the youngest on the ground and covers it with some dirt and bushes. The beast moves its gaze away from him. Starts chewing grass. He finds a rock nearby the size of both his fists and picks it up without making any sudden moves. It feels heavy enough to kill whatever it strikes but light enough for him to lift and throw. He cannot throw the rock from this far away. He must get closer. He leaves the youngest to serve as a distraction and gradually makes his way around the beast as it keeps ravaging grass. His heart is about to break free

from his chest. He only has one chance at this. He lifts the rock to the side of his neck and holds its weight on his shoulder. He squeezes his eyes almost shut and gathers all his strength in a long huff and with a shout he throws the rock at the beast but loses his footing and falls to the ground and rolls a few times before landing on his back. It takes him a few moments to find his place again in the world. He gasps at the sound of the beast moaning and hustles back to his feet. The beast lies struggling on its side. Crawling and kicking dirt.

See that father? My first kill.

He rushes over to his prey with every breath filling his chest with a grand sense of accomplishment. He thrusts his fists in the air and rejoices. A glorious and joyful moment at first turns awkward once he passes by his rock. All dry and bloodless. A long way off the blood trail the beast has left behind. As if it never left the ground.

Did I miss? he wonders. Wait. Father, please don't look yet. He follows the blood trail to a wound on the beast's side. A small and broken piece of wood sticking out. A stone tied at the edge of it half shoved. Grass drenched in blood and the ground wet with piss where the beast lies. His eyes might be fooling him. He lowers his fists and wipes the sweat dripping from his lips along with his smile. He kneels over the beast to take a closer look. Stuck deep in its side the sharp end of a broken spear. A shadow cast from behind his back overwhelms him and the beast. He turns around. Eyes wide. Mouth opens halfway and stays open.

There's more like me.

He always wondered whether there were other men out in the drylands besides father. And now he knows. The man's gaze skims past him as if he were nothing but a stone in his way and the eldest rushes to cover his naked manhood for no reason he can explain and for the first time in his life he has ever felt the need to do so. The eldest stares at the man as if he were a walking tree with a face and limbs. The man emits the smell of piss and shit and a swarm of flies has made a home of his head. Hair long and dry curls and dense as spears made of thorns. Even the wind can't move the man's hair away from his shoulders. A rough beard hides most of his face and falls to his chest. Thick fur covers his body from neck to knees while other small pelts hang from his sides and the skin of his limbs is lost under many layers of filth and dry shit. The man's gaze lands on the beast and stays there. Neither of them speak. No other sound but the cries of a dying beast.

Herae, says the eldest, trying to keep the worry out of his voice. This is the word mother taught him to utter whenever he sees father returning from the hunt.

The man stays silent. He reaches to his side and grabs one of his pelts. The eldest swipes his tongue across his lips and his eyes lit up at the sight of water dripping from the pelt. Father is always gone for many days before he comes back with water. Often comes back with barely enough water to last us for the days he's gone. The man drinks some and wipes his mouth and straps the pelt back to his side. Waterdrops trickle down his beard and fall to the ground. The eldest gasps at the waste. Every fallen drop skins his dry throat. He points at the pelt and craves for it. The man ignores him and starts walking down the beast's trail. The man returns holding the rock of shame and with a smirk on his face he drops it at the eldest's feet. He kneels by the beast's head and rips the spear out of its side. Blood spurts. Some drops land on the eldest's face. The beast shakes and kicks and groans and the man stabs its neck so hard and deep his fist gets lost in its throat. He cuts it from edge to edge and puts an end to its suffering. The eldest wipes the blood from his face and pays attention as the man picks up the rock and holds it over the beast's half severed head. He imitates throwing it first and shakes his head. Then points at his spear and nods. He shows the eldest the proper way to kill things with a rock. Up close. You strike them on the head and smash their skull. He slices a piece of meat from the beast's thigh and tosses it at the eldest's lap along with an empty pelt with straps for him to hide his manhood behind. The eldest covers himself and starts eating with relish.

Hyda, he mumbles through a mouthful of meat and points at the man's water.

 The man points at the same pelt while shaking his head and says a different word. The eldest has never heard this word before. He reaches out for the pelt and the man shoves him back and lifts the dead beast on his shoulders. Hyda, the eldest yells as the man walks away, hyda dide. The man speaks a few words with clear annoyance in his tone but the eldest can't understand any of their meaning. Dide, says the eldest once again and the man answers back, but no common words exist between them. With a chunk of meat still hanging from his mouth the eldest rushes back to the youngest and picks him up without strapping the pelt around his chest and runs after the man. Once he catches up with him the man turns with no warning and throws the beast to the ground and pulls a sharpened stone from one of his pelts. The eldest dashes back thinking the man might slice his throat but the man draws a straight line in the dirt between them instead and waves him away while shouting. He points the sharp stone at the youngest with one hand. Taps his own ear with the other and starts making rapid wavy gestures. Imitating noises flying across the land. The man seems to know the rules of the night. Infants are too loud. The eldest lays his brother on the ground and steps over the line. He must get water. He tries to snatch the pelt from the man's side and a quick hard slap sends him face down in the dirt. Blood spurts from his split lips as he huddles like a wounded beast. He shuts his eyes and covers his head while the man gives him a pounding of fists and kicks that could have made a grown man weep. Cut and battered and shaking and hurting like never in his life the eldest dares not to uncover his head even after the beating ends and the man steps back to catch his breath. With a sidelong glance through the gap between the inside of his elbow and his head he sees the man walking away with the beast. He still won't uncover his head. All things around him are moving when they should be dead still. Like the hills and the giant rocks down the field and the ground itself. Spinning and twisting and bending as if the whole land was light as a hair. He stumbles back to his feet with great struggle. Every part of his body hurts. Legs are sticks. Arms bruised and sore. Can barely lift them. He leans onto a nearby rock spitting blood and wobbling and watches the man as he drifts further away down the field. His eyes get watery. Only one reason for getting up. His brother. He would have stayed there on the ground if not for him. Let Aeos take him away too. He lets the youngest suck on his finger and turns his back at the man. Starts walking in the opposite direction. Wondering how long he can keep going.

It doesn't take long for him to notice the dryness on his brother's lips. He gets the sense that the youngest wants to cry but chokes himself. Unable to. He pulls his finger out and finds not even a hint of spit on his finger. My brother is dying, his first and only thought. He turns back with grit in charge of his pace and urgency in his stare. He can still see the man far ahead in the field. Nothing but yellowed grass and dead bushes between them. He follows the man from afar. Barely keeping him within his sight. He thinks he can stay undetected at this distance. He has no idea how long an infant can last without water but a mouth so dry before even a day's passing scares him. His brother is all he cares about. He must get water.

A haze of dust and heat dims the drylands in pale orange shades. Aeos gets closer to his resting place at the edge of the sky. The man has disappeared after passing through a path forming between two massive rocks many times his height. The eldest wants to get closer but the youngest makes noises at unpredictable times. He moves his gaze around the area until he sees a tree not too far away in the direction of the mountain. He's not sure if the beasts can climb trees but doesn't know what else to do. He reaches the tree and climbs as high as he can. Its trunk splits into two large branches spreading out like arms. There's life still left in the tree but the leaves it bears are sick and falling. He lays the youngest on one of the tree's joints and takes a last tender look at him before he climbs down.

He approaches the rocks from the direction Aeos sleeps. They form a roofless shelter of sorts for they come together at one end and spread apart at the other. Blocking the wind from all sides except the one Aeos rises. He gets closer. Mindful of the noise he makes. Close enough to hear the man coughing and slicing and moving things around. Sounds like the ones father makes when he skins a beast. He hides behind a bush and waits. His lips and cheeks have swollen. The blood running from his mouth all the way down to his bruised chest has long dried. It hurts to breathe. He waits there. Still like a stone as the shadows all around him grow. Another hot night approaches. The eldest is sweating as if running for his life. Quaking as if bitter cold.

Night falls. Aeos surrenders his place to a moon sliced thin like a beast's claw. He can't even see his own nose at first but his eyes gradually adjust and allow him to see a few steps ahead. The man's coughing has stopped. All he can hear now is something sounding like a snore.
Now you must move, he thinks.
A few moments pass and he has yet to move. He remains hidden behind the bush instead. Visualizing all the cruel things the man will do to him if he catches him.

You must move.

He keeps taking ragged breaths through the nose.

Move now.

He starts breathing through his mouth. Caressing his forefinger with his thumb.

Move.

He dashes up. Sneaks around the rock and creeps into the shelter. Wide space gets narrower with every step. He passes by what seems like a carcass. The buzzing of flies over it louder than the man's snore. He can barely tell through the dark the man lying right under a bunch of pelts hanging from a branch at the end of the shelter where the two opposite rocks meet. The branch has an edge jammed in each rock and the pelts are high enough for the struggling moon to reach and the soft breeze to tingle. One pelt hangs stubborn. Too heavy for the wind to carry. He moves with caution. One slow step at a time. He must get to the pelts with the man lying in the way. A rock near the carcass. Probably where the man sits. Seems too heavy to throw far but light enough to carry a few steps. He loses himself in his thoughts. Expecting the man to wake up any moment now. It won't be just a beating he will get this time. And no way he can outrun a grown man. His brother is as good as dead if he doesn't make it back.

Do you risk it, he contemplates, or do you make sure?

He lifts the rock with both hands stretching down while biting his lips and lays his back against the wall. With short sidesteps he moves within a few steps of the man who's lying on his side with his head facing the entrance. Facing him. The man knows the rules of the night well. Never turn your back on your only way in or out. The eldest's knees are trembling. The weight of the rock too much for someone less than half a grown man. Arms start shaking. He stops and lays the rock on his legs for a while. The man could be looking at him right now. Might have been watching him the whole time. Laughing within. The sound of the man still snoring gives him enough courage to take another small step but then he stops again. He hesitates. The man could be faking it. Patiently waiting for him to get closer so he can snatch him with not much effort. The man moves his head and startles him. The faintest and shortest of gasps comes out of the eldest and even though it didn't carry much sound and only lasted for a breath's moment it sounded like a scream to his ears.

He wouldn't move like that if he was faking his sleep. Would he? Why would he do that?

He takes a shy step. And then one more. With the next step the man's hair gets caught up in his toes. One more step and now he's standing right over the man's head. He takes a deep breath and holds it captive. He lifts the rock up against his chest and clenches his teeth pushing himself to lift it higher and just as his arms are about to give in all his grief and all his strength come together in a single scream as he slams the rock straight down on the man's head. All four of the man's limbs jump up for an instant. The rock is so heavy it never rolls over his face. The man's body starts trembling in short bursts. A stream of blood slides from underneath and gathers around the eldest's splattered feet. The man's hair feels like wet fur under his toes. He rolls the rock over to the side and sees the man's face smashed into a bloody mash of skull and hair.

I don't understand. Why is he still trembling?

He kneels in the pool of blood and keeps smashing the man's face with the rock again and again till the trembling stops. Once he makes sure the man is dead he wastes no time. He leaves the shelter without ever giving another look at the pelts and hurries back to the tree.

Thoughts of the worse run faster than him. The beasts might be tearing his brother apart right now. He hears no crying as he approaches. Not sure what the silence means. Is my brother well, or is the slaughter already over, or has the thirst drained his eyes of tears and left him skin and bones? He finds the youngest exactly where he should be. As he should be. And finally. Some ease of mind.

He takes the youngest back to the shelter and finds the pelt full of water. Little by little he pours water in his brother's mouth. Careful not to choke him. He then quaffs until he's full and splashes some on his face and cleans his wounds. The youngest goes to sleep while the eldest watches over him. Father never slept while he slept. Mother never slept while father slept. Distant howls take the night. He stays awake. For him.

Darkness. Stillness. Safe. Tiny creatures keep crawling all over him. Myrme, mother calls them. So many of them live in the dirt that if you gather them in a pile they might reach Aeos. Annoying and stubborn and larger here than the ones up the hill. Their bite leaves an itch and their teeth are like thorns.

All night he weeps but silently. Choking back his tears. Forcing himself to obey the rules of the night. The first chance he has had to lay his back against the wall and morn in peace. A night without father watching over him. The cold skin of stone caressing his back instead of mother's warm hug. He sits there contemplating. Staring at the corpse before him. The man was right. There is a proper way to kill things with a rock. So much hidden still in a land with so little to offer. So many habits to learn from the living. And even more from the dead.

The early light of dawn comes shy through the shelter's opening and reveals how much blood has been spilled. The ground around the man's body has turned to mud and the blood splattered on the wall has dried and meshed with the grey shades of rock to create random shapes. The eldest even left a trail of bloody hand impressions on the wall by accident. All unintentional creations and yet the eldest finds order and meaning in their form. One splatter seems like a tree with roots in the sky. Another like the head of a beast with many eyes and teeth twice the size of its head. He sees a woman's face. She has a mouth and a nose but no eyes. He gathers some red mud and paints a set of eyes on her face. He creates a body for the beast. Four legs and a tail. Heads don't move around on their own. He fills in the gaps of his hand impressions. Two of the fingers were incomplete. Painting brings him calm. Meshing the shapes on the wall with his imagination helps him think of the many lessons he has learned today. There might be more of his kind out there. An ignorant boy and a crying infant are too heavy of a burden for any stranger to carry. If there's a choice between taking a risk and making sure you always make sure. A spear from afar. He paints a spear. A rock from up close. He paints a rock.

He discovers more trees and bushes and mutilated creatures all over the wall. Something is missing. So many of the small things are here. Micro, as mother calls them. But where are the grand things? Mega, the word for them. He gathers more blood and stands on the man's chest to reach higher. He wants to paint the sign of Aeos as he can see it in his mind. Above all else on the wall. Where it belongs. Early at dawn and late at dusk Aeos becomes kind enough to allow the eyes of his children to take a glance at his real shape over the world. The same shape the mouth forms when his name is spoken. One might stand upside down on his head and still see the same absolute sign.

O

After a brief nap, the eldest wakes up to the youngest's cries. He looks around the shelter. A dead beast. Killed by a spear instead of a rock. A pile of sharpened stones next to it. Further down a spear lies upright on the wall opposite another pile of bones and claws. A man's corpse with a flattened head. Many damp pelts but just one full of water. The rest empty. All hanging from a long branch with both edges crammed in the jagged corners of the two opposite walls. The skins of many beasts in the far corner where the two rocks meet. The fur the eldest wears smells sweat and vomit. The man's blood all over him sticks like flesh over flesh. He scatters the many skins in the corner looking for a dry one for himself and one for the youngest who has spent the night in a pelt drenched in his own body's waste. He lifts a thick dark fur that seems perfect for him and finds four eggs wrapped underneath. Of all the things hc has found in the shelter these eggs are the most impressive. Eggs slightly larger than his joined palms and heavy. Much larger than the eggs father brings home from the hunt. Three are cracked at the top and hollow. Only one untouched still. The eldest first licks his upper lip and then bites the lower. He grabs a sharp stone from the pile and cracks the last egg. He tastes the eggs yolk and his eyes roll back for a moment. It's refreshing and cool and his belly stops moaning after swallowing half of it.

My brother should be able to eat this. No need to chew on anything.

He feeds the youngest some with the tip of his finger. Afraid he may choke if he gives him too much. The youngest stops crying and the eldest heaves a sigh of relief.

The man must have been getting these from somewhere close.

The food and water he found in the shelter can last them for a day. Maybe two. The beast holds enough meat on its bones to feed a man for many days but it quickly becomes a

home for flies and worms. So many of them gather after just one day that you struggle to see the skin underneath. Repulsive to eat and smells of rot. He must throw it away by tomorrow at the latest. That's what father does. He wipes the sticky yolk from his lips and waves his hands over his face irritated by the constant buzzing of flies around him. They have made a home of the carcass. Now circling over the man's head too.
I should get rid of him first before all else.
The man's body. Heavy. So many odd wounds on him. Fresh cuts whose lips should be apart yet something keeps them together like a mouth forced shut. Tiny black claws of sorts or thorns they seem like. He takes a closer look. Myrme. But just their severed heads. Their teeth can keep wounds sealed. Interesting. Another lesson learned, faceless man. But no time for this now for he must carry him a great distance down the field. Not enough to just drag him outside the shelter. His scent will bring the beasts on them. How far is too far or how close is too close? I have no idea. Not going to risk it. I want to make sure. Too far is better than too close.
He only manages to drag him a few steps outside the shelter before collapsing to the ground. Exhausted. Rapid breaths hunting air as if it was more precious than water. He moves his gaze at Aeos. So early in the day and already beating him down. Heat makes the blisters on his back and shoulders cry. His face is dripping with sweat. He rushes back to his feet. Aeos looming over his head is a burden he doesn't need but his presence makes him try harder. Father and mother are watching him.

He's dragging the man through the dirt by holding his feet. Moving further and further away from the shelter. He looks back after great struggles at the distance he has covered so far. Too short. He could run it in just a few breaths. Frustration takes over. He drops the man's feet and kicks him in his sides and shouts at him. Wishing he could kill him again. Stones could have moved him faster and further than me if they wanted to. He knows they're watching him so he grabs the man's feet and struggles on. Never looks up at Aeos again. Never utters so much as a groan for he knows they're listening. The youngest strapped to his chest. Always. Sometimes crying. Sometimes silent. And as he makes his way down the field he accepts the inevitable. This task will take him all day to complete.

Aeos comes down from his highest point and finds the eldest dropping the man as far away from the shelter as his legs have allowed him to. He's full of concern still. But even if he could carry him to the edge of the world it still wouldn't feel far enough. He spends the rest of the day covering up the blood trail he has left behind in his way. Hoping the beasts won't pick up the scent.

He returns to the shelter with all his strength long gone. He gives the youngest water and only has a sip himself. He needs it at night to keep him quiet. He feeds him first. Eats the remaining yolk and closes his eyes to rest as Aeos drowns the land in the evening shades.

The youngest's cries wake him up. Loud. Intense cries. He opens his eyes and sees darkness in all its might. A sense of dread takes over him as he rushes to give the youngest some water and then lets him suck on his finger hoping he can make him quiet. Nothing but blackness around the shelter. His eyes are struggling and searching for the faintest shades of grey to grasp. Desperate for any outlines or shapes he looks to the moon's claw. Anything to break the totality of the dark. To make keeping his eyes open worthwhile. The air feels like it could slice skin. The walls around him not forming a shelter anymore but a trap. The thought of staying in a confined space like this with his brother crying. His mind takes him back to the cave again. Mother. Father. I'm sorry. I wasn't enough.

He heads outside with just his brother and the pelt of water. A strong wind instantly dries the sweat on him. He dwells around the rocks that form the shelter looking for a way to climb them but can't find a safe way to get more than a few steps off the ground. Mother not here to lift him up anymore. He remembers the tree. He may be wrong but being trapped high off the ground feels safer than being trapped in the shelter or out in the open fields. Distant howls and cries spread everywhere as if they were the darkness forcing him to quicken his pace and no longer be mindful of the noise he makes as he heads to the tree that has kept his brother safe the previous night. He can't see more than a few steps ahead but knows what direction to take. The wind helps him find the tree as he gets close enough to hear the faint rustling and whizzing of its branches and the crackling of twigs grinding against each other. As he's climbing the tree a man's cry startles him and he almost falls over. With one leg already over the sturdy branch he manages to keep his balance. The cry only lasted a breath or two. The same as father. Their teeth sink in your neck. Hunting for your last breath. It takes them a breath to find it.

All night he rests his back on the tree's trunk with legs tied around its sturdiest branch and his brother wrapped in his new fur. Giving him water and his finger to play with at the first cry of need. It keeps him calm and quiet long into the night till he finally sleeps. More screams and roars and squeals burst out of the unforgiving dark. Some from afar. Others closer. Much closer. Some sound like the desperate final cries of men or of other weaklings perhaps. Not enough time to tell for their squeals only last a breath too.

Then they become the silence in the night. The smell in the gusts passing through the tree's branches.

He can't sleep. He needs to stay alert. Father stays awake all night watching over him and mother and sleeps only during the evening. So he does the same. Another sleepless night full of horrid sounds coming from the drylands. He focuses on the sounds of the tree. All night the rustling of its leaves keeps him calm. The tree watches over him. Like father does.

At the first light of dawn the eldest returns to the shelter not knowing whether they are still alive because of a wise choice or mere good chance. He stares down at the empty bottom of the last egg less than eager to start eating crawlers again. Less than half a pelt of water left.
Father never finds these eggs. So maybe the beast that lays them lives in the fields, far from the hills where father hunts. And water. I need to find where he gets water.
He straps the youngest to his chest and grabs the spear and a sharp stone and the last pelt of water and some empty ones and makes his way down the field further away from the hills he has spent his whole life.

Raaaaaaaaa

Aeos shines well into the morning when he hears this sound coming from the sky. A shrieking cry. Long and lasting. His gaze moves across the sky in search of what might be

making such distinct noise. Right on the edge of Aeos' circle he finds a shadow roaming free of any burden. Untamed by the hideous world beneath and unscarred by the ruthless oppressor above. His widened eyes suck all the light out of the day. He stands still as his mind drifts away in awe of how close to Aeos this shadow wanders. The son of Aeos. He must be. He's the only one who can touch him. The eldest has seen flying creatures before drifting just above the scarce trees of the hills. But they were tiny and frail and none could ever reach so high. No wings of theirs could ever get so close to the one above all.
Tell me your secret. How did you get all the way up there? Is my family yours now?
The eldest can barely see him. A distant shadow in the sky to the eyes of men with Aeos shining in the background. A glorious shape. Easy for the eldest to imitate. He stands straight. Feet touching each other. Arms stretching outwards at shoulders height.

†

It comes and goes as it pleases. It roams the skies for a while and then flees on a straight path leading to the mountain. A glow of admiration and jealousy shines in the eldest's eyes every time this shadow appears. The sound of absolute freedom in its cries. The skies are for him to play with and the mountain must be his home, the eldest reckons as the son of Aeos gradually fades away in the sky's blue haze once again.
He can touch Aeos, so he knows how I can get there.
A cracking sound from under his feet startles him. He's standing over a shallow pit in the dirt. Eggs like the ones he found in the shelter lie everywhere. Immersed in his thoughts he has walked into a nesting area without realizing

it and out of nowhere a bizarre beast comes dashing into the pit. He steps back. His eyes become guarded and he raises his spear and points it firmly at the beast which keeps moving back and forth and making erratic growls like it can't decide where it wants to go. After taking a closer look at it the eldest has doubts whether this creature is even a beast. It stands on two feet like a man. It has wings like a bird and a long thin neck like a slithering crawler. The creature seems more frightened of him than he of it. More of its kind are moving in circles around the nest. He grabs some eggs from the ground without making sudden moves and starts walking backward out of the nest. Never losing sight of the creature. Once he gets a safe distance between them he swiftly turns and runs away and never looks back.

He makes it back to the shelter just as the evening settles. Exhausted and soaked in sweat. Aeos hasn't been kind to him. He has covered a long distance around the shelter. In all directions. So thirsty after the long walk but only has a sip. An itch on his back and when he pours some water over it the drops feel like they're cutting his flesh. He wipes his shoulders and moans for he can peel his own skin right off. He cracks one of the eggs and feeds the youngest as he gathers his thoughts. Pleased to have found the eggs. Equally concerned about not finding any water. Nothing. Not a drop anywhere. The youngest falls asleep in his pelt. Decides to spend the night in the shelter. No tracks of any beasts on the ground after a whole night of screams from the land and a full day of them absent. It must be safe to spend the night here. The man could have carried all his belongings with ease except the piles of stones and claws. Large piles. It shows the man has been living here for some time now. Gathering them. It can't be less safe than being stuck on a tree.

We're staying here. Obeying the rules of the night is what matters most. All else is chance. He watches over the youngest all night.

At the break of dawn he falls asleep and wakes up with Aeos still on the rise. He feels a sudden urge to paint. Somehow it helps him think. He glides a sharp rock inside the egg and gathers the yolk that got stuck on the inside of the shell. He mixes it up with dirt and uses his fingers to paint, filling the lines he carves with the stone on the wall. A creature with a long neck and wings walking on two legs like a man. It has made an impression on him. He imagines and paints other oddities. Half men. Half beasts. A man with a pair of horns and one eye. Another with the head of a howling beast and four hands.
Questions collide with memories in his mind. The man has been getting his water from somewhere but that somewhere is nowhere near the shelter. It used to take father at least three days to come back with water. For some reason they both chose to keep a great distance between themselves and their source of water. Walking under this heat is no easy task. So why did they choose to stay so far away from it? Where could it be and how am I supposed to find it? This he ponders while jiggling one of the cracked eggshells in his hands. His eyes following the eggshell from left to right and right to left and left to right and back to the left when a sudden moment of clarity strikes and the jiggling stops.
These creatures need water too, he thinks while staring at the eggshell with utter focus. They seemed harmless yesterday. They will get thirsty at some point. Perhaps I should follow them today.

The youngest wakes up and the eldest rushes to comfort him. He managed to finish a new shape. Aeos stands above all in the real world and so does his sign on the wall. Then right below comes the son of Aeos. His sign belongs between his father and the land but the land has been broken and formless. Until now. So many shapes in the land to choose from but none greater than the shape of the mountain. The highest point of land. Proud. Unyielding. Like the tip of a spear piercing the sky. Everything that touches the soil gathers under its sign in unity. Hills. Trees. Men. Beasts. Crawlers. Everything.

Λ

The walk from the shelter to the nesting area seemed longer today. The distance harder to cover. The eldest used all the water to keep the youngest calm during their journey. Now he watches the creatures from far afield and waits. The morning passes with the creatures taking turns sitting on the eggs and meandering around the nest and not doing much else. The heat has made the eldest queasy while his brother sleeps in the soothing shade his shadow provides.

Aeos at his strongest. The eldest doused in sweat. Tired of waiting. Just as he's about to give up and settle for some eggs he sees many creatures leaving the nesting area and heading towards Aeos' resting place. He picks up his brother with care and follows the creatures. He wants to keep a safe distance between them. The same he kept when following the man to the shelter. But these creatures are much faster than the man even while strolling. He walks as fast as he can. Struggling to keep up with them and trying not to wake up his brother. He starts running once they move out of sight. The sweat pouring down his face hurts his eyes and the youngest wakes up crying from the constant shaking and bouncing of his run.

He's out of breath and on the verge of collapsing when the creatures disappear behind a hillock. One short step after the other he scuffs his way to the top and halts. A long stare. Lips start shivering. Rubs his eyes for he might be imagining things. A lake rests on the other side of the hillock surrounded by a field of tall grass. More hills rise beyond the lake scattered in all directions as if the land itself keeps the lake in a nest. Could have never imagined so much water gathered in one place. The lake glimmering in the mean light of Aeos seems unreal. Doesn't belong here. His eyes. Unworthy of such glare. The field around it yellow and dry like the rest of the land but coated with a far denser fuzz of bushes and grass. The lake lined with lively trees and the harsh yellow of the field gradually turns to soft green the closer you get to its shores. He imagines the hills as sleepless guardians keeping the lake safe from giants falling from the sky trying to steal the water and return it back to the clouds where it belongs. A clash between the creatures of land and sky. A thought worth painting later. He sits on a nearby rock and rests for a while. He sees the creatures with their long necks and fluffy bodies approaching the lake. It's another long walk all the way down there but he has time now. His struggles are over.

These creatures. So easy to spot even from afar, I wonder how they managed to stay alive for so—

A beast leaps out of the grass and claws one of the creatures down. He jumps up and goes hiding and peering from behind the rock. The creature kicks and wags its wings unable to free itself. Cries of agony dissipate in a cloud of dust as two more beasts appear and overwhelm the helpless creature. Visions from the cave scourge his mind. He watches the slaughter as if every bite on the creature's body was a bite on his own. Every gush of its blood a stain on his face and every thought an open wound that still needs time to heal. He wipes away the sweat running down his forehead. Shivering all over. It feels like he's wiping blood. These are different beasts than the ones from the cave. They look strong enough to rip a man apart with just a single swing of their claws. They have light fur in both color and thickness and they all look the same except one. Bulkier than all the rest. With a distinctive long mane falling over its head and shoulders. The rest make way for it to pass as it approaches the dead prey. All the other creatures manage to reach the lake while the beasts feast on their fallen brother. They drink water from the shore and turn around in a hurry. Another one gets slaughtered on its way back. And then another. The rest pass by the beasts feasting on their dead like nothing has happened. Most of them make it out of the field and up the hillock. Everything looks more and more like a swap to the eldest's eyes. Take some of our own. Give us some water. The creatures are coming straight at him. He runs down the hillock the same way he came from. Full of worry that the beasts are still after them. The creatures dash right past him as if he was standing still. Reminding him how insignificant a man's legs are. Whether the beasts are far away in the fields or just a step away there's no way he can outrun them.

He stops running when he can run no more and only then he looks back. No beast has bothered to chase them up or down the hillock. He's not sure why. Perhaps three creatures are enough to feed the pride. Or maybe the beasts don't need to hunt so far away from the lake since their thirsty prey will eventually come to them. Maybe there's a beast prowling in the bushes right now. Right next to him. Within the same day the lake has turned from a true marvel of bliss to a cunning trap. Waiting for the fools and the desperate to follow its tender whispers. He knows he must get to the lake but he's too shaken to do so right now. So he gathers some eggs instead and heads back to the shelter.

Shoulders curling forward the whole way back. Dragging his feet in the dirt.

The night comes with the eldest in a constant state of turmoil. Now he understands why the man refused to give him any water. Now he knows why father beats him with a stick whenever he unintentionally spills some. It's too precious. Too dangerous to get. He must go back. No way around it. The pelt once full of water now only holds air. This is a risk I must take.

The image of the great beast that rules the lake lingers in his thoughts all night. He has no word for it. But a creature so grand and daunting deserves a word all on its own. And a sign to go along with it. The one who stands ruler over everything in between the mountain and the land.

A

The next day he has a lot of time to think during his long and laborious walk back to the lake. Aeos is at his highest point when he reaches the hillock. He finds a tree nearby in the fields. The only one within sight. He leaves the youngest on one of its highest and sturdiest branches. Guilt flutters through him as he walks away. To abandon his brother again at the mercy of chance. Cruel. Necessary. But cruel.

His legs can barely hold him as he makes his way up the hillock. Approaching the lake will take a lot of planning and effort and he's already tired from the walk here. Sight. Smell. Sound. The three senses he needs to be wary of. Taste and touch are not a concern. If the beasts can either taste or touch him that means he's dead. Dirt. Shit. Piss. Rot. The most prevalent smells in the wilderness. Abundant in the air everywhere one goes. He remembers the man and how much he stunk. The eldest spots a swarm of flies circling just ahead and finds a pile of shit there. He takes off his fur and drags it through the shit. He pisses all over it and on himself. Struggles to get anything out. Then rolls naked on the ground a few times. The piss and the sweat make the dry dirt stick to his skin like mud. He straps the fur back around his waist and moves on. Covered from head to toe in the smells he considers common and undesirable. He gets help from the wind carrying his scent away from the lake today. Fortunate for him but it won't matter if he gets spotted. He must stay low. Doesn't know how far the beasts can see. A risk he's not willing to take. So he starts crawling while still ascending the hillock's peak.

He makes it down to the grass field. The smell of rot. Suffocating. He never raises his head to see how far the lake lies. Or if he has drifted in the wrong direction. A peek of curiosity. That's all that separates the clever living from the foolish dead. The shadows guide him. Aeos' path to his resting place leads to the lake.

He crawls all day long. Mindful not to make any striking noises or sudden shifts in direction. His moves are so painstakingly slow and gentle the wind disrupts the grass more than he does. Hair crawls between his fingers while reaching through the bushes. He pulls it towards him. His stomach judders into a mouthful of vomit. He tries to crawl away with numbed arms and legs and slithers a few steps away using just feet and elbows and empties his stomach along the way. A man's severed head. Rotting. Covered in flies and ants coming out of every hole. A large chunk of the skull is missing while a swarm of crawlers fills the gap inside. He stays still and flat on the ground until he calms down and starts crawling again once the numbness goes away. Nervous. Uncertain. And even more cautious.

Aeos has passed over him. Now well ahead. His elbows and knees are bleeding but he keeps moving. Countless thorns trapped in his flesh. He can feel the wetness. Dirt getting stuck under his nails. There's more green around him than yellow and the touch of grass feels gentle and soothing to the skin. He must be close to the lake.

Sssssssssssssss

 A hissing sound. Coming from the bushes just ahead. Or from the ones next to him. Hard to tell. He holds his place and waits for it to go away. The sound persists. Getting louder. And closer. The bushes in front of him scatter. His eyes widen when he sees a crawler's head coming out of the bushes. A head twice the size of his joined palms staring back at him with the unblinking eyes of the dead. It flicks its tongue out as if to taste the air and gradually reveals its thick and limbless body as it slithers towards him. Skin dark as night and hairless. Not the kind of crawler you find hidden under rocks or in the dirt. This the kind mother finds slithering in the cave sometimes and yells at father to get rid of it. Even father seems afraid of their presence. But the ones they come across in the cave are short and thin. Neither long as a spear nor thick as the eldest's leg like this one. Father taught him to stand still when he sees these crawlers so he lies flat on his chest and covers his head and touches the ground with his forehead. He shuts his eyes and welcomes the ignorance of darkness. Trying to stay completely still. Heart pounding against the dirt. His whole body stiffens when he hears the crawler's hissing tongue passing by his right ear. He takes in a breath and holds it and if he could squeeze his eyes shut even harder he would. Its body leaves slime on him as it creeps over his right shoulder. It slides down his backline and slips back to the ground from between his legs. It moves past his ankles while more of its heavy body keeps rising over his right shoulder. Much longer than he first thought. Two spears for sure. Might be longer. Its weight forces his stomach further down. He couldn't lift himself up even if he wanted to. He opens his eyes once the weight leaves his back and only takes a deep breath when the crawler's tail slips off him. With the crawler gone he feels an overwhelming urge to stand on his feet and run. But he can't move. Its weight. Somehow crushing him still. Keeps his face in the dirt. He wants to gather all his pain and grief in a shout that will smash the sky. Cry tears of rage that will drown the world. He hears the crawler hissing away while fear has him stripped and gagged and bound. Blind. Deaf. Limbless. He weeps silently. Pushing his mouth against the dirt and wallowing every sob till it hurts to breathe. Every heartbeat chokes him. Even finds dread in the soft breeze messing about with his mane.

Raaaaaaaaaaa

He turns around and lies on his back. The son of Aeos is gliding through the deep blue of the sky above him but nothing can ease his grievance. The shadow in the sky only reminds him of his weaknesses. Men exist to suffer. Wherever he looks he finds nothing but new ways to die. He stares at the shadow that rules the sky with a grudge and a charge trapped in his mind he needs to unleash. A voice he never knew he had.

Why is your father doing this to me? asks the inner voice. Why has he taken everything from me and yet he still wants more? He wipes his tears away, for he won't allow it. His eyes narrow. What is your secret? What makes you so worthy of freedom and me so unworthy? Tell me. I need to know.

The son of Aeos drifts out of his sight. The moisture on his back clears his thoughts. Brings his purpose back into focus. There's a reason why he has been crawling all day. He must be getting close. Still alive and so close.

He kicks and pulls. He slogs and staggers through the field till the ground becomes mud. The sound of water sloshing makes him shiver. He peeks through the bushes at the lake just ahead and finds a safe way to reach its shore and the moment he gets there he drags his body out of the bushes and dives his head in the water. Never done this before. He stays underwater relishing the coolness for as long as he can hold his breath. He soon pulls his head out. Ripples dissipate. Revealing a new world. A mystical world. With different rules and no bounds on what may be possible as water falls back and leaves him breathless gazing in awe at the unthinkable in the lake's natural serenity. His own face in the water.

Not possible. Our eyes can only see the faces of others. Is this who mother sees in me?

Water drips from his mane and distorts his image in the lake creating smaller ripples and tiny circles. He stays there for a while. Tilting and turning his head. Exploring the lines of his face. He finds Aeos in the lake as well and the clear sky and the surrounding hills. He had no idea water could do that.

So it's possible to see yourself as others see you. Interesting.

He fills three empty pelts with water. Halfway through filling the last one he is met with a challenge. Up until now he had them strapped to his side. He can't do that anymore. He would if he could walk back. But he can't. Water spills out when the pelts are not kept upright. He tries to seal them shut with straps by tying their necks tight but water still finds its way out when the pelts lean sideways. He realizes he can't carry more than two pelts. One in each hand constantly clenching their necks tight and not letting them fall. He must crawl all the way back by dragging himself with just knees and elbows as if his forearms were ripped off. And the pelts are heavy. Aeos is about to touch the hills as he heads back. Pushing his body forward with his knees and dragging himself with his elbows. Careful not to let the pelts slip from his hands. Every time he shoves his knees and elbows in the dirt he leaves behind a gap with blood.

Aeos has moved across the lake and beyond the hills. An orange shade that fades into black at the edge of the sky is all that remains of him. The eldest wishes he could move faster. His mind constantly drifting away from exhaustion. Warm memories of mother get swept away when a man's scream disrupts the whole field like a backstab. Stunned initially and then curious the eldest forgets all about keeping his head down and peeks over the bushes. It turns out he's not the only one crawling for his life today. A man not too far away. Stumbling around in the field and waving his hands and screaming and battling with a long crawler wrapped around him. The man has lost all sense of composure. No way he won't attract the beasts. The eldest doesn't know what to do. Keep crawling? Make a run for it? Further ahead another man rises out of nowhere and hurries down the field. He's making a run for it. The sight of these men out in the open reminds the eldest he needs to stay low so he lowers his head and before he can gather his thoughts he hears screams coming from the direction of the running man. The screams only last a breath or two.
You don't make a run for it. You keep crawling.

He peeks through the bushes at the other man as he crawls without raising his head much. Many beasts have circled him but none attack. Odd. As if they're waiting for something. The man manages to free himself from the crawler's tight grasp and as soon as he tosses it aside a beast jumps at him from behind and takes him down instantly. More beasts run over him and suffocate him in a cloud of dust and roars. The eldest lowers his head again and moves on. There's not a great distance between him and the slaughter. He hopes it's enough to remain undetected.

Horrid darkness takes the land as the moon hides scared behind clouds as rare as water. The kind of night everything from rock to grass to beast blends into one shadow of a world feeding off such blackness that can break the bravest of hearts. The eldest makes it over the hillock and tries to stand but falls to his bleeding knees and almost drops the pelts. He straps them around his shoulder and finally frees his sore hands and sits with legs crossed. Resting arms on thighs. He drinks water till he can drink no more. More than half of each pelt has been spilled on his way back. One long breath after the other. His body slow to recover and he can't wait on it for the night's eerie silence breaks when his brother cries. He jumps up and hobbles down the hillock. He can barely see so he follows the cries with his mind swaying between fear and hope.

Howls and roars coming from every direction compete with his brother's cries as he reaches the tree. The youngest sounds weak. Nowhere near as loud as he should be. His weakened cries might be the only reason beasts have yet to gather around the tree. He climbs up and finds the youngest quivering in his filthy pelt and soaking in a whole day's worth of his body's waste. He gives him water and makes him silent with his finger. He hangs his legs around the branch. He lets out a sigh that makes him feel as though he left half his weight up the hillock just as a howling beast comes charging out of the darkness and takes that sigh and every other sigh he has and swallows it. He almost falls over the side but barely manages to keep his balance as the beast keeps jumping up and down the tree's trunk and ripping it with its claws. The youngest starts crying again. More beasts gather in a clamor of howls and scratches and grinds. Trying to climb the tree from all sides. The eldest cries too. He can't hold it inside any longer. Since the night in the cave he's been swallowing his sobs. Pushing them down and holding them in his stomach like a vomit of grief.

Don't make any noise, a voice in his head kept saying. Cry since you must, but quietly. Keep yourself and your brother safe.

Now it's all pointless. Trapped as he finds himself. No more use in silence. So he unleashes all his sorrow. All pain and anger gathered inside in a single burst of tears and screams that skins his throat and starves his chest from all breaths. He cries so loud he strangles his heart and brings every other sound down to a hint of a whisper while the beasts rage under his feet and jump even higher and shred whole chunks of wood from the tree's trunk and even bite each other.

The beasts keep creeping around the tree throughout the night. They take turns jumping on its trunk every now and then and slide back down every time. The eldest has found calm in the warm breeze. If the beasts could get to them they would have done it by now. A flash of hope finds a corner to rest in his watery eyes as if fallen from the stars. He may be able to wait this out. He lays his head back on the tree's trunk and finds the stars through the gaps in between its swinging branches. Cracks on the roof of the world too high for him to reach out and crawl through.

Cracks leading to a world of light where mother and father wait for his arrival. He shuts his eyes. And as his weary body gives in he finds a way to crawl through the cracks in the night sky. For there is nowhere the mind can't go.

The light of dawn on his face. Warm. Tender. He opens his eyes to the shifting shadows of countless sticks cast all over him. No beasts lurking around the tree anymore. Not sure if he's asleep or dead but one moment the beasts are here and it's dark and the next they're gone and it's dawn. He drags his legs over the branch thinking it's safe to climb down but not before he makes sure. When there's a choice you always make sure. He breaks a large stick from the side of the branch and throws it as far as he can. Two beasts dash out of the bushes and jump all over the stick and once they realize it's not made of flesh they take turns sniffing it. Another one rushes out from the side and tries to climb up the tree. They lurk around for a while before running away. Sneaky howlers you are. But Aeos is rising, hot as ever and strong. That fur on you looks thick and warm. I have two pelts of water. Tell me, fools, how much water do you have?
He goes back to sleep as if the world was his.

Halfway through a still morning he breaks another stick and throws it out in the open again. Same result. The eldest gets it now. They run far away. Making you think they're gone and then cunningly prowl back through the bushes. No worry. No rush. He carves a new sign on the tree's trunk to pass the time. The sign of the long crawler. He thinks of a word for it too. Based on the sound it makes as it slithers. Fis, he speaks. This is the word for snake.

S

As Aeos gets close to his highest point he tries again. The beasts jump at the stick once more and try to climb the tree. This time he splashes some water on their desperate faces thinking it might make them thirstier.

Long into a typical hot day the eldest throws another stick. Nothing jumps out of the bushes this time. He throws a bunch of sticks all around the area. Still nothing. He leaves the youngest behind and climbs down from the tree with nothing but suspicion creeping into his eyes and picks up a stone as big as his palm and throws it straight with not much curve in his throw. Making it bounce many times off the ground before it halts. Nothing reacts to it. He brings the youngest down from the tree and begins his long walk with confidence in his stride.

As he heads back to the shelter the cries of the son of Aeos give meaning and purpose to the mute sky. The eldest looks to the sky with excitement but can't find him anywhere at first. Then his sharp stare catches a glimpse of the glorious shadow heading towards the mountain. He looks in the direction of the shelter and sees himself rotting away. His brother turning to dust. Two bleeding hearts trapped in a heartless land with no meaning. No purpose. You hunt to eat so you can have the strength to gather water and you drink so you can have the strength to hunt and eat so you can gather water and just the thought of living this endless futile mess makes the muscles in his face jitter and the nerves on his neck stretch like tight leashes and his eyes twitching so hard the wounds on his face start bleeding again in shame. He moves his gaze to his brother. Sleeping calmly in his pelt. He turns around. Now heading towards the mountain.

Don't worry, brother. Mother and father are safe with Aeos, waiting for us. You see that shadow up there? If someone knows the way to Aeos, it is him. And his home is the mountain.

Aeos' haze comes late where the land is flat. His heat blends everything into a vast blur. A strong wind is sweeping the field ahead. Raising clouds of dust from the distant plains and through them the mountain barely visible like a dark stain on the sky's skin with roots at the edge of the world. In between the dust clouds and the mountain lies the unfamiliar. He will gather more eggs along the way. When he runs out of water he will follow harmless beasts and they will show him the way. The rules of the night are clear and he knows them well. It won't ever get any easier but now he follows the mountain with determination and trust in himself for he has done the killing and the gathering before. Therefore he can do it again. This is the way of the world. You search. You watch and listen and when you have a choice you make sure. You bleed and cry and suffer. You find the ways that keep you alive and make a habit of them. Hunt. Gather. Kill. Endure.

Habits in time birth order. Order forms structure.

II

EXODUS

C

The loud clatter of stone striking against stone disrupts the day's calm. The youngest has a firm grip on the stone he wants to sharpen. Keeps rubbing and grinding its hard skin with another smaller stone while resting its side on a flat rock. He chips away its corners till a sharp tip forms. Awkward. Kind of leaning heavier on one side but as jagged as it should be.

He has seen father do this many times but never tried to make one himself until now. It takes time and patience. Focus. Strong and steady hands. He has none of these things. But he may be able to get it done with sheer will.

Except for time, he thinks. Time, I have plenty.

He lifts the newly sharpened stone and puffs the dust off its edge. He turns it around sideways. Checks if the stone is sharp on all sides and rubs the tip with his fingers. Warmth crawls over from the stone to his thumb.

This is odd. He tracks its form with narrowed eyes. Why is the stone warm? He moves his fingers across the whole surface of the stone. The tip and the chipped sides are warm while the bottom unscathed part is still cold. He then picks up the smaller stone and notices the same thing.

There is warmth in the living things. This he knows for sure. Like the warmth he finds when he sleeps in father's arms or when rubbing his own hands together. But a stone? Only Aeos can do that. Things get cold at night while Aeos sleeps and warm again during the day.

Hmm, he utters rather loudly, even though father isn't around to hear him. It seems there is warmth hidden in all things. Even the lifeless.

He places the sharpened stone at the top of a pile of many others father has made. He lays it with cunning care. The obvious one to pick first. This is the task. To see if father can tell the difference between his stone and the others. He wants to surprise him by showing him how well he has learned the way of the stone. It might bring a rare smile to his face.

Father left at dawn. The youngest once again alone in another hole on another rock of another hill. They've been here for two days now. Father coming back late every evening with empty pelts. When they're not heading towards the mountain father finds high shelter and leaves him in the shade as he roams in the drylands searching for food and water. One day father will take him along but that day seems far away still.

He goes wandering outside looking for more stones. Not just any this time. They must be flat. One smaller than the other. The largest one must be as wide as his joined palms. He needs six of them.

He picks them up counting and murmuring the words father has been teaching him.

Alfa lih, one stone, when he picks up the first. Bea lih, two stones, when he picks up the second. Gaa lih, dea lih, ene, h—

He scratches his head for a while. Can't remember the word for six. Five will do. If father has six, then I can have five. I'm smaller.

Once he has all the rocks he needs he stacks them up in front of the shelter's entrance next to father's stack of six rocks. Largest rock at the bottom. Smallest at the top. He gathers many small stones and dashes back inside the shelter and takes position behind the line father has carved on the ground.

They play this game every day. On a good day it's just a fun way to pass the time. On a bad day it helps take their mind off the thirst and the hunger for a while. It never matters where they are. Whether down in the dreary fields or up at some barren hill they may have neither food nor water but they always have rocks. Rocks are aplenty.

The goal is to hit the pile with a stone thrown from behind the line and make the rocks crumble. The first to take them all down wins.

He throws a stone and whines when it bounces ahead of the pile and lands to the side. He throws another stone. Just the one at the top falls. He has yet to drop all of them in a single throw like father does but he's getting close. He needs more practice.

He tries again. He fails. He tries again and gets two of them to fall. His next throw isn't even close. It skims past the rocks and ends up somewhere in the thornbushes. He finally gets them all to crumble but not before he has thrown more stones than he could ever count. He gathers the rocks back into a pile. Not ready to quit.

There must be a way.

He frowns at the rocks as if they had a mind of their own and could talk back. Deliberately trying to embarrass him. He grabs one and squeezes it tight. It's the smallest and the lightest. The one that falls most often. He wonders whether it's possible to balance the rest on top of this one instead. He places the smallest at the bottom and then one of the heavier ones on top. It falls over. He tries again. Tilting it a little to the right and a little to the left. The rock stays.

He finds a point after many tries and failures. A single point on every rock where if he's careful enough and patient and precise enough he can stack them up in a way that at first sight seems impossible. Smallest at the bottom.

Largest at the top. It's a very fragile pile. A gentle rise to the wind or even a sneeze might be all it takes to bring the whole thing down. That's precisely what he wants.

All the rocks fall on his first throw. Not even a good throw. The stone barely touched the side of the pile. He throws his arms in the air victorious for he has found a hidden balance in the rock. A secret no one else knows. He rushes outside to gather more stones overjoyed with his findings and wondering whether there's a balance in all things around him. More secrets that are well kept out of sight in the land and the sky. The dead and the living.

His gaze catches a man's figure coming up the hillside. Too far away still to be anything more than a moving shadow to his eyes. The only man in the world.

Herae apa, yells the youngest and keeps waving both hands in the air as father gets closer.

Father replies silently by lifting a finger to his lips and waving his hand downwards. The youngest knows he shouldn't be yelling but there's no greater joy than seeing father come back from the hunt.

Long before father reaches the shelter the youngest rushes to him and hugs him tight.

Elthe apa, he says and pulls his hand and drags him inside eager to show him how much better he has gotten at the game. Lave lih. He picks up two stones urging him to take one. Let's play.

Father lays his spear down and crouches next to the pile of rocks and chuckles.

Alfa, bea, gaa, dea, ene, he says, as he counts every rock on the youngest's pile one by one. He then points at his own pile. Hea? It has a sixth rock.

The youngest smiles. Hea, of course. That's the word. Hea, hea, hea. He lifts his eyebrows as far as they can go while shaking his head and shoulders. Pretending he just noticed the missing sixth rock.

Father grabs his spear and signals the youngest to follow him as he heads back down the hillside. The youngest rushes after him. His brows gathered in a frown of many questions. No play? Father never takes him out in the fields. Too excited to notice before but father came back much earlier than usual and with nothing to show for. He never comes back early unless he finds food early.

They leave the hill behind and walk through thirsty fields of nothing but thornbushes and scattered patches of yellow grass. The youngest stays by father's side and seldom wanders a few steps ahead whenever he sees something interesting. He stumbles upon a pool of gore and a swarm of flies and crawlers torturing the dead after death. Something has eaten everything but the bones and the parts that stink.

He rushes back to father's side and grabs his hand. Never leaves his side again. Te apa?

Therios, father says.

Man-eaters. Never seen one. But every night he hears the howls. He sees how agitated father gets because of them. He knows their sign. A pair of sharp teeth on either side of a pointy nose.

M

Their walk ends when father halts and instructs him to get down. They crouch and hide in the pale grass as the midday heat drenches their bodies in sweat. Father gathers him in his arms and gives him a slight lift just enough so their heads are right beside each other as they gaze over the grass.

Ore, father says, urging the youngest to look at a herd of beasts just ahead. Five of them. Horns on their heads. Harmless grass-eaters with flat teeth. Like the ones they usually eat. Father has a sign for them too.

Y

Ora apa. Father will teach me how to kill them, the youngest assumes.

Father leaves his spear on the ground and instructs him to follow his hand as he points to the herd. Two of the beasts are old with long horns while the other three are young and half their size and with horns too shy to grow. Father guides the youngest's gaze to the three young beasts. Delf, he says. Gaa delf.

Delf apa? What's a delf?

Father pulls a sharpened stone and draws a straight down line in the dirt. Apa. The sign of father.

I

He then points at the three young beasts and draws three more lines flat. Shorter. They would have been three separate lines if not for the sign of father. Father unites them. Delf. Gaa.

E

Sy delf.

I'm a delf? Like the three young beasts? Now the youngest understands. He's here to learn his place in the world along with some new words.

Father wipes the dirt clean first and then hops his finger from one young beast to the other and draws three similar signs next to each other. Alfa delf. Bea delf. Gaa delf.

ΓＣＥ

Sy te? Father hovers his hand over the signs like a passing cloud and asks the youngest to choose a sign for himself. The youngest chooses the first one. I'm the only son of father.

Father shakes his head. Oun. He points at the second sign. Sy bea delf.

The youngest narrows his eyes and tilts his head in utter confusion. I'm the second one? And before he has a chance to grasp what he's being told father taps his own chest and points at the first sign.

Mon alfa, father says. Mon alfa delf. He lays one hand on the youngest's chest. The other on his own. Mon alfa, sy bea. He brings his hands together in a clap in front of him. Delf.

The youngest's eyes jump from narrow straight to open wide. Shivers take his whole body. Leaves of grass are scratching him like claws. Sy oun apa?

The eldest shakes his head. Oun apa.

Te apa? asks the youngest in a brittle voice. His stare begs for an answer. If we are two delf, where is our apa?

The eldest points at Aeos. Aeos elthe. Aeos lave apa. Aeos lave ama.

Ama? Te ama? What is this ama?

The eldest draws another shape. It starts as the sign of father just like the others. He drags another line flat and turns it into the sign of the son. Then he completes it by adding another line of father at the other end. Two fathers that would have been separate lines if not for their son.

Ama.

H

Moments ago father was all the youngest ever had. And father was all he ever wanted. Because of him his heart was complete as the day is complete when the dawn becomes dusk. A lie. His heart is dark and broken in two and apa is just half of it. The other half is this ama. Another kind of father it seems. An empty heart he has and empty it always has been for he's a dawnless and duskless day missing them both.

The brothers share a stare in silence. Nothing between them but the rustling of the grass.

Apa ama te Aeos lave? the youngest asks, for he doesn't understand why Aeos has taken them away. He keeps pulling at the fur covering his brother's body. Te?

The eldest says nothing and turns his gaze at Aeos and keeps it there for as long as he can stand the light. His eyes turn red and watery. Some tears run down the side of his face and he's quick to wipe them away.

Thoughts standstill. The youngest's mind. A land of dead bodies. He sees his brother fighting back his tears and feels an urge to deny his own too. But he's not as strong as his brother is. Not the man that he is. The feeling of loss inside him grows teeth and claws. A monstrous beast swallowing whole chunks of the son in him and spitting out the broken bits of a brother in need of care. Fatherly. Motherly. Brotherly. Any kind of care.

He breaks down in tears. The eldest takes him in his arms and caresses the back of his head. The youngest feels his brother's warmth overwhelming him. Not like a son feels his father's warmth anymore. The eldest is holding him tighter. Warmer. Like all there is to love in the world.

ГІН

The eldest keeps scratching his face. Itchy by the early signs of beard. His filthy long mane smears the ground as he hides squatted behind a thicket of thornbushes. A spear rests in the firm grip of a palm with skin rough as wood unbothered anymore by the pokes of thorns or splinters. Countless scars all over his slim body admit of flesh torn apart and tacked back together again over time. A testament to the failures of days long gone and lessons learned by the hardest ways.

His eyes reflect awareness. Controlled aggression. His stare is sharp and focused and teeming with the ways of the old. Habits that grew as the eldest grew as strict and averse to change as the midday rejects the moon. He parts the leaves of the bushes and looks out into the field.

The beast is unaware of its stalker. Chewing on sparse and half-dead grass. A stubborn creature. He has been following its tracks all morning without ever managing to get close enough undetected. Until now.

He rises over the bushes and strikes the beast down with a swift throw of his spear. The beast moans and crumples to the ground and gets back to its feet before the eldest's pounding heart gets any chance to settle. It tries to run away limping and struggling to gain speed while kicking dirt and changing directions as if lost or sightless.

He chases it down the field through rising clouds of dust. A good strike with a spear is enough to hurt a beast but not enough to take its life. It might slow it down. Bound to make it angry. Only a perfect strike to the head or the heart can kill a beast from afar. No easy task. Most often he must make the kill with his hands.

A wounded beast will push and claw and kick and bite with fury and it won't stop until it's either free or dead. He catches up to the beast and drags it down by the horns. He kneels on its throat and pushes all his weight on it. It tries to bite him but its flat teeth get caught in the gaps between the large bones strapped around his legs.

Bone is lighter than stone and tougher than fur. It keeps him quick and agile while protecting the most vulnerable parts of his body. Large bones fixed with straps over pelts tied to his limbs keep the bites and the claws away. Pelts cover his knees and elbows while a smaller pelt swaddles his neck bearing bones the size of a man's fingers.

He pulls a sharp stone from the pelt on his side and slashes the beast's throat. There's a moment in every kill when your prey's heartbeat comes crawling up your arms like shivers begging for mercy. As the shivers fade you become the cold in their dead eyes. You become the darkness every living creature fears.

Blood spews all over him. The struggle ends. A good kill. He senses small creatures dashing through the bushes all around and running away from him. It feels good to be feared.

With the dead beast hanging over his shoulders he passes by the remains of another man like him on his way back to his brother. The meat scraps left on his gnawed bones are still fresh. Wastes from the previous night. He has no pity for him. Time heals the wounds of the hunt and he carries the scars of such wounds with pride. But the scars of man's cruelty are a burden he carries with shame and anger. Such wounds time can never heal.

Days pass all the same. Countless. Aeos rises. Aeos falls. A day might have passed for every hair on their heads since they left their homeland. How many. How long ago. How often. How impossible to know. Time is days killing nights and nights killing days in an endless battle between light and darkness. Two immortals trapped in the vanity of their own grudge for they will never stop fighting and they will never kill each other.

Beyond the wretched fields right at the edge of the world the mountain rests. Elusive. Careless. A giant dipping his toes in everyone's shame. The one above all once rammed a sharpened stone through the world's throat and left the broken tip jammed in the wound. A constant reminder of Acos' undisputed rule. Yet still nothing but a distant shadow taunting the eldest's eyes.

They should have passed through the mountain's haze by now. They should have been able to see it clearly by now. He was wrong in all his assumptions. It's as if the haze moves with them.

Lands ahead empty of all grace. Rain is rare and brief. Only enough to create a few small puddles. A short-lived enticement. More of a tease than a comfort. The ground sucks the water dry and turns it into mud faster than the eye can spot a lone tree in a flat land of nothingness. Sometimes they find water hidden in the cracks of rocks. Aeos doesn't allow such comforts to last for long.

They keep heading towards the mountain. But not always. They go wherever hunger takes them. Sometimes tracking beasts for days on end. Thirst forces them to go out of their way and roam the dry fields looking for ponds. Long gone are the days of the great lake he found as a young boy. The ponds are so small and scarce even the beasts struggle to find any.

The thought of reaching the mountain has never left his mind. An unfulfilled desire with roots in his childhood. One he can't get rid of. But as he grew older he began to wonder about things that once eluded him as a young boy.

The mountain rises high. Remarkably high. The closest thing to Aeos his eyes can find. All this suffocating heat comes from Aeos. The closer you get to him, the greater the heat, he imagines. What if the heat over there is so fierce, it turns our bodies into a mash of meat and bones? What if the pond I found yesterday was the last drop of sweat left on this dying wasteland's wretched body? Do I take that risk?

If he had nothing to lose he would have taken these risks without a second thought. A chance to reunite with mother and father again is worth every risk. But he has everything to lose. Hiding in a hole in the rocks just ahead. Waiting for him.

The first word he taught the youngest to speak was apa. The boy was struggling to speak and was pointing at him and looking at him. It didn't matter which word it was. Any word I teach him now will mean father, he thought then, so I might as well teach him the right one. From his first steps to his first sharp stone, every time the boy called him apa was a joy and sorrow like a smile in tears. The boy still calls him apa sometimes. Out of habit. Perhaps. Out of need. Apa or delf it doesn't matter. His brother depends on him to make every decision and make it the right one. Was it the right decision to leave the great lake behind? He's not so sure anymore. A terrible brother he might be. And an even worse father.

The land around here is flat. Treeless. No high ground within sight. The eldest had to leave his brother under the shade of some massive rocks. One might mistake them for the tiniest of hillocks from afar but they're just a pile of giant rocks with no roots to the ground. They seem so out of place at first sight. As if they fell from the sky one day and landed in the same spot. The gaps between them form shelters and tonight will be the fifth night they stay there. It took him four days to find water. They now have all the food and water they need after today's kill. All they need to keep moving.

He reaches the shelter and finds the youngest meandering outside. The boy is rolling rocks and gathering sticks and raising dust and making all sorts of clumsy noises. Everything he has instructed him not to do. Days are more forgiving for the man-eaters avoid the heat and only hunt during the night. But this is not the kind of world to take things for granted. The long crawlers especially are unpredictable.

Elthe, the eldest shouts and signals the youngest to come.

Oda, replies the youngest. He throws away the sticks and runs back to him.

The shelter is long and narrow. Its opposite walls are two separate rocks leaning onto each other. Spread your arms wide and you can touch both walls while the roof is high enough for a grown man to stand inside with ease.

The eldest drops the dead beast inside and waits. Determined to give his brother a few slaps for being so careless during his absence. The youngest comes dashing into the shelter and jumps on him and hugs him. He's getting heavy. And stubborn. Was I so stubborn? Can't remember. Should ask mother when I see her.

He carries him at the far end of the shelter and nods at him to stay still and silent as he skins the beast and if he does as he's told there won't be any slapping today. He drinks some water and pulls a sharp stone from the pelt on his side.

The youngest drags him from his pelt and shows him another stone. Honed today while he was away. Lave lih, he says, urging him to take it and use it instead.

It's a fine effort. Sharp at the top and smooth on all sides. Rough corners at its bottom for straps to hold. A little too short for his liking but would make a fine tip for a spear. The youngest is getting comfortable with the way of the stone. The eldest shuffles his brother's hair and gently pulls his cheek.

He kneels over the carcass and turns it over. Belly up. He points at the beast's genitals and looks to the youngest with a silent question in his stare. Expecting an answer.

Gyne, says the youngest, omio ama.

The eldest nods. Yes, a female. Like mother.

He splits its hide from tail to throat. Careful not to pierce the stomach. He peels the skin back on each side and cuts a piece of meat from its chest. He takes a bite and hands over the rest to the youngest. While he's emptying the beast's belly the youngest mishandles the piece of meat and drops it. The eldest groans for the waste and frowns at his brother who has wrapped his arms around himself. Doesn't bother picking up the meat. Face gone pale. The boy's widened eyes stay fixed upon the eldest and an even wider mouth can't find words to speak. It takes the eldest a moment to realize his brother isn't staring at him.

"Maim," speaks a man's voice. Coming from behind the eldest.

The eldest turns around. A cold wave of urgency overwhelms him as he signals his brother with a subtle gesture to move further back. A man has sneaked his way to the shelter. Now standing at the entrance holding a spear.

The youngest backsteps until his back meets the wall while the eldest picks up his spear and stands facing the man. He has forgotten how to blink. Old wounds reopen. Scars all over his face and body bleeding memories.

An older man in his prime. Hairy and filthy and unremarkable like all men except for an oozing wound around his left eye. Eyes hiding under the shadows of wild thick brows. The eldest has come across only a few men who were neither dead nor about to die. It never ended well for him. Every brief encounter he's ever had with men was full of hostility and suspicion and cruelty. Afraid of the world around them almost as much as they were of each other. Was never any true understanding between them. No coherency in their tongues. They either take what they want and leave him with nothing or they beat him for having nothing.

The man tracks and measures everything in the shelter with his one good eye. The carcass. The pile of stones. Spears and eggs and hanging pelts and especially the two brothers. His gaze passes by everything twice before landing on the pelts. The eldest tightens his grip on his spear.

"Av?" A soft voice coming from outside. The eldest sees a shadow of long hair waving in the air and sliding forth from the corner of the entrance. At a snake's pace a little girl appears and peeks inside. A child around the same age he was when. When.

The eldest loosens his grip. He has never seen another woman other than mother.

The man shouts at the sound of her voice and strikes his spear against the wall and kicks dirt at her. "Habat," he says, "asham," and gestures for her to stay outside. His hand movement is sharp and with no subtlety. The girl keeps gazing inside. Gradually walking towards him with shy steps. "Habat," the man keeps saying with annoyance growing in his voice and then yells at her a trail of words spoken too fast for the eldest to make out as she goes hiding behind the wall outside.

The man shifts all his attention back inside. The eldest raises his spear again. Rising over the hostile silence between them the sound of faint waterdrops dripping down from the bottom of the pelts to the rocky floor stands out like Aeos would if he had woken up in the middle of the night.

"Maim," says the man. He points at the pelts and signals the eldest to hand them over.

The eldest understands nothing of the man's words. It's clear maim means either water or give me. He shakes his head in defiance and says nothing.

"Maim." The man strikes the bottom of his spear down so hard he finds stone under the dirt. He repeats this word many times. Every time raising his voice as if the eldest is without ears.

The eldest hears him just fine. He shakes his head once more and thrusts his spear forward and points with its tip outside. Go get your own water.

The man makes a move for the pelts but the eldest gets in the way. The man steps back and leaves his spear lying on the wall and draws a sharp stone from the hide around his waist. He moves closer. The eldest thrusts his spear at the man but the man dodges his strike and swings the stone at him and cuts him across the chest and hits him in the face with the bottom of the stone. The eldest falls on his back. Dazed. Tasting blood gushing out of his busted nose. He hears his brother screaming. He tries to get back up but a kick in the stomach sends him crumbling back to the ground spitting all the blood out. The man starts kicking him like a piece of meat so rotten even a starving beast would have spitted out its chunks in disgust.

The youngest jumps at the man screaming and biting and scratching him like a wild beast. The man screeches from a bite to his arm and pulls the youngest by the hair and slaps him down hard. The eldest finds the chance to crawl towards the pile of stones and reaches out to grab one. The man kicks him in the face and drags him away from the pile and spreads his arms. He kneels on the eldest's shoulder joints and starts pounding his face.

Punch. The eldest sees red. Punch. Then mother. Punch. Arms stretching outwards at shoulder height. Punch. His ears are a nest of flies. Punch. Legs straight. One foot over the other. Punch. He hears father's voice. Punch. The pain is gone. He can touch Aeos with his bare hands. Punch. White light whispering with a man's voice. A deep voice. So familiar yet not of any man he has ever known. Punch. Bursting through the light comes a shadow. The son of Aeos. The light shifts like wild hair blowing in the wind. Punch. The light becomes bright red. Blood drips over his eyes from the man's torn knuckles. He hears his brother's wails and the little girl's anxious voice. Punch.

Raaaaaaaaa.

The whisper rises to a deafening endless cry. The shadow spreads its wings and blocks the light. Red dissolves into a blazing dark blur. Punch. He senses the little girl or something or someone pulling the man away from him.

Punch.

The blackness becomes him.

CIH

He lays his hand over the eldest's blood-covered chest hoping it will rise. "Ano," shouts the youngest, gasping out between tears. Shaking his brother's shoulder and urging him to get up. "Ano." The cold shiver taunting his heart wanes once he feels his brother's heart beating.

The man is leaning on the wall out of breath. A few more punches and he would have killed his brother. The man grabs his spear and wipes the eldest's blood from his beard and stands over the two brothers staring down at them. He starts tapping the bottom of his spear on the ground. Thinking. One tap for every nervous breath the youngest takes. Consistent. Recurring. He moves his gaze at the little girl and after a few more taps he lays his spear on his shoulder and heads to the pelts.

"Habat," he says, and the little girl goes to him. She's trembling whole. Holding tight at her own wrist. Hair shadowing her face.

He hands her over one of the three pelts of water. And the little girl drinks.

Mouthfuls of it she gulps in a hustle like she hasn't had water for days. Once she's full she wipes her mouth and offers the pelt to the youngest. The youngest leans forward to take the pelt but the man shouts at her and snatches it from her hands sending the youngest rushing back to his brother's side dreading what the man might do in his rage.

This time the girl talks back to the man and the youngest watches their argument in silence unable to understand any of the words they speak. Amazement and fear have his thoughts split between them into equal shares for he has never seen others of his kind and he has always been curious to meet them because of how his brother paints them and now he wishes he never had.

The girl points at him and his brother. The man keeps pacing up and down the length of the shelter while the girl talks to him. Shaking his head and shouting at first and then calm and silent as he ends his back and forth by standing over the two brothers.

The youngest raises his head. The man's stare is a slap. The youngest lowers his head and sinks his gaze back in the dirt almost instantly. The girl comes up to him from the man's side and offers him another small pelt. Not one of his brother's. He hesitates for a moment. The girl encourages him to take it. And so he does with the man's silent approval. The pelt emits the smell of green. He finds the blood of trees and some leaves inside still fresh. The man then gives him another pelt full of water and heads back to the far end of the shelter.

With a little less worry painted on her face the girl returns to the entrance and stands by the wall. Shuffling the edges of her long hair while waiting for the man to finish his task.

The man takes all the other pelts and the eggs and the fresh carcass and everything else he can carry and leaves the shelter with the girl holding his hand. She takes a sneak glance back at the youngest as they walk away into the field side by side.

Relieved to see them go the youngest splashes some water on the eldest's swollen face and tries to shake him back to his senses. He can tell his brother's eyes are moving under his eyelids as if trying to escape his own face. The youngest can't even recognize him. His face lies hidden under a red land of bloody cuts and bruises. All his wounds are oozing blood.

The youngest wipes his tears and pushes his hands against his own cheeks. Glances dash about from the roof to the walls to the floor. Outside. Inside. Trying to shake off the blame. This is all my fault. I was the one facing the entrance. I should have seen the man coming from the field sooner. They probably heard the noise I was making earlier. All my fault.

He must focus. He knows what to do for he has seen his brother treat wounds many times and has been treating the cuts on his brother's back since forever. He starts washing wounds with water one by one filling the gaps between split flesh with the blood of trees and a mush of leaves. The tree's blood slows down the bleeding and makes everything stick together while the mush becomes flesh over flesh.

Lively trees are just as scarce as ponds. So whenever his brother finds one he waters it even if he hasn't got much water to spare. A way to show his gratitude for the many healed wounds of the past.

Nurturing wounds is a painful task. The youngest hurts himself a lot by being clumsy out in the fields. He knows well how much pain he's causing his brother right now.

The eldest comes back to his senses. Groaning and taking labored breaths. His weakened body reacting to the pain in every way it can. He keeps spitting out blood. Then a tooth. The youngest spreads his lips apart to have a look. He's missing two teeth. One on each side.

Just by touching his lips the eldest's eyes sink in tears but he stays mute as a stone. The youngest sees sadness rising over pain in his red-blooded eyes. He drags a thick piece of fur close and helps the eldest lie on his side and shoves the fur under his head making it easier for him to spit out the blood without moving his head too much.

After nurturing all his wounds the youngest sits by his side. Ready to care for him for as long as he must. Aeos moves to his resting place and brings a shy end to a day of shame.

Darkness descends. A moonless night. Hollow stars. Harsh to the thoughts and accusing. The youngest keeps cleaning his brother's wounds. The dark has made the task trickier.

Perplexing whispers. Anxious breaths and sudden gestures. All night the youngest at his brother's side is in a constant state of unrest for the eldest keeps reaching out to grab things that aren't there and shoving his nails in his head as if his thoughts were something he could rip out of his skull. The youngest keeps washing his wounds with shaky hands. Fearing for the worse. Trying not to waste any water. Less than half a pelt of clean water remains.

Every time he touches the eldest he feels intense heat. Heat so fierce it belongs in the day. Aeos has found a way to sneak under his brother's skin tearing his insides out with claws of light. The eldest is shivering and grinding his teeth like he's cold. Yet drenched in sweat from top to bottom like he's hot. The youngest can't explain it.

Howls spread menace throughout the night. Man-eaters kill until death's belly is full. His brother only keeps enough meat from a carcass to last them a few days. He tosses the rest out. Neither too close nor too far away from where they spend the night. Hoping the man-eaters hunting nearby will feed on the dead beast instead of them. Tonight the youngest has no such means. Panic comes surging through him and sends his heart leaping into his throat with every howl the wind carries to his ears. A sleepless night. Drenched in the youthful sweat of ineptitude. The longest night of his life.

Please don't leave me, brother. He wipes away the sweat from the eldest's forehead with a trembling hand. I'm here by your side, eager to care for you, just like you have cared for me all this time.

Dawn. Light begins to creep on the walls near the shelter's opening. The eldest is asleep. The wounds all over his face are no longer bleeding but the cut across his chest is stubborn and oozing still. The heat inside him is getting stronger.

The youngest stares down at an empty pelt with weary eyes. There's a pond hidden somewhere in the fields and he must find it. And the ants. Myrme, his brother calls them. He has seen him treat deep wounds with them many times.

One step out of the shelter and the newborn light makes him dizzy. His eyes begging for sleep. He goes wandering in the fields with wobbly legs. Reeling towards one direction for a while. Changing direction once he goes too far without finding any water. The hissing of snakes all around him makes him wary of his steps. Avoiding the patches of grass and bushes. He drifts far but never loses sight of the shelter.

He roams the fields for most of the morning. He finds the ants he was searching for under the rocks and gathers aplenty in one of his pelts. No sign of water. Covered in sweat and with no more spit in his mouth to soothe his dry throat he heads back to the shelter with worry in his pace and a mountain of guilt on his shoulders.

As he enters the shelter he falters at the sight of his brother standing and facing the wall with one hand leaning on the rock and breathing fast as if the air was filled with the blood he lost and now he wants every single drop of it back.

"Delf," says the youngest with a tentative smile. He staggers back a step and holds a hand over his chest. Relieved his brother is up and moving again. A few steps forward and his eyes widen. Smile fades. "Delf?" he says once more, with relief and anxiety in quarrel over his voice.

His brother is painting the wall with his own blood.

The eldest says nothing. He spits more blood in his hand and keeps painting. The youngest remembers his brother's mouth stopped bleeding during the night and he's certain his wounds had been calm when he left at dawn. So much blood on the wall. Some of his cuts like new. Brother is hurting himself.

The youngest gets closer. He breathes air so brittle it could snap into bits and slash his throat. Cold shivers creep back to his heart. His brother is painting strange things. Shapes and forms you don't see in the wilderness.

Twisted lines mesh. Wild hair around Aeos' circle. At the far end of the wall a man's body with a beast's head and wings instead of arms. The eldest starts an outline of the mountain close to the entrance. The lines fade as he drags his hand over the rock. He sticks his fingers back in his mouth and moans as he gathers more blood. The lines turn vivid again. Dark red. He colors the mountain and drags a line across the wall to the man-beast at the other end. Mountain and man-beast bound by a stream of blood.

"Myrme," says the youngest while lifting the pelt high but his brother's mind is elsewhere. He gets closer and lays his hand on his brother's shoulder. Barely touching him. His patched wounds are still one sneeze away from bleeding again. His flesh remains hot like fur left out to dry all day after skinning but the swelling on his face has calmed down a bit.

The eldest stops and turns his gaze at him for a moment finally acknowledging his presence. He lays his forehead on the wall and starts weeping and scratching the paintings with his nails as the youngest stays still and silent for he doesn't know what to do. Soon the eldest has no more tears to shed and goes limping outside and the youngest follows him. The eldest sits slumped on a rock nearby. Facing the direction of the mountain. And the youngest stands by his side. Ready to care for him.

"Bea delf, ode," the eldest says, with the faintest of words stumbling over his torn lips as he points to the mountain.

"Ode?" We go now? Shouldn't we rest first, get some more of our strength back? He doesn't dare argue with his brother so he keeps his thoughts mute.

"Nae. Ode. Aeos."

"Aeos?"

The eldest gives a blank stare back at the shelter. He takes the youngest's hand and makes him touch his forehead. To feel the heat that grows inside him. He then brings the youngest's hand over his chest and makes him feel his heartbeat. "Nae. Aeos lale es."

Aeos speaks inside us?

III

CHIMERA

ГН

There was never a need to shout before. Roaming the fields searching for food and water has always been a loner's pursuit for the eldest. Now his brother is old enough to hunt and gather, able to hold his own in the wild. A natural need has gradually developed. The need to let each other know from afar of what they see and hear.

The few words the eldest once knew have become many. Trails of them come together now to express his thoughts, often too many for a single breath to carry. With every new word he creates, the voice he hears coming out of his mouth sounds more and more like the one he hears in his mind.

He walks through dry grass, looking for any signs of water, like the mud left behind by the wet feet of beasts. He swats away the flies hiding in his beard. A beard that has met his chest. He is bones covered in scarred flesh with not much else in between. Strapped around his waist, a soiled pelt covers his manhood and his legs down to his knees.

The taste of blood in his mouth is constant. His teeth are colored like the late dusk. Great pain flows back and forth from teeth to ears as if something inside his mouth is trying to rip a hole in his skull and chew his brains. The pain comes and goes as it pleases, more intense during nighttime. Sometimes it's subtle, but most often, the pain is so fierce it shadows his vision, torments his ears and bleeds his teeth. Headaches make it difficult to stand and walk straight. Chewing meat has become a frustrating task, almost unbearable. He has learned to deal with it. Live with it. Bleeding is as natural as breathing.

"Elthe delf, hyda," shouts the youngest from not too far away.

"Oda," replies the eldest and follows his brother's voice.

The land is awkward. Uneven. With newborn hills aspiring to rise from mother soil but too shy to leave her womb. The dirt he walks on as hard as a stone and with on-again-off-again patches of pale grass as far as the eye can see.

It's been a while since they last found a shelter in these lands. The endless fields have become their home. Two brothers a shelter to each other. The eldest longs for the safety of knowing where everything is and the reassurance things will still be there the following day. He misses his paintings. Watching something of his own creation grow over time. He used to carve the stones wherever they would settle for the night. But after a long while, he stopped painting, for they were always on the move and leaving them behind only brought him sadness.

Instead of painting, the eldest now creates more words. A new word for every new thing he finds. One for every type of beast, of rock and tree. A word to match every way there is to act is especially useful when his brother is far out of sight but close within a shout's reach.

He teaches his brother most of these words, but there are some he cannot. He has words in his head for things his brother has yet to see, like leondas, the giant beast with the long mane near the lake. It's impossible to teach the youngest a word for something he has no experience of. And even though the eldest has always tried to keep his brother away from danger, danger sometimes comes to them.

Nevertheless, the way of words, just like the way of the hunt and the way of the stone, has become a vital habit. The eldest points at a thing. The eldest speaks. Whatever comes out of his mouth becomes the word for that thing. A way to show to each other whenever they like and as many times as they like, things the eye only needs to see once. Simple. Effective. Rearing.

He steps out of a long patch of grass and finds his brother stretching over a small pond overwhelmed by flies that leave a nasty rash on the skin wherever they bite. He covers his head with a pelt as he approaches and waves his hands in the air to keep them away. Their buzzing sound overtakes the rustling of the grass and almost mutes the splashes of water the youngest makes while washing his face.

The eldest smiles at the sight of his brother scratching his cheeks, trying to get rid of a nasty itch under a beard that is barely a few days old. Because of him, the passing of time makes sense. Every new day matters. Every new day, another chance to watch him grow. Grow when all else falters.

He crouches next to the youngest and gulps down a handful of water and clears his throat. The pond is barely a hand deep. Water smells piss and tastes dirt and is full of dead flies. He gargles a mouthful to wash the blood from his teeth and swallows it. Water too precious to spit out. Along the pond, a burden of snakes stepped over and chewed to pieces. Bones covered with gore and black clouds of flies scattered everywhere. They shouldn't stay long. The eldest gets the sense they're lucky to still be alive. This pond belongs to the fast and the strong. The slow and the weak are not welcome here.

They drink more water and eat whatever half-rotten meat scraps they can savor from the bones. The eldest can tell some of the bones are of men but doesn't tell the youngest. It hurts to chew, so he swallows chunks of it whole. The taste of his own kind stays in his mouth and strangles down his throat. They drink and eat to vomit and vomit to drink and eat some more and once their bodies can take no more punishment, they fill their pelts and move on.

After many days without, the initial relief of drinking water soon wears off, leaving their aching bellies grumbling and stretched thin. They spend the rest of the day in sickness, heading towards the mountain. Always.

No longer a mere shadow in the distance, they have come close enough to the mountain to be able to see clearly what a massive chunk of land it is—many times the size of the most prominent hill they've ever come across. It has been elusive and unreachable to them for the longest time, but now reaching the mountain seems like a much easier task than returning home.

"Pafs. Ous." The eldest halts and gestures for his brother to do the same. For a moment, he thought he heard someone wailing. The faintest of cries coming from the direction where Aeos rises. He looks at the youngest with narrowed eyes, unsure whether this sound was real or in his mind. "Sy ous?" A startled look on the youngest's face to match his own is all the sign he needs to pull the sharp stone from his pelt.

They move through the dry grass with caution. Their steps, as silent as the slither of snakes. Aeos behind their backs, heading towards his resting place. The wails grow stronger with every step they take and soon become loud and clear enough to track.

Moments later, they find a woman crawling in the field, turning rocks over and messing the dirt, searching for something, crawlers maybe. She's crying and mumbling as if in grievance with someone. No one else around but her.

The eldest signals the youngest to stand still and silent as he walks up to the woman. She's so immersed and raucous in her ways, she only notices the eldest after his shadow creeps all over her.

Her mumbling ends. She stops dragging her hands in the dirt and looks up at the eldest. He can barely see her face, for it hides behind long curls of wretched hair, brown like the dirt and just as soiled. The fur over her skinny body is old and hole-ridden, her skin heat-slashed. No spear near her. Wary of her at first, the eldest now slides his sharpened stone back into his pelt. *No way she belongs to a man,* he ponders. *A man would have skinned new fur for her to wear and no man would ever leave his woman wandering in the fields.*

"Gyne?" the youngest says.

"Nae, gyne." The eldest found a few women while alone on the hunt but none since his brother began to hunt by his side. All dead. A couple with half-chewed heads and no meat left on their bones. Could barely tell they were women. And one who had no wounds on her. Young. Her body hadn't stunk yet. No signs of struggle. She was just dead. He couldn't explain it. Mother remains the only woman he has seen alive. And that little girl, that one time.

"Omio ama?"

The eldest nods, just now realizing his brother has never seen a grown woman before. If only he could rip the image of mother out of his mind and give it to him. If only there was a way to carve her face in the stone, so his brother could see her.

The woman crawls towards the eldest, gasping and mumbling strange words. The eldest takes a step back. Her gaze is fixated on the pelts hanging from his shoulder. They are still wet, dripping water. She reaches out to grab them, but the eldest slaps her hand away.

"Te delf?" the youngest says, "gyne lave hyda?" He walks up to the eldest's side, takes one of his own pelts of water and when he tries to give the woman some, the eldest stops him.

"Pafs. Oun hyda." The eldest would have given her some of their water if the pond hadn't been so close. They're not going back and there's no telling when or if they will find water again. The pond is an evening's walk away. She can take her chances there. He snaps his fingers to get the woman's attention and points to his pelt. "Hyda," he says to her.

"H—hy—da. Hyda?" She pulls the hair away from her face. Her chapped lips are trembling. Her eyes heavy-lidded and dark, starved of sleep.

The eldest nods. He points towards the direction of the pond and by using two fingers, he imitates walking.

The woman answers with reaching hands of despair, mumbling and shaking her head erratically. The eldest takes another step back and points down the field once more, but the woman persists. She slides one hand between her legs and starts rubbing her womanhood; she points at the pelt of water with the other, then draws her hand back and starts caressing her breasts while giving the eldest a pleading stare, sending brief gasps of pleasure towards him. Deliberate. Pretentious. Enticing.

He remembers father coming up to him in the evening, covering him up with fur and instructing him to stay under and silent. Not to peek. The woman's gasps remind him of mother's, though mother's gasps sounded spontaneous and honest. He has come across grass-eaters mating many times while hunting and that's all the experience he has with the act.

Strong urges have been trapped inside him for the longest time. Urges he has learned to either subdue or ignore completely, for he could never fulfill them, never able to settle the urge on his own. Mother was the only woman he has ever known and for reasons unknown to him, his mind could never paint the image of an imaginary woman. Whenever the urge was too great, he would try to please himself in his loneliness. And every time he failed, for the faces of mother and dead women were all he could see in his mind and it filled his heart with guilt and shame for what he was trying to do.

The woman crawls on her knees and gets closer to him, close enough to touch him. The eldest lets her. She slowly slides her hand under his pelt, whispering the word *hyda* in-between voluptuous gasps as her hand slithers upwards between his legs. She starts caressing his manhood. The eldest closes his eyes, losing himself in the sensation, unable to resist her ways.

He turns to the youngest and gestures for him to walk away, to look elsewhere for a while. The youngest does as he's told.

The woman slips both her hands under his pelt, urging him to come down to the ground with her. He sits and she slides over him, rubbing her female against his male and she lays her head on his shoulder, whispering *hyda* in his ear constantly while rubbing herself up and down his manhood. He unstraps his pelt and the woman strokes him, pushing her waist against his waist as he crawls inside her. Mind goes blank, free of thoughts. Her long gasps overwhelm his neck. His hands shiver. Sweaty palms reach out and fill with her breasts. He closes his eyes and gives in to the warmth of her body, feeling no shame. No guilt. Nothing but a mountain of pleasure and tension rising to new heights and when he reaches its peak, his eyes open wide, looking over the woman's shoulder at her wild hair loving the wind. And the wind loves her.

She rests her head on his shoulder. Her gentle voice gradually slows down his pounding heart, filling his ear with gasps of passion and recurring whispers of the same word.

"Hyda."

He brings one of the pelts forth and lets her drink till she's full. She must have spent days without water, for she drinks half a pelt with ease. He then points to his brother with his head and shakes the pelt, making the water splash inside. The woman nods. She gets to her feet and walks up to the youngest, who still has his back turned at them. He turns around as the woman lays a hand on his shoulder. He looks over her shoulder at the eldest. She starts touching his manhood. His gaze is asking for approval.

The eldest gives him a nod of consent and smiles as his brother follows the woman down to the ground. The youngest is still young, barely a hint of a man, but if he can feel the urge, then he's old enough to mate. The eldest moves his gaze to a pale sky flooded with the dark evening shades. They have covered enough ground for one day.

The night finds them resting in the field, exhausted, with nothing around to use as shelter. The wind carries no other sound but its own howl. The moon is a claw, faint behind gathering clouds. Clouds are a good sign.

The woman and the youngest sleep in each other's arms, while the eldest stays awake gazing at the night sky like he often does. His mouth full of growing pains, with roots to both edges of his upper jaw, spreading to his ears like spiky twigs.

He used to see visions of the mountain and bright and strange amalgamates of creatures. Now when he sleeps, all is black. All is darkness and nothing else. The light inside him, caught from the day he faced the man and the little girl, has long abandoned him. It stuck with him for a few days and faded away as soon as his wounds healed.

The light was real. He's sure of it, for he felt it. As real as pain and sorrow and rage and all else that comes bursting out from within. The visions he had were real—he saw them. Everything the eye can see is real, like stones and grass, the dirt and all living things. But what if the light was just Aeos' way to torment him, like the heat, the hunger and the thirst? Perhaps what he heard that day was the skies hating on the soil. The cunning whispers of eerie creatures, luring fools of flesh to a lake of light and ripping them apart before they get the chance to dip their toes in its bright shores. Perhaps he is one of those fools and his brother now suffers for it.

The clouds move with caution, hiding as many stars as they reveal. Eyelids are getting heavy. The eldest is still alert but barely. The moment he decides to let his brother sleep a little while longer, he sees something in the night sky that invigorates his eyes, instantly draining him of any urge to sleep.

"Delf ano," the eldest says and taps the youngest's shoulder. The youngest lifts his head and swiftly reaches out to grab his spear. The woman wakes up too, but the eldest gestures for them to stay calm and silent. He shows them the sky. "Ore."

The youngest and the woman track his hand at a star left behind by the moving clouds, as bright as nothing else but the moon. The star is low, more ahead than above them, close to the line at the end of the world. So bright it captures your gaze and makes the rest of the stars seem pitiful in comparison.

The brothers stare at the star in awe. It wasn't there the night before. Or was it? The eldest looks at the youngest, trying to figure out his expression through the darkness. The youngest knows the night sky well and he seems just as stunned by its presence. The eldest then turns to the woman, but she has already gone back to sleep. *Odd,* the eldest thinks, *she doesn't seem to care for it. She's used to it being there. So how come we haven't seen this star before and she has? Clouds have been constant for a few nights now. Was it hiding there? And what about during the countless other nights the skies were clear? All this time, no way I wouldn't notice a star as bright as this one. A new wound on the night's flesh. For us. Aeos hurts the darkness for us.*

Neither of the brothers can sleep for the rest of the night. They watch the star put to shame whatever else flickers in the dark. It still shines stubbornly through the early light of dawn while all the other stars fade around it. Shades of orange lit the sky as the line at the end of the world becomes clear. Right below the star lies the mountain.

Horos is the word for mountain. Aste is the word for star. But you are not just any star, are you? You deserve a word of your own.

"Horaste," says the eldest.

"Horaste?"

"Nae delf. Horaste." This is the word for the mountain's star, the brightest of them all.

The eldest wakes up the woman with a nudge. They will keep her, whether she likes it or not. But judging by how fast she gets to her feet, she probably wants it more than they do. Another mouth to feed in a world that offers so little is challenging, but the rarest of pleasures she hides between her legs. A well-earned reward for a man's struggles at the end of the day. And a motive at the start.

They take their pleasure from the woman in turns. Once their desires are met, they gather their belongings and start walking towards the mountain. No rush in their pace, with the eldest leading the way.

He takes no more than a few steps and halts the moment he hears the woman's shouts coming from the back. He turns around. The woman is dragging her feet away from them with crossed arms, reluctant to follow in their set path. He waves for her to come along and points in the direction of the mountain. She answers by shaking her head many times, slurring words in a quavering voice.

"Te?" says the youngest and looks to the eldest for guidance.

The eldest briefly lifts a shoulder and instructs his brother to stay where he is. As he walks up to her, she finds a thornbush nearby and snaps a small branch off it. She shows it to him, points at Aeos and imitates things falling from the sky with sharp, rapid gestures. Things that look like branches? Maybe? Or maybe not. The eldest is struggling to make sense of her ways and he knows nothing of the strange words she's saying. Her anxious tone speaks louder than any words she can utter.

What do you mean, woman? Have you been to the mountain? I can't understand your signs. The only thing that falls from the sky is rain. And what does Aeos has to do with some twigs snapped from a bush?

She pulls her hair behind her ears, exposing the fright that has taken over every subtle movement of wrinkled flesh on her face. She stops speaking words and continues by making roaring noises in between quick, loud gasps. She snaps some more branches and tries to reproduce the sound of them snapping with the high stretches of her voice.

The eldest tries hard to find meaning in her sounds and gestures but gives up once the woman starts repeating them, seemingly unable to find better and more coherent ways to express herself. He shakes his head and points to the mountain once again. *That's where we're going woman and we're taking you with us.* He reaches out to grab her hand, but she slaps it away. Her eyes are bulging, horrified, as she takes a few more backward steps.

He thinks about forcing her to stay. Her will is not necessary for the pleasures her body grants them. But the last thing he needs right now is someone running when they should be hiding, shouting when they should be silent. The pleasures she holds are not worth the dangers of disobedience. He returns to his brother, annoyed by what has happened, dragging the burden of countless unanswered questions in his stride.

"Te delf?" the youngest says. "Gyne elthe, nae?"

"Oun gyne elthe. Horos ode e mon e sy." The eldest walks right past him without stopping and the youngest follows in his steps. After a while, the eldest takes a quick glance back at the field; the woman is long gone, nowhere to be seen.

Ahead of them, the mountain awaits. And even though he tries to stay calm for his brother, he now worries more than ever. The woman has chosen loneliness over the safety of two men looking after her. She has chosen hunger and thirst over men who could have provided her with food and water. Her ways were confusing and hinting at absurd things his mind cannot fathom, but the horror in her eyes was clear and striking.

Hunger. Thirst. Loneliness is what she chose over them instead. A senseless choice the eldest tries to reconcile with. He tries to put himself in her place, to think of a good enough reason for him to make the same choice. Did she meet the gods? Were they cruel to her? Is he guiding his brother to their inevitable downfall?

For food. Water. Safety. The woman was ready to accept anything. To follow them anywhere.

Anywhere but the mountain.

ᴄs

One day as a young boy, the youngest asked his brother to explain the stars to him. The eldest took a pelt and pierced small holes all over it with a sharp stone. He lifted the pelt over their heads and made a roof of it. The midday light shined through the holes like stars.

The night rewards the shelter-less by showing them secret habits that would have passed as arbitrary otherwise. The youngest noticed the stars were moving a long time ago. After tracking their path for many nights, he realized they follow Aeos as if trying to sneak up on him, wanting to slice his throat while he sleeps. To kill the night-killer before he kills the night. And with every new dawn, Aeos cunningly appears on the other side, laughing at the stars as they fade away in shame.

The youngest sees no cracks in the night sky. Cracks don't move. The mountain star just came to be one night out of nowhere, as bright as no other but the moon. It wasn't there the countless nights he slept as a boy on his brother's lap, clenching on his pelt, in dread of everything around him. It wasn't there as he grew old enough to hunt on his own.

Now Horaste is the last to fade once again at the break of dawn. His brother is fascinated by the connection between Horaste and the mountain, but the youngest is drawn to it for other reasons. The mountain star isn't moving. Its place in the sky is constant. It shares no habits with its countless brothers. Nothing else in the sky behaves this way, not even Aeos.

He never understood his brother's urge to reach the mountain, but he would happily follow him to their deaths if he had to. Besides, the mountain's grand presence in the distance has made him curious. He wants to find its balance in the world, to uncover its secrets. But for now, they need to eat.

His brother is in agony, moaning constantly, complaining about his teeth. Odonda, the word for them. The eldest has been unable to hunt for days now. The youngest has left him under the shade of a tall tree on the slope of a nearby hill, easy to spot from afar. He's tracking a herd of grass-eaters with toeless footmarks, like two sharp claws facing each other.

The mountain soars before him as if determined to pierce the sky's blue skin. It dominates in every which way he looks except back. The closer they get to it, the more common and lively the trees become. The ponds easier to find. It's as if the land feeds off the mountain, gathering food and water from its rising slopes.

As the day grows, even the trees become desperate for shade. He finds another kind of footmark mingling with the ones he's tracking. Many times the size of his own feet, round and going deep in the ground. Whatever creature leaves behind these marks is large and heavy. He tracks the grass-eaters until their trail disappears along with the dirt as the ground turns craggy and sharp. A rough skin over the soil made mostly of rock, full of sharp corners and bushes rising through the cracks. He walks down the rocky field blind of trails, feeling like he's stepping over the mountain's roots.

He sees a herd of massive beasts ahead with long, hanging noses. Two teeth, or maybe horns, coming out of the side of their mouths, sharp edges facing upwards. The largest horns he has ever seen. They are heavy and slow in their steps. Even the young members of the herd are larger than any other beast he knows. Their feet are round. The grass-eaters he has been tracking all day must have passed them.

As he gets closer, they seem unbothered by his presence. He keeps a safe distance from them. One of the herd's younger beasts, with half-grown teeth, suddenly gets agitated. It raises its heavy legs as if trying to stomp something, moaning, waving its head. The youngest hears a hissing sound and a long black snake rises swiftly over the rocky ground and bites the beast on its foot. The beast tries to squash it, but the snake bites it again before crawling back into the cracks it came from.

The youngest sees a fool in the snake. Its tiny fangs are near useless against a beast of such massive size. He walks away, amused by the idea of something so small having the nerve to challenge something so big.

The ground becomes dirt again. Grass as vast as any eye could wander. The mountain rests far to his left. Some lonely trees are scattered here and there, healthy and vigorous despite the excruciating heat. He wonders whether the land draws strength from the mountain through its roots in the ground. Midday, he finds the herd of grass-eaters feeding on the grass and claims one of the young ones.

On his return, he takes the same path he came from. A challenging walk back, now that he's carrying heavy prey over his shoulders. He hears a beast moaning not too far ahead and follows the moans until he finds one of the massive beasts he came across earlier, abandoned, lying on the ground and suffering. The rest of the herd is gone.

The youngest drops his prey and gets close to the beast. He recognizes it. Teeth half-grown. He caresses the side of its belly. Its skin is warm and mellow. It lifts its long nose and swings its head as if to take the scent of its last breath. He feels its skin turn cold and stiff. Its belly getting low, never to rise again.

He sees no wounds. No blood. If the wounds are on its bottom side, there's no way this beast was hunted down and left untouched with no one to claim the meat off its bones. The snake comes to mind. *A beast so massive can't drop dead from just a couple of tiny snake bites to its feet... can it?*

It becomes apparent to him that this creature died of sickness. He wonders whether there's something about the snake's fangs that can make a beast die from sickness. He searches through the cracks and the bushes to find another snake. He wants to know. He needs to find its secret.

He has come across many snakes in his life. His brother taught him how to handle them when he was young. Sometimes they would slither in their shelter and he was instructed not to kill them. They eat the furry crawlers. The irritating, squeaking little pains that are difficult to catch and kill. Mys is the word for them.

It took him many days to learn how to catch a snake. And many bites. But the snakes he's familiar with have tiny fangs. Their bite is painful but harmless. If this snake's bite can kill a beast of such grand size, he needs to be careful. The pelts and bones protecting his limbs might not be good enough protection.

After meandering around the area for a while, he finds a snake slithering through the rocks. Black, long and thin. He uses his spear to distract it by slowly waving the tip in front of its head. The snake starts swinging its head along with the spear, following the movement of his hand. He first guides its attention away from him, then swiftly pinches it behind its skull. He squeezes it at the back of its jaw, tight, allowing no room for it to turn its head. It opens its mouth and the youngest sees two sharp fangs coming out of its upper jaw.

The snake squirts its waste and writhes its body. It releases a horrendous smell, hard to ignore. The youngest forces the tip of the spear into its mouth. It clamps its fangs on the stone and drops come out and run along the rock's curve and fall to the ground like sweat.

The youngest watches with widened eyes and a pair of raised eyebrows as one drop after another stains the soil. *So that's your real weapon, you sneaky one. Now I know your secret.*

He hikes his shoulder to scratch his beard, still holding the snake firmly, as he contemplates ways to store this sickness. A pelt won't do. He needs something smaller and less absorbent. Bones are the only thing that comes to mind, for they become hollow after you suck their pulp from inside. They've never used bones in such a way. There was never a reason to save so little of anything.

Now there is.

The more he gathers the more he ponders about faceless and shapeless things. Coincidence. Chance. He's been bitten by snakes many times. Some carry sickness it seems. Some do not. It's astonishing how arbitrary life is. How frightening one's ignorance can be of things mystical and ethereal. Who lives? Who dies? One moment too late you die. One moment too soon you live. Many right guesses, you live a long life. You hesitate for a moment or rush too soon, either way, you take one wrong guess and you die young.

So many hidden secrets in the world to unravel. So many qualities to discover. Who gets to decide what's right and what's wrong and who can you trust to pass a fair judgement, when some traits inside us all are cussed and anathema and only there to keep you blind and deaf and mute to the true form of things. Some men get bitten by snakes and die.

Some others, fortune favors.

†

Harsh soil. Ankles tumble left and right over volatile rocks. Aeos shines strong at his highest point. The mountain rises in the distance to claim authority in the sky. Its slopes seem covered with the fur of trees. The walk to get there is over long ridges of broken rock and through steep, craggy paths, like scars over barren foothills.

Deep, jagged crevices hold the night captive during daytime. The eldest peeks over one and finds depths of darkness with no end. He stands there for a moment, wondering whether to fall inside is to fall forever. Or that one might find the mountain's roots at the very bottom, if one can find enough courage first to descend into blackness so thick it could scare away night itself.

Raaaaaaaaaa

The eldest hears the son of light through a gathering of echoes. A wild light comes into his eyes like a glow stolen from stars as he captures its shadow with his stare, flying towards the mountain's peak. An unexpected chill in the wind dries the sweat running down his forehead. Layers of piled filth all over his face. Fresh air fills his chest with determination. Mother and father are calling for him.

His brother, not too far behind, messing around with another snake again. He has been catching them for days, draining the piss from their fangs into a hollow piece of bone he has strapped around his neck. He then seals it off by jamming a smaller bone inside, sharpened to fit perfectly and covered with the blood of trees so it sticks to the inside. It holds the piss from spilling out, even if he turns it upside down. His brother speaks of death to large beasts, but the eldest has yet to see any actual use for it. Reckless. Dangerous.

The eldest sees in his brother a fascination with the how of things. A noisiness that grows as he grows, getting louder with every new day. It worries him. It makes his brother too eager to act, making decisions more out of curiosity than of need. Or sometimes too slow to react, willing to forego time and safety under dangerous circumstances. No words or gestures the eldest knows can make his brother understand. It doesn't matter how things came to be as they are. All that matters is they are.

It takes two days for them to pass beyond the mountain's rocky foothills. Safe for them to move only during the daytime. They leave behind barren lands of no food and no water and once their feet meet soil and grass again, the eldest shoves his toes in the dirt with great relief. Unlike the piss-colored dry ground they're used to, the mountain's slope is covered with a different kind of soil, deep brown like a man's skin and humid as if the mountain sweats.

The brothers slip and slide and stumble, the incline getting more burdensome with every step they take. The eldest notices a pleasant scent in the air coming from the trees. He was expecting excruciating heat. Heat so intense that would make a man rip his own eyes out in despair. To his astonishment, the higher they climb, the cooler it gets.

Trees thick about them, remarkably tall, with trunks of immense girth and branches barely swaying despite a strong wind. Their shade hushes Aeos' bright but does little to make the steep incline any easier.

The dim evening light finds them exhausted at the lower ends of the mountain's slope. They come upon a clearing, where the dirt now hides under a fur of leaves. Small creatures dash through the bushes around them, fast and agile. Their presence brings forth the old, great hunger, for the brothers haven't eaten anything in days. Suddenly, new spectacles matter not.

The youngest climbs one of the trees and picks up some of its fruit. He takes a bite and tosses one down to the eldest. The eldest hesitates to take a bite. He can barely chew anything anymore without getting in a world of pain. The fruit seems full of taste and freshness but unkind to the teeth. He sees overwhelming pleasure all over his brother's face, too tempting to ignore. He takes a bite. His mouth fills with flavor and sweet sap. A burst of joy turns all other senses mute, forcing his eyes shut. He chews for the sweetness to last, but all taste becomes blood the instant his teeth meet the crunch. He spits it all out in pain and coughs himself to his knees.

The youngest rushes down from the tree. He gives him water from their last pelt to wash his mouth and puts some fruit in one of the other empty pelts. He places it on the ground, mashes the fruit inside with a rock and hands it over to him. Little by little, the eldest eats as much of the pulp as he can, groaning and squeezing his eyes to tears as if chewing thorns. The youngest leans over, caressing the back of his head while he eats.

For the eldest, every bite is torment. With every bite, he sinks his head between his knees and groans. Even thoughts hurt by the time he's done eating. Unable to endure any more pain, he taps his brother's shoulder, grateful, gets back to his feet and urges his brother to do the same. They need to keep moving.

The shadows grow strong around them as they reach higher ground. Fallen leaves crunch beneath their feet while they look for shelter in unfamiliar lands, adorned with outgrown twisted roots and food-bearing bushes of many colors and kinds new to their eyes.

They walk until the last light. Nothing but trees and dirt around them. They gather bushes around a tree to hide and rest their backs against its trunk.

Staying on the ground makes the eldest uncomfortable. He has thought of spending the night on the trees, but he senses creatures moving above their heads, dashing from branch to branch. Man-eaters, grass-eaters, who knows?

Darkness covers them. A night so different, but like so many others where the brothers sleep by taking turns. The eldest stands guard first. Always. The night brings an awkward kind of blackness and coolness. There's water in the air that sticks on everything, making wood, stone and flesh shine in the dark. Stars appear behind branches swaying with grace in the heavy wind. Trees are arms with many hands and fingers with a life of their own. The wood is soft like flesh.

The eldest hears the mountain speak in menacing tongues. Growls and howls, barks and whines. Creatures large and small, moving on the ground and on the trees, screeching and crying with no end, hissing and whining enough worry in the eldest's mind to keep him sleepless. He never wakes up his brother to take his turn. This is not why they came here. There was enough fear back home to last a lifetime. All night, his grip on his spear never loosens.

He shakes the youngest's head off his shoulder at first light. Reaching the mountain's peak his only thought. Nothing else matters, neither sleep nor food nor water.

They walk till the tall trees make way to smaller trees. The smaller trees make way to low grass. Aeos shines over them through clear skies as the world grows bigger. Hidden valleys and distant peaks appear in the far distance.

Breathtaking views of their past blend with the wind's howl beating against the mountainside.

The eldest sees the way to the mountain's peak is through stone. *The wind is cold. Why is it cold when everything else is warm?* The walk becomes a steep climb from now on. Any kind of a slip or a trip would mean certain death. He looks at the youngest, holding his knees and breathing heavily, just as tired as he is. It's too dangerous. He doesn't want his brother to follow him to the peak. He looks around to see if there's another way to the top, but he finds no other way.

"Delf," says the eldest, "ode," and points to the spot his brother is standing.

The youngest shakes his head and tells him with an angry stare how he feels about staying behind. The eldest grabs the back of his brother's neck, shuffles his hair, kisses him gently on his forehead, repeats the same words straight to his face and squeezes his neck a little. The youngest finds the ground with his eyes and nods in compliance. The eldest begins his ascent, leaving his brother behind sitting on a rock and waiting for his return.

Feet tremble over skin-slicing rocks. The raging wind breaks his balance and throws dust in his aching eyes. The mountain, just as obsessed with keeping him away as he is with climbing it. Stones plummeting all around him make him shiver more than the cold. The blood from his arms and knees stains the stone red. Whatever comes, he keeps going. Pulling and dragging himself, sliding and slipping, clinging and hanging from whatever hole in the stone or sharp edge he can find. Breaths feel empty. He looks over his head. The mountain's peak rises as a spear through Aeos' heart, shedding his bright blood and drenching everything in light.

He hears the son of Aeos calling for him, louder than ever. This is the moment he has been waiting for all his life. Tears of excitement dry out before they have a chance to leave his eyes. He pushes himself through the light and he drags himself over the top as his fingers grasp at the edge of the last rock. He gathers all his will and lifts himself onto a vast, bright world. A ridge that leads straight to the peak, now a short walk away. Not much strength left in him, but he stands up with confidence and grows stronger with each step. Finally, he can see the world as Aeos sees it.

The bright gradually dissipates as he walks up the ridge. His eyes adjust. He sees Aeos as high in the sky as he has ever been. Nowhere near the mountaintop, where he thought he would be. *Where are you, son of light? Come to me. Teach me how to get there.* Clouds of dust are flying off the ridge, stones falling off on all sides. Bushes have managed to flourish through the cracks. It's like any other place only higher and colder.

He makes it to the peak and sees a new line forming beyond Aeos' haze over the other side of the mountain. A further edge to the world, as far away ahead as where they came from. His face turns bloodless. The heavy air chokes him down to his knees.

Small sticks scratch his face as he struggles to breathe. The sticks are flying off the side of a naked rock close to the edge. He looks over the side and finds a large nest within an arm's reach, hidden in a deep hole in the stone. Three eggs inside, equal to a man's fist. One is cracked and a creature is hobbling around in the nest. A tiny bird.

He reaches out to grab one of the eggs. He hears the son of light tearing the wind apart with his cries. The eldest tries to track him in the sky, but the echoes make it sound like he's coming from everywhere. Just as his fingers touch the egg, the cries rise to deafening heights and a creature plunges down and lands with fury on his back. The impact sends him a step away from falling off the edge. He yelps as the creature sinks its talons deep in his shoulders and starts whirring its wings with fury, biting and ripping away chunks of flesh from his neck. He writhes away from the nest, yelling and waving his hands erratically. The creature bites his ear, but he manages to land a slap on its head. It takes off, gliding through the air, blood dripping from its beak and talons.

The eldest tracks the creature as it starts circling the mountain's peak, becoming the shadow he has been following all his life. He hears its cries. The cries he has thought to be the sound of the holy. He looks down at the nest and the eggs and the newborn beast with wings. He then moves his gaze around, lost, looking for something more, anything more. There's nothing else.

Nothing more to find here. Nothing worth seeking for. No heavenly paths to follow. No way to reach the light above, and in a moment of sheer anguish, he screams in hate of the light. He hates Aeos and his bastard son. He hates this wretched world and everything in it. And most of all, he hates himself.

A long echo of his rage drains the distant wastelands of their still calm. He leans over the nest, grabs the infant beast, bites its head off and spits it out and over the edge. *Aeos has no sons. Just another damn beast that eats and cries, shits and breeds. There is nothing new for us here. Only struggles.*

He takes the eggs from the nest and stands up.

No hope.

He lifts his arms to the air and unleashes a scream full of rage at the beast as he crushes the eggs in his palms.

No freedom.

The beast stops circling, dives straight down and descends upon him with fury in its cries.

No mother.

He covers his head as the beast flaps its wings, biting and scratching and tearing his flesh apart.

No father.

The eldest feels its talons deep in his shoulder. He reaches over his head, snatches the beast from its neck and slams it to the ground.

They're gone.

The beast tries to fly away but he shoves it back down. He swiftly grabs a rock the size of his fist and keeps smashing its wings until they break.

Gone.

With one hard, final strike, he crushes its head, ending its cries.

Gone.

He weeps, but the wind dries every tear. This world doesn't want them. He stays on his knees for a while trembling and hugs himself as the cold crawls under his skin, trying to drink his blood. It gets fiercer with every passing moment, punishing him for choosing to stay still. He straps the corpse of the beast to his waist and begins his descent with its broken wings hanging from his side.

Horos is the mountain. *Ra* is the sound this beast makes. The beast rules over the mountain. He lets the two words hover naturally over his tongue, allowing enough distinction, so they can grow into a new sound.

A

Aeos' warmth dissipates and his shine sets over the mountain like orange skin. The wind has settled down. The treetops down the mountainside stand still as the youngest grows impatient. He has bitten away his fingernails down to the meat and has scratched the skin red under his infant beard. It will be dark soon and his brother has yet to return.

Up here, even the slightest noise becomes intense. He throws another stone down the mountainside, the last of many. The mountain echoes every knock of every roll the stone takes before it disappears through the trees below. If the world has a tongue, it speaks in echoes. A calm voice over the harsh land, soothing to the ear. A peace that matches the stillness and the fading colors of the evening.

But if you focus hard enough, you can hear the true, pretentious tone of the mountain. If you close your eyes and allow your ears to grasp at the farthest sounds they can find, you can hear the howls and the squeals lurking under the lie of peace. The hunters and the hunted, trading lives.

He hears water sloshing. The faintest of sounds but constant. A stream it might be, somewhere to his left, not too far from where he is now, hidden in a mess of awkward cliffs and stubborn paths. His brother will need water when he comes back. He will be back and he will be tired, thirsty and joyful after finally reaching the mountain's peak. He will be back.

The youngest follows the sound of water to what seems to be a very unfriendly side of the mountain. Steep, with no clear pathways. Now the trees have thinned and he can gaze far over the mountainside and into the wastelands of his past. Everything appears so tiny from this height. The hills and valleys are dull and still, like markings on the stone, but lacking his brother's peculiar way of breathing life into the lifeless and movement where things should be unmovable. He always had a way of making things more interesting than what they really are.

Flat, thorny bushes grow over unstable soil, rocky and moist, easy to slip and lose balance. No way to pass without using his hands as an extra pair of feet. He crawls and slides across until he reaches the bottom of a small cliff. He finds water running down from its lower side, splashing on the rocks and gradually spreading into many small streams, splitting further and further away from each other the lower down the mountain they flow.

He climbs up the cliff and finds the water pouring out of a massive wall of rocks. It flows straight through some cracks on its lower part, while the upper side seems dry. The space between the wall and the edge forms a narrow, steep path, no wider than three men standing side by side, leading straight to the highest end of the cliff. There he finds an opening. A cave's mouth, at least three times his size in both height and width. A clearing of nothing but low grass just ahead of the cave leads to a crag extending high over the mountainside. He walks close to the edge of the crag and looks down at the bottom of the cliff he came from. Not too high, maybe five or six times his height distance from the bottom of the cliff to the edge of the crag, but utterly precipitous, challenging even for the most agile beasts. The side path he took to get here seems to be the safest way to reach the cave.

The sound of water he has been tracking is now fierce and clear and coming from inside this cave. A warm breeze is rushing out of its blackened mouth as if the mountain breathes through it. A cave with water flowing inside it is the best shelter anyone could ever hope for, but the youngest unties his spear from his back and approaches the cave with worry and caution. The breeze carries a smell from the cave's dark depths. The mountain's breath stinks of rot.

Aeos' light fades behind him as he enters the cave. A flock of winged creatures sweeps across the roof and sends him down to his knees covering his ears. Loud and nasty black beings screeching and raging over his head before gliding out in the open. He gives his pounding heart a moment to settle down, then continues to venture deeper into the growing darkness of the cave.

His shadow dissolves. It's getting much warmer. The sound of water smashing into water obscures any other sound. The stench grows. The tight grip he has on his spear gets tighter.

A few more steps ahead, the cave's passage expands into a wide space, sealed all around by jagged and uneven walls. Light bursts inside from a large hole on the roof at the very end, from which pouring water enters the cave and enough light shines through. His eyes adjust quickly. The water runs wild and forms a pond stretching across the far wall, covering almost half the cave itself. It keeps flowing through the walls to his left, probably feeding the streams he came across earlier from some cracks below the water surface. It's a beautiful sight. A perfect shelter, at first sight.

The stench comes from the right side of the cave, where the floor breaks into another higher layer of flat stone. There he finds the insides of many scattered all over. The severed heads of beasts, large and small, grass-eaters and man-eaters. Piles and then piles of bones, stripped from all flesh and meat. The whole stone is covered by a skin of dry blood. A killer's home of slaughter.

The youngest bites his lips at the sight of all this gore, regretting the moment he stepped foot in this cave. Something has already made a home of this cave. Something that can kill anything and anyone. It eats everything but the bones and the heads. Not much meat on a head, by far the most useless part.

Coming here was a mistake. I should leave. He turns and heads towards the exit and no more than a few steps later and just as he's about to quicken his pace, he stops. A roar, coming from outside, fills the cave with the threat of something large and heavy on its way here. His legs turn into dead sticks. Every strand of hair on his body stands. A shadow appears on the wall at the cave's passage. He takes a few backward steps, never taking his eyes off the looming shadow. As the shadow grows, his feet meet water. After a moment of hesitation, he retreats further into the pond and doesn't stop until the water reaches his waist. He kneels, bringing the water level just under his nose. He's shivering all over. The cold water covers him like new skin.

The shadow creeps from the wall down to the ground. The beast enters the main area of the cave. It purrs and hums as it heads to its slaughtering ground. A powerful, massive body hiding under light-colored fur, with a bushy mane falling over its broad shoulders and another small beast hanging from the sides of its blood-drenched jaws. A man-eater that kills man-eaters.

The youngest tracks the beast with widened eyes. His trembling breath is skimming the water's surface. The beast leaps on the flat stone with ease, drops its dead prey and hops back down again near the pond's shore. It takes a few sips of water and halts as if the water could speak to it. It raises its head and catches the youngest in a direct stare.

Its eyes glow, cold and rough like a smooth stone, slicing light. Its sharp stare can make your heart stop beating before its teeth and claws can rip it out of your chest. The youngest goes numb. He'd ask for pain just to feel his own body again. The beast glowers at him, stripping his mind naked of all courage. How many hunters lost their pride in its jaws? How many lives lie trapped under its claws? The brief moment of its stare feels everlasting, for he can hear their screams in its long sniffs. The desperate cries of so many other fools like him. The slow and the weak, forever caught in its impenetrable gaze.

The beast releases an ear-crushing roar. The youngest jumps back and slips on the rocks. He falls underwater in panic, sinking in a pond black with terror. He loses himself in the confusion of his own frenzy, choking on water, desperate for balance.

He rises to the surface, coughing out water like vomit and finds himself with his back against the wall. The beast is walking back and forth down the pond's shore, growling and breathing heavily, shaking its mane and scratching the ground with its paws. It roars forward, raging towards the youngest and pounding its feet in the shallow waters, but the moment water comes splashing all over its mane, it pulls itself back and continues walking up and down the shore.

The youngest finds some calm when he sees the beast reluctant to advance beyond the shallows. Water is all that separates them and it seems to be enough, remarkably so. He hears a recurring knock at the end of the pond to his right where the flow of water carries everything—his spear afloat, banging against the wall. He looks around. The rocks are climbable, leading up to the hole in the roof. He leaves his spear behind and starts the slippery climb while the beast returns to its prey, lays its forelegs on its chest and takes a few hefty bites.

The crackling sound of its teeth smashing the prey's ribs rattles the cave as the youngest continues to climb. He stops midway to catch his breath and looks down at the beast. Disappointment drags his breathing. *Fools we are.*

There's nothing for us here. Nothing but the ways of the old. The light comes pouring down shame over him. For being a part of this world. For coming here, looking for a new way. *Am I saving myself now,* he wonders, *or am I heading to my downfall? Is this why we came here? A life of running and hiding and crawling and eating the rot off the scraps of the land and drinking from its piss-full ponds. All this to get here and for what?* He starts rubbing the bone of sickness dangling from his neck. *For the chance to keep running and hiding? To keep crawling through holes of light leading to the same old struggles, begging of vile creatures to grant us a silent death, for there is nothing else to hope for. Nothing more to strive for.* He pulls the bone and cuts the straps from around his neck.

No... I want more.

He climbs back down into the water and unseals the bone. Relieved to see no water has found its way in, he moves with caution to the edge of the pond, grabs his spear, rubs the sharp stone on the wall until it's dry and covers its tip with the sickness. He stares at the beast, contemplating. The fangs of the snakes he has been harnessing the sickness from are half a finger long. That's how deep he must pierce its skin. The cave is too dark to aim from afar with precision. The water makes his legs wobbly, challenging to keep his balance. The beast, being aware of his presence, is too unpredictable. If he throws his spear and misses, he loses everything.

The beast is ripping through the insides of its prey. The knocking starts. Steady knocks, repetitive and provocative. Out of the pond and now standing right at the edge, the youngest is pounding the ground with the bottom of his spear.

You are the fastest and the strongest in a land that favors only the fast and the strong. I am just another prey for you and the head of a prey is worthless to you, for the meat around the skull is rough and thin. So go ahead.

Come and take what you yearn of me if you can and leave my head and my bones to rot. But know this. I'm not here for your meat, your fur or your bones. I'm here for glory.

Water splashes as spear strikes stone.

I want your head.

His eyes speak of challenge, demanding the beast's attention. His mind sharp, repeating one thought. *Stab half a finger deep, then jump in the water. Half a finger deep and jump in the water. Stab and jump in the water.*

With jaws soaked in blood and a mouthful of meat, the beast leaps off the flat stone and roars to the challenge. The youngest rushes back into the pond where the beast is reluctant to chase him. It halts for a moment as its paws meet water. The youngest tightens his grip, aims, takes a few steps to gain speed and screams his throat dry as he stabs the raging beast in the side of its neck.

The tip of the spear snaps instantly. The beast moans and gets rid of the sharp stone stuck in its neck with a swipe of its paw, giving the youngest a breath's chance to jump back into the deepest area of the pond. The beast leaps through the air with the force of a mountain and plunges into the water faster than anything the eye can track. The sheer power of its charge sends waves crashing all over the youngest as the beast's rage grows stronger than its dislike for water.

He thought the pond could protect him. How wrong he was. He fights against the waves to reach the rocks, but the beast is too fast, even in water. One giant leap and it comes within reach of him. Too far away from the rocks, he has nowhere else to go except down. He holds his breath and goes under with his back touching the rocky bottom, hoping the beast can't dive. The beast sinks its head to take a bite. Its jaws can't find him, but its claws can. Swipes of its paws tear the flesh on his arms and chest and when he whirls away, its claws get tangled with his long hair. He's struggling and choking and swallowing his screams. Every swipe is anguish. Water keeps most of the beast's weight afloat and slows down its attacks, but its claws are long and sharp. Whenever they find flesh, they rip straight through it. Red is all he sees. Violent waves of pain and water take turns suffocating him. Heart pounding a storm of memories. He can't hold his breath any longer. The beast keeps swiping and cutting him, but its attacks are getting weaker. Loud roars turn to muffled groans. He slides away from its reach and bursts out of the water near the shore. He spits out all the water and takes in the fullest breath of his life as he crawls out of the pond. The beast comes after him, but the power in its legs is gone. It moans and stumbles, trying to get out of the water. The youngest rushes to take the broken tip of his spear and sees blood all over its sharp edge, a finger long. He sees the beast, aching and struggling to get out of the pond. Its jaws are trembling. Its shiny stare lost behind dull, half-lidded eyes.

Overwhelmed by oozing wounds, the youngest stumbles around the cave, waiting to see if the beast can track him. It seems lost and dazed, unable to hold its own weight. It charges at him with just a shadow of its true strength. He gets a hold of its neck and stabs it under the jaw. The beast moans and stands on its back feet, shoving its claws in his shoulders as he sinks the stone deeper in its throat and drags it down on its back. Blood flows like mountain streams from the deep wounds on his shoulders. He keeps stabbing the beast in the neck while it keeps swiping its paws and ripping his flesh. Man and beast bleed each other till there's no way to tell which gush of blood comes from whom or where. The youngest screams in agony, landing one ferocious stab after the other until the beast stops moving. Its paws collapse to the ground, but the youngest doesn't stop. He takes the stone in both hands and keeps stabbing its throat, screaming and raging and stabbing harder and harder until he can lift his hands no more.

The blood-drenched stone hits the ground. He falls on his back, utterly exhausted, shivering from head to toe. The bright from the roof has already faded into an evening blur. He dips his hands in his soaked pelts, looking for the blood of the trees and the plants that can treat wounds. All he finds is a muddy mush. Pain follows his every move like the grass follows water. No way to make it through the bleeding if he stays here. He must return to his brother but can't even lift his back away from the floor, let alone stand up.

He stares at the cave's roof, wondering whether to die is to sleep forever. Soon his eyelids become too heavy to lift. The darkness comes soothing. The sound of water falling on water. The cold touch of the cave's rock-strewn floor. Cold as still as time.

Sweat. Pain. The familiar sting of ants mending his flesh. The scratchy warmth of wounds stuffed with the blood of trees all over his body. A hand caresses his forehead, gently slapping his cheeks a few times.

The youngest opens his eyes halfway. The eldest looks at him and smiles, just as the dim evening light flees from his face and on its trail, the night settles. The youngest tries to speak but a groan is all he can mutter.

"Shush delf," the eldest says. "Sy zon, keme."

"Te? Pos elthe sy?"

"Hyda ous." The eldest taps his ear a few times. "Hyda ous, ore en spelaon."

"Ore… ore therios en spelaon."

"Nae, mon ore." The eldest points with a nod of his head to the dead beast lying a few steps next to them. "Leondas."

"Leon—das?" says the youngest in a faint voice. The young night allows him one decent look at the beast before it swallows the last of the evening's dim breath. The waterfall gathers the faint light left in the sky and paints the walls around him with shades born from the pond's waves.

The eldest smiles. "Nae, leondas." This is the word for *lion,* the lake's teeth. "Keme delf, oun lale." He places a pelt under his brother's head, urging him to sleep. He cuts a piece of meat from the lion's thigh and just as he's about to take a bite, the youngest stops him with a shout of worry.

"Oun pafs," the youngest says. He first tries to grab the bone of sickness from around his neck but then instantly remembers he had taken it off before. "Fis delf, fis. Fis es creas leonda nekron." *The meat carries the sickness. I have no idea what will happen if we eat it.*

The eldest tosses the piece of meat and moves away from the lion.

"Te?" The youngest points at a weird, dead beast with wings hanging from the eldest's side, wondering about it.

The eldest takes a moment to think. "Hieras," he speaks.

This is the word for *hawk.*

ΛΓΕ

Branches of light lit the dark sky in rapid, consecutive strikes. Their deafening roars can humble the bravest of hearts. A furious wind runs through the mountainside as if chasing prey over swaying treetops.

Standing outside the cave, the eldest is gazing far as livid clouds overwhelm the mountain. All that was once green and blue has turned grey. He reaches out, palm facing upwards, embracing the first drops of rain with a sense of melancholy in his stare. It has taken most of his life to get here, only to find the heavens still mocking him. As far beyond reach as they have ever been. *You can never come to us,* they say with every drop of rain, *but we can always come to you.*

Another strike of light rips the sky apart. A flash so intense, it steals his vision for a while. The woman they found in the fields comes to mind. *Branches of light falling from the heavens,* he ponders. *Her clumsy ways make sense now.*

A rumbling blast makes him cover his ears. The world turns pure white in a glance. The sky spits jagged flashes of light that cut through the clouds, crashing deep amongst the trees at the side of the mountain far opposite the crag. The eldest ducks and covers his head, fearing the white light has just cracked the world in half. Light appears on the ground where the strike hit. Yellow and bright like Aeos. On the ground.

That's... not possible. He blinks a few times, struggling to believe his own eyes. *Light only lives in the sky.*

He rushes back to the cave to grab his spear and some pelts. Two days have passed since they settled here. He finds the youngest, still hurting but getting stronger, sitting by the pond holding the lion's head in between his thighs. He wants to keep it. He has ripped off its lower jaw and emptied its skull through the hole of its neck. Now he's wiping off the remaining brains stuck inside with fresh water and clean pelts. The eldest grabs everything he needs and instructs his brother to stay in the cave, but the youngest grabs his things, eager to follow him.

The eldest stands at the edge of the crag in awe of the impossible becoming possible before his eyes. The light is a tree of blinding violence growing fast. There's a dark cloud rising from it as if trying to reach its brothers in the sky. As the youngest scuffs to his side, he gasps at the sight of light growing in the trees. The eldest taps his brother's head and instructs him to get back in the cave. There will be no debate. He sees in his brother's eyes the same childish sense of adventure that almost got him killed a few days ago. He doesn't know what dangers await in the light. All he knows is that his brother is still too weak to either run or fight if they must. So he heads down the mountainside alone, leaving behind the youngest, utterly fixated on the light.

Trees sway, humbling themselves before a wind strong enough to scatter thick bushes. His breaths fill with the fresh smell of the coming storm as he tracks the rising dark cloud under the constant pattering of infant raindrops. He could still tell it was daytime from the cave, for Aeos finds ways to puncture the dark clouds suffocating the sky. But down here, walking through the dense trees, the darkness thickens and the night comes early.

He walks at a fast pace but cautious of his surroundings. Glimpses of light appear far ahead, behind the blackened trunks of trees whose shadows fall towards him. All sounds of the mountain vanish. A crackling, whooshing sound, hectic and violent, takes over. He feels warmth over his whole body and for a moment, he's a child again sleeping in mother's arms. As he gets closer, the warmth grows as the light grows, now reminiscent of the hot days hunting out in the fields with no shelter.

Pass the trees, the area clears. He drops his spear and stands open-mouthed at the sight of pure, raging light. Blinding violence engulfing a tall tree, leaping like wild hair off the back of a running beast as dying branches and twigs tumble to the ground all around him. Wooden corpses. Wherever they fall, they spread light. Smoldering, tattered flashes of intense heat moving rampant, destroying everything they touch. Relentless and famished, devouring the green of the grass and the bushes and belching out black clouds.

Mother? Father? Is that you?

The air chokes him. The clouds carry an acrid smell. He's sweating as if he never stopped running since birth. The light is too intense, too ferocious for his eyes to focus on. It punishes him for staring too long, just like Aeos. Shadows slither against the surrounding tree trunks, fighting each other like dark creatures with no form.

"Delf?"

His brother's voice startles him and he turns, thinking the shadows have come to life creeping up on him from behind. The youngest, too curious for his own good, walks towards him past the trees, with new heights of astonishment pouring out of his wide-open mouth. The eldest sighs and shakes his head at the sight of his brother. Momentary anger turns to relief.

They stand by each other's side, admiring and fearing the mayhem unfolding. Power overwhelming. The absolute destruction of everything. To be a man is to be afraid of the dark, for no man is born to live in the dark. Now lies before them the killer of darkness. The nightmare even nightmares dread.

The eldest tries to match the sound he hears coming from the light with a spontaneous roll of the tongue. "Fos," he speaks. This is the word.

"Fos delf?"

"Nae. Fos." This merciless, glorious thing or creature or state, hissing and roaring as it destroys everything it touches. A new word for a new thing.

The eldest signals his brother to stay back. He approaches the light reluctantly, with slow, measured steps. He gets close to one of the fallen branches covered with light and reaches out to touch it. He can feel the heat growing at the tips of his fingers. He tries to caress its bright leaping tongues, but the heat hurts him. He falls back stunned, groaning and holding his hand. The pain of a bite or a stab, he's not sure. A new kind of hurt.

He tries again, not to touch the light this time, but to lift the whole branch instead. The light has yet to spread to its edge. The wood is warm but not harmful. He manages to lift it and hold it tight with both hands like a short, shining spear. He keeps it upright and the light starts spreading downwards, crawling towards his hands as if it can't stop feeding and it won't stop feeding until there's nothing left in the world to devour. His eyes glow as bright as the light. He shakes and twists and turns the branch, trying to see if he can control it. It soon reaches his hands, so he drops it before the heat hurts him.

"Elthe delf," says the youngest, asking for his attention. The youngest breaks a small branch from a healthy tree and dips its edge in the light. Fos leaps to it with ease, first at the size of a glowing fist, but grows stronger fast, slithering down the shape of the branch. They cannot touch Fos, but it seems they can carry it from branch to branch.

The eldest cautiously picks up the branch from his brother's hand. He notices the raindrops make a hissing sound as they fall in the light. It reacts by switching into even more jittery shapes as if annoyed by their presence. He finds a muddy spot on the ground with no grass, lays the branch there and waits. The light gradually fades away, struggling to spread over the dirt. He lifts it high and watches as the raindrops beat down on the fading light until there's no more left. The light is gone. Water hurts it. A storm is about to fall over their heads.

We need to move now.

The eldest sets a branch alight while the youngest gathers more sticks and bushes. They rush back through the woods, moving from tree to tree, using them as shelter from the rain. Whenever the light spreads too close to the eldest's hands, they move it to a new branch.

They reach the cliff right under the cave. There are no more trees left between them and the cave above, so they strip themselves naked of their pelts while heading up the path on the side of the cave's wall. The eldest carries the light with one hand, holding fresh branches with the other, ducking under the roof of pelts the youngest holds steady over his head. The wind torments them, but it somehow breathes strength in the light, helping it spread faster down the branch. The few drops of rain that pass through the torn pelts have little effect.

They stumble over slippery rocks, grunting their way up the path as the rain becomes relentless. The eldest remains low under the cover his brother provides, struggling to keep the light alive and confined while switching branches on the move. The light, too unpredictable in its movement, jumps on his hair and beard and hurts him. He picks up wet mud from the ground, covers his face and wipes the light off his hair.

By the time they reach the cave, the storm is thrashing the mountainside. The youngest can barely stand and the eldest is holding a near-dead branch in his hand with the light gasping on its last breaths.

He hurries inside the cave and lays it carefully on the ground before rushing back to the entrance, where bushes lay scattered along the walls. Small but dry, deep enough inside the cave so the storm can't reach them. No more light is coming from the woods. A dark cloud dissolves in the rain. He rips some of the bushes from the ground and carries them back into the cave. He takes a handful of leaves and small sticks and one by one, he drops them over the fading light. With every leaf, the light grows strong again, then retreats ever so slightly. Always demanding more.

The eldest sighs in relief and smiles at his brother. The youngest is sitting in the corner of the cave, where the cold breeze can't reach, shivering, drying himself with the lion's fur. Some of his shoulder wounds have split open.

"Fos delf, elthe," the eldest says, inviting his brother to come close to the light's warmth. He takes the fur from him, hovers it over the light until it gets warm, then squats down behind him and lays it over his back. He hugs him tight over the fur until he shivers no more.

"Aeos omio Fos," he whispers to his ear. He brings both his arms over the youngest's shoulders, points to the light and brings his hands together, joining his fingers in the shape of the mountain, with the light in the center. "Ama apa es Fos."

He shuffles his brother's hair and gets up. He cares for the light, throwing handfuls of leaves and sticks in its hot bowels as it grows and grows and grows…

The same way the glow in his eyes grows and grows and grows….

Φ

The days rush into the nights as dark clouds plunge the mountain in full shade. The cold is persistent, getting harsher. Storms have drenched the mountain's skin. The brothers struggle to adjust, coming from the hot drylands, where every rare drop of rain was like a hug from Aeos. The mountain's erratic weather has changed everything they know about the way of the hunt.

The mud gathers tracks with ease, but one must hurry, or the rain will wash them away. It used to take all day, or sometimes even days, to find a kill. Here the way of the hunt is different. Tracks or no tracks, if you follow one of the countless, endless streams running down the mountainside, you will eventually find prey along their shores. What was once so rare only the strongest and the cunning could claim, now lies so abundant and common all creatures can share.

Three days have passed since the light came to them. The brothers get more familiar with its wonders every day. The first night was just pure admiration. Enjoying the warmth it emits, scratching their heads in confusion and wiping their eyes in disbelief. The eldest is more concerned with nurturing it, like a third brother, while the youngest is more occupied with learning its secrets and controlling it, like a tool. The light turns everything into white dust and never stops wanting more. It holds many ways and is willing to share them all, just as long you keep feeding it.

All the bushes outside the cave are no more. The brothers have gathered all the grass down the cave's path, all the tall plants creeping over its outside walls, leaving behind nothing but mud and stone. As much dry food the light needs, it demands twice as much when food is wet. Now they must gather bushes and branches from the woods below the crag.

Fos must always be nurtured, so the brothers sleep by taking turns. When one must hunt or gather, the other stays behind to keep it safe.

It's the youngest's turn to watch the light. His brother left at dawn to gather all the wood needed for the day. A lot of wood. The storm outside has settled down. Clouds still hold the sky captive, but Aeos finds paths to shine through them. All is wet and muddy and finding anything dry is a difficult task. His brother must hurry or else they risk losing the light.

The youngest is feeding the light as much as he's feeding his curiosity. He already knows dirt can stop it from spreading and water can outright kill it. He tosses a stone in the light. After a while, he drags it out using two sticks. The stone is hot, darker in color now, but hasn't lost its shape. It seems it can withstand the light's power more than anything else. It might even be able to keep it confined.

He picks up a few rocks the size of a fist from outside, takes them back to the cave and places them in a circle around the light. He then drops a small patch of fur in its bright grasp. It instantly grows vivid and furious but calms down soon after. The branches seem better at keeping it alive longer, but fur helps it grow faster. *Interesting,* he thinks.

Meat comes next. He cuts a piece of meat from the grass-eater his brother brought from the hunt yesterday and throws it in. The light goes wild making hissing noises. The scent it excretes catches his attention. He takes a deep breath over the light and amongst the bitter smells of dead wood and white dust, he finds a new pleasure. A delightful smell. He pulls the meat out, now harsh and dark, as if he cut a chunk from the night's thigh. The pleasure in the air is gone. It stinks of white dust. If he had left it a little longer, the light would have probably turned it into white dust too. But that smell…

He takes a small branch from the last remaining bush, sticks a piece of meat on its edge and hovers it over the light. This time he won't let the light too close. Just close enough to hear the hissing sound again and long enough to force out that enticing smell. The meat slowly darkens in color, blistering and scrunching and soon it releases the scent he wants. He pulls it away, brings it close to his nose, takes a long sniff and rejoices.

He wonders about the taste of it but hesitates to take a bite, for the same reason he has yet to eat the lion's meat. The lion's corpse should have stunk the place with rot by now and it baffles him why it hasn't. Meat spoils slower up here. He will throw it away once it starts to smell, but he needs to find out somehow if the sickness kills you when you eat the carrier. He has an idea, but he must fully heal first. It's a risky idea and he doesn't want to involve his brother, who is often very judgmental of his ways.

He keeps sniffing the meat. The scent makes him hungry, even with a full belly. *The light hurts whatever it touches. What if the meat carries the light, like the lion's meat carries sickness? What happens when the light crawls inside you?*

Despite his worries, the scent is too enticing, so he finds the courage to take a small, reluctant bite. He chews and the meat turns into mush in his mouth with astonishing ease. It has a grand taste. A warm, deep flavor. Every bite makes his jaw shiver. He swallows with an urge to close his eyes and to keep them shut. Just to revel in the moment.

He thinks of his brother and how grueling it has been for him to eat, especially meat, often swallowing whole chunks of it and choosing the hurt of the belly over the hurt of the teeth. He remembers the joy he felt as a child every time he saw his brother coming home from the field. Safe, holding water or prey or sometimes nothing, but it never mattered. Nothing, coming from his brother, was still a joy for him. That's what the meat tastes like. The joy of a loved one returning home.

He has endured many sufferings, yet he knows of no heavier burden than the one his brother has had to carry by having a child under his care. The youngest can look back on his childhood and see glimpses of joy, all because of his brother, who suffered every beating, every malice, every ill chance of luck this unforgiving land has had to offer. For food and water and to keep him safe, always. No matter how hard any given day was, he always felt safe by his side.

This is my chance to make my brother happy.

"Deeeelph therios!" The eldest comes rushing back into the cave, yelling a warning of beasts, dropping branches left and right in panic.

Just as the youngest gets to his feet, a pack of man-eaters storms the cave. Five of them, with fur black to match their eyes and slavering mouths, growling and howling. The youngest takes a thick branch of light and starts thrusting it towards them, waving it close to the ground. The beasts shuffle their feet and hold their charge, unwilling to get any closer. Fos keeps the beasts at bay, giving the eldest a chance to take a fiery branch of his own.

The eldest dashes towards them, shouting, waving around the fiery branch and kicking white dust in their eyes. The beasts get agitated with discomfort, scared even. He forces them further back towards the cave's entrance.

"Pafs," says the youngest and signals his brother to hold his charge for a moment. The eldest looks at him with a query and the youngest gestures for him to stay calm. It's time to test his idea.

He slices a large piece of sick meat from the lion's belly and tosses it at the feet of one of the nervous beasts.

"Te?" asks the eldest.

The youngest wiggles the bone hanging from around his neck and tilts his head. *Let's see if they get sick.*

The beast takes a few sniffs at the meat and starts eating. The youngest throws another chunk of meat to one of the others. Then another. Once enough time passes by without any sign of the beasts getting sick, the youngest chuckles. It's time to get rid of them.

He tries to strike one but overextends his spear and misses. One of the other beasts jumps at him and bites his leg before he has a chance to withdraw his spear and he falls to the ground moaning, while another beast jumps over him. He covers his head and the bones strapped around his arms take the bites for him.

The eldest comes to his aid shouting and beats them down with the light and scares them off him. He bashes them hard, burning their furry backs and chases them out of the cave. The last one stumbles down the cave's passage with light dashing from its shoulders, groaning and wailing its way outside.

Another deep wound to recover from and another lesson learned. The youngest limps to the pond, leaving behind a trail of blood in his path. The eldest drops the fiery branch in the circle of stones along with some other sticks and bushes.

The youngest's mind runs wild as his brother takes care of his wound. He can't even look him in the eyes, for he knows his brother's frowning gaze will slash straight through him if he does.

How could I be so careless? A few days ago, I killed a lion. The fastest and the strongest of all living things in the world. What went wrong today? How did a pack of slower, weaker beasts get the best of me? His brother ties a piece of fur tight around his wound to stop the bleeding. A rush of pain silences his inner voice. As the pain settles, he realizes the answer lies hidden in the question—a *pack* of beasts.

The sickness is effective against the loners, but the packs are more dangerous than any other beast on its own. Their strength is in numbers. Even if you manage to strike one, the rest leave you no chance for a second move. The light can keep their home safe, but they can neither track nor hunt prey with it. It draws too much attention from too far away. The only reason he's still alive is because of his brother. What if this pack of five had been of six or seven, or ten or more?

His brother helps him sit by the light, then cuts a piece of meat from the grass-eater to eat, with the youngest still gathering his thoughts.

"Oun delf," says the youngest and holds him off from eating it raw. He takes the meat from his hands and shows him the effect the light has on it instead.

The eldest takes his first bite and the youngest smiles at the sight of great relief across his brother's face. The eldest tracks his teeth with his fingers looking for blood and finds none. His lips are trembling. Eyes get watery. Unable to utter a single word, he wipes the tears sliding down his rough cheeks and covers his face. Shivering hands match the shiver in his breathing.

Their foreheads meet as the youngest brings his hands around his head and hugs him. They share the moment, which might be the only moment of true comfort the eldest has had in a long while. The last time his brother had an effortless meal, too far hidden in the past to remember. The habit of suffering is the hardest to unlearn, for even moments of joy are still painful, when pain is as part of you as your eyes or your limbs.

The youngest prepares another nice, warm piece of meat for his brother. The eldest eats slowly, relishing every bite as his last. Once he is full, he caresses the youngest's wavy hair and lays on his back to rest.

While the eldest sleeps, the youngest returns to his thoughts. He keeps nurturing the light, throwing one stick after another in the pile of branches, pondering over the finds of the day.

Fos the untouched. Fos, bringer of warmth and comfort. Fos, the killer of night, the one all can see in the darkness, even from a great distance. A strong beast is weak against a pack, for the many overcome the few. Loneliness is a path only fit for the strongest amongst us. The true strength of the weak is unity.

True strength lies in the numbers.

The thought of using the light as a sign sticks to his mind like dry blood over flesh. When the sky is clear, they could move the light outside and make a massive circle of stones close to the crag. If they keep the pile of branches large enough, men and women roaming the wastelands are bound to see it. Men will have its shine to lead them during the night and the dark cloud it sends to the sky during the day.

Men are cruel, but things have changed. Fos has changed everything. He imagines the mountain as the home of all men. Everyone coming together in numbers so great, they can finally claim this land as their own. A new way in an old world. The way of man and it all starts with Fos.

"Oun." That's all the eldest says after the youngest expresses his thoughts with combinations of gestures and words. That's all he says the second time the youngest tries to explain his reasoning. And the third. And every time the youngest asks for a reason why, he finds only silence in his brother's angry stare. "Oun delf. Pafs." The eldest tosses branches in the light with complete disregard of where they land, as if in a quarrel with the light itself.

"Te?" The youngest persists. He takes two small stones and knocks them together. "Bea lih," he says while tossing them from one hand to the other, showing the eldest how weak the two small stones are, how easy it is for him to throw them around. He then gathers more stones and starts counting them as if they were men. "Alfa aner, bea aner, gaa aner, dea, ene…" he gathers many of them in a pile so large he can no longer move them all together. Single stones move with ease. Make a large enough pile of them and stones become unmoveable.

The eldest throws another small branch in the light. It skims off the pile of wood and lands outside the circle of stones. He doesn't bother picking it up. Remains silent

Frustrated by his brother's resolve, the youngest starts walking in circles around the light. "Gyne elthe," he says, for he knows his brother loathes men, but he's also fond of women and the pleasures they hold. "Fos mega, gyne elthe horos."

The eldest stops throwing twigs in the light, looks to the youngest and starts patting his palm with the twigs. The youngest has caught his attention with the mention of women coming to the mountain. The youngest stays silent, giving his brother time to gather his thoughts. A long time goes by with nothing but awkward silence between them, so the youngest lies down to rest as the night unfolds, hoping his brother will change his mind by the time his turn comes to nurture Fos.

Deep into the night, the youngest wakes up. The light is gone. Dead. Left to fade, only blackened twigs and white dust remain within the circle of stones. His brother is missing. He jumps up in concern and moans as he tries to stand. The pain reminds him of the fresh wound he carries on his leg. The cave is the darkness of the old world. His brother never woke him up to take his turn. There's light coming from the cave's mouth. Wild shadows crawling and shifting on the walls.

He hobbles towards the entrance as fast as he can. A shadow looms over him as he moves down the cave's passage. He sees a black figure outside overwhelmed with light, his brother a shadow casting a shadow towards him three or four times his size. He steps outside. The eldest is standing with his back turned, facing the mountainside. Fos just ahead of him rising high, confined within a large circle of rocks, close to the edge of the crag. It grows in strength and fury, gathering the cold wind in its frantic, slithering tongues and snapping the tormented thick branches deep in its scorching belly.

"Delf te?" he wonders, but the eldest says nothing. The youngest limps to his brother's side. He looks at him and sees the stars in his eyes, his stare fixated on the light. A face as bright as dawn.

No words are spoken for a while. The youngest, unsure of how else to react, watches as the light grows to a height twice their own. The heat bursting out of it makes the cold night sweat.

"Fos mega," finally says the eldest and throws a few more branches in the light. "Nae delf, aner elthe horos."

The youngest smiles. The night has managed to change his brother's mind, but the eldest wipes his smile away instantly by lifting a finger of warning straight to his face. Men can come, but his brother seems to have a firm condition.

"Aner oun lave Fos," the eldest says. "Fos delf e mon e sy. Fos mega. Delf mega."

The youngest looks briefly over the crag at the total darkness covering the mountain, thinking of his brother's intentions of not letting other men take the light. *Why keep people in the dark, brother, when you can turn the night into day at will?*

The eldest lays a hand on the youngest's cheek and pulls his gaze back to him, demanding his attention. "Nae delf?" He points at his own two eyes with one hand, holding the youngest's chin firmly with the other, forcing direct eye contact. "Nae?"

The youngest nods and agrees to his brother's terms, feeling the grip on his chin getting stronger before the eldest finally lets him go. He watches as his brother starts chucking small twigs in the growing light, counting them as men. Men, eager to follow the bright sign at the top of the mountain.

"Alfa aner, bea aner, gaa aner…"

Twigs falling in the light, one after the other.

IIII

ARITHME

ONO

As the evening sets, the eldest heads back to the cave with a heavy load of branches strapped on his back, enough to keep the light strong for one more night. The hawk's skull lies strapped around his head, extending from his forehead; its wings fall on each side of his face, tangling up with his hair. Blood from a split lip runs down his long beard. Markings painted with white dust all over his face and body, covering the scars he hates the most.

He had to gather everything the light needs from the woods down the mountainside, for they have long stripped the slope below the crag of its green. Now only naked, thick trunks of trees still stand and if they could cut them down too, they would. Six times a day, they take turns and go out to gather wood—Fos demands it.

He shuffles his feet through the white dust covering the once green path leading up to the cave. All the grass and the shrubs around the cave, the colorful flowers and the creepers growing on its walls. All gone.

He stops by the giant pile of scorched wood at the edge of the crag and drops the fresh batch right next to it. White dust everywhere. Four whole pelts the light lays waste of it every day. At first, they were throwing the dust off the crag, letting the wind have its way with it. Then one day, the eldest thought of a better use for it.

He enters the cave, passing by shapes and figures and signs painted all over the entrance walls. Most drawn in black with dead wood; some in white with the light's dust. An old habit of his, reinvigorated by a fresh set of interesting tools at his disposal. It soon became clear the beasts despise the smell of white dust more than anything else. Their attacks on the cave had been frequent, tiresome for them to deal with, but the beasts have yet to return since he started painting. Sometimes he sees shadows at night lurking outside. He hears long whiffs, searching for the scent of meat and sweat and blood in the air, only to find the light's sour breath bursting through the cave's dark throat. The stench of scorched wood and flesh all over its walls.

The black he uses for signs mystical in form, for they are things no one can see in the world, birthed in the depths of his mind. Symbols that stand for all sorts of things: numbers, feelings, actions, attributes, sounds. An attempt to bring his words and paintings together under the shelter of a strict, consistent structure. He'd like to assign a word to everything there is to feel, hear and see. Every word to have its own sign. He imagines one day expressing his thoughts to his brother with clarity, silently, using just these signs. But that day is still far away, for there are too many things in the world still unassigned and only so little the mind can hold in a day.

The white he uses for his broad paintings, for it's easier to use and there's much more of it. Words and signs are great but limited by a strict condition—their meaning must be explained to you by someone who already understands them. So, the white dust marks the walls with things kind to a stranger's eye, like the shapes of many different beasts, man and Fos; Horos and its star, Horaste. Things he imagines one day, long after he's dead and gone, other men dwelling in the cave will be able to grasp their meaning at first sight.

Aeos' circle is the most lucid and yet the most time-consuming sign to make. Free of sides and corners, beginnings and endings, strict in its smooth curves and an action unbroken. The eldest has ascribed the same sign to represent time, for Aeos turns the day into night and without the switch from bright to dark, the world would be still and timeless. Father Aeos and mother time seem to share the same body and their lone child is the weather.

Cold weather. Warm weather. Each has its turn as ruler over the mountain. Trees shed their leaves, then flourish again. Back in the drylands, there was no noticeable change in the weather. Every day was as hot as the next, with rare and unpredictable exceptions. But here, all things around him run in cycles. Aeos' cycle lasts a day and a night; the weather's cycle lasts much longer.

Counting days is harsh. A word for every number up to ten is all he knew and that's all he ever taught his brother. There was never a reason to create new ones, for there was never a reason to count anything in such great numbers. Now they can track the weather and as many days pass from the warmth to the cold as there are trees on the mountain, it seems. It's easier to count the full moons, so he added two more words for two more numbers. Twelve is the last number of the world. Twelve full moons pass, from the time the first flower blooms, until the warmth and the cold have settled their argument and the flower blooms again.

Marked on the wall at the end of the corridor, leading to the main area of the cave, are the twelve faces of Selene—the full moon. Two complete cycles and one more face to start the current cycle. In a few days, he will add another with the arrival of the new full moon.

Fos welcomes him by casting his shadow on the wall. The black figure of the one who has the body of a man and the head of a hawk.

He finds his brother sitting by the pond, washing the lion's skull.

"Fos ex," says the youngest and points to a pelt on the floor close to Fos. "Lave creas emon peaeo." He sets the lion's skull firmly on his head and walks towards him. The light casts his shadow on the floor as he passes right by it. The black figure of the one who has the body of a man and the head of a lion.

The eldest sits close to Fos but not too close, for he needs its light more than he needs its warmth. His brother joins him. Warm chunks of meat lie primed on a pelt, so they eat. The pain in his teeth is bothersome still, but Fos has made it possible for him to eat in peace as much as he wants of whatever he wants with not much struggle. Moreover, the warm meat and the fruit of the mountain have induced great strength between their skin and their bones and he has grown stronger than his brother, for he eats more. A lot more. And so he carries more.

Once their bellies are full, the youngest picks up a long, fresh branch from a pile and sets it alight. They head outside walking side by side, with the youngest holding the fiery branch, casually tossing it from one hand to the other.

"Pafs delf," the eldest says, takes the branch away from his brother and smacks the back of his head. *Mother and father are one with the light, brother. When you disrespect the light, you disrespect them.* "Fos omio ama, omio apa. Sevo."

The youngest lowers his gaze. They resume their walk, with the eldest just ahead and the youngest following right behind him.

They reach the circle of stones at the edge of the crag. A young night skins the treetops from the faint remains of the evening haze and the dark comes to them fast and unforgiving. They clear the white dust from the circle of stones and place a large pile of fresh wood in the middle. The eldest sticks the fiery branch at the bottom while the youngest drops leaves and shrubs through the cracks, a small enticement for the light to find its way to the top.

Fos takes over the whole pile, dashing high to break through the dark's thick skin. Every night, the eldest watches his brother as he nurtures Fos with excitement, taking frequent glances over the crag, expecting men to arrive any day now. Every night the eldest takes white dust and paints over the scars on his body, hoping the day never comes. All he needs is a woman. Once a woman arrives, he will end this recklessness.

They eat some fruit and drink and play the game of stones they have been playing since childhood. It never gets old. They have been deprived of many things throughout their lives, but there has never been a shortage of stones.

It's the eldest's turn to throw. He must make at least three stones to fall from his pile, or else his brother wins. Long gone are the days he could win with ease, often losing deliberately to give his brother some joy. The youngest's aim has come to be as good as his own now, if not better; the game more fun and challenging than ever. He places one foot ahead of the other right on the edge of the line and just as the stone is about to leave his hand, a voice startles him and ruins his throw. A faint echo of a voice coming from down the mountainside.

Is it...? The eldest turns to his brother at once and sees the same astonishment in his stare. *It is.*

They rush to the edge of the crag and look down, trying to put a face to the voice they've just heard, but the night won't allow it. The voice persists, getting louder and closer. Silence must never be broken at night. Not out there where the light can't reach.

Soon after, the eldest sees a figure coming up the mountainside, pass the tall, shadowy trees and into the naked area underneath the crag where the bright of Fos makes the night seem like dusk. It gets closer. No, two figures—a man and a young boy. No woman.

The man raises his hands in the air and instructs the boy to do the same. He sighs and utters many words, of which the eldest understands none, but the man's relief and awe are evident in his tone.

"Aner delf, aner oda." The youngest points to the side of the cliff at his right, where the strangers can find the path to the cave and signals them to come up. He starts warming up two chunks of meat to welcome the man and the boy.

As his brother prepares the meat, the eldest keeps walking around Fos, back and forth in half circles. His narrowed gaze is fixated on the light. *Don't worry, mother, I won't let these beasts come anywhere near you.* He grabs his spear and starts dragging it through the dirt.

The moment the man and the boy reach the cave, they both cover their untested eyes from the bright of Fos. Strange words struggle to pass through gasps and lost tongues. A man typical of their kind—hairy, filthy and skinny—and so is the boy, though still too young to carry a beard. The youngest raises a hand and encourages them to come close to the light, but the eldest grabs his arm and stops him.

"Pafs," says the eldest. "Oun."

The youngest cocks his head. "Te?"

The eldest moves assertively towards the newcomers. The light casts his giant shadow over them as he points with his spear at the ground under their feet, a few steps before they reach the open area in front of the cave. "Pafs," he says with a stern voice, signaling them not to come any closer. He sees the man shifting his gaze from the light to the youngest to himself and back to the light like his eyes cannot decide which is more worthy of focus. The man falls to his knees weeping and drags the young boy down with him, who has had his eyes and mouth wide open since they came up the path. The man's body is nothing but skin and bones, covered in filth and old wounds, but the boy is scarless, well-sheltered. Their foreheads meet the ground as they bow before him. He hears no sorrow in the man's cries. Every tear speaks of deliverance and gratitude.

The youngest walks up to his side. The newcomers raise their heads at the sound of his steps and the boy reaches out to touch him, but the man holds him back and speaks words of fright in a trembling voice. The youngest calmly waves his hand up and down, showing the man it's safe for the boy to get closer. He reaches out as well, rests his palm over the boy's palm and the boy's face instantly shines with an awkward smile—the kind of smile that can't decide between fear and excitement. The man exults, wipes his eyes and rejoices when the youngest smiles back at the boy and shuffles his hair.

The eldest sees in them the same excitement he had when he was about to climb the mountain's peak for the first time. They both seem just as mesmerized by him and his brother as they are by Fos itself. His brother gives them each a piece of warm meat and their faces go bright with the light's favor. His mind dwells on the kind memories of their own first practices with the light, unravelling a new secret each day.

The youngest goes back to the cave and comes back soon after with a pelt of fresh water and some fruit. The man and the boy mutter strange words to each other while reveling in the joys of warm meat. When the youngest tries to give them some water, the eldest holds him off and takes the pelt from his hands. He wants the newcomers to speak his words.

He offers them the pelt. The man reaches out to take it, but the eldest pulls it back and pours some water in his palm.

"Hyda," he speaks. This is the word for *water.*

"Hyda," say the newcomers in one voice as they reach out and the eldest hands them over the pelt.

The eldest repeats the lesson again. More words follow. The newcomers repeat every word he says and he points at whatever every word stands for: Fos is the word for *light*, lih is for *stone*; aner is *man*, omma is *eyes*, arche is *head* and many more. Then they do the lesson again. And again, and again…

Well into the most unusual of nights, the eldest has grown from overly cautious to laying his spear down and enjoying teaching the newcomers the words of all they can see around them. Hearing his words uttered back to him with admiration and humility is a habit he can easily get used to. The night flies by quickly and not all words stick, but the eldest relishes every moment. The boy tries to pronounce another word and lets out a loud yawn instead and wipes his eyes. The youngest chuckles and looks to his brother for advice. The eldest shows them the area below the crag, for he has no intention of letting them sleep near the light—his one condition. There are small caves on the side of the cliff for them to find, good shelters for the night.

Before they leave, the boy repeats every word he has learned. He gets most of them right, but in the end, he points at the eldest and speaks a word that sounds like a question. He points at the youngest with the same inquiry.

The eldest stays silent, for the boy has caught him unprepared. There was never a need for names. They have always called each other *delf;* there was never anyone else to call out for. His lips move to say *aner*—that's what they are after all—but the word refuses to come out. Just doesn't feel right. Then he tries to say *delf* —that's how they call each other anyway— but once again, he hesitates. This word doesn't feel right either. Too generic for his liking. Finally, after a moment of deep thinking, he points at the youngest.

"Leondarche," he speaks—the man with a lion's head. This is the word from now on that will only belong to the youngest. Then, using the same logic, he points to himself and says, "Hierarche."

The boy tries to utter both words but struggles with them. The eldest realizes the names he has just come up with are hard to pronounce, hectic and unfriendly to the tongue. He looks to the mountain's peak and after another brief moment of silent contemplation, he picks up his spear, raises the boy's chin and makes him look straight into his eyes. "Leos," he speaks and guides the boy's gaze to his brother first, then back to himself. "Ra."

He finds the light in the boy's eyes and his own dark figure, reminiscent of the day he first saw his reflection in the lake. *So, it's possible to see yourself as others see you,* the boy in him thought back then. Now another boy stands before him with eyes soaked in the waters of dread and as bright and reflective as lakes of pure awe and Ra can't help but wonder:

What if others see a god in you?

Ω

Two weather cycles it took for the first man and his boy to arrive. And now, two full moons after their arrival, the two men became five. Faces grim. Bodies weak and scarred. Tongues soaked in incoherence. The brothers keep the light strong out in the open during the night. The guide of men in the dark. They keep it confined in the cave during the day when the mountain itself becomes visible again from afar. One brother rests, the other protects Fos. No one else gets close. No one. Ever.

A sign for every number up to twelve and then one more, marked on the wall opposite the faces of Selene. All are painted with the black of scorched wood. All except the last—the one beyond the twelve. Ra is almost done carving this number's unique sign. White dust is what it deserves. Just like Aeos is the one above all things, Ra imagines a number above all numbers. One sign to describe the end of all things. Gods, men, beasts… everything.

Leos is outside, nurturing the light. "Elthe delf," he shouts, "Fos mega, aner elthe lave creas." It's time.

Ra ignores him. The men will have to wait to receive their blessed meat this evening. The new number is almost done and he can't focus on anything else right now. It will represent the ultimate sum of all things. A circle that rises above all that exists. By far the most beautiful sign he has ever created—rightfully and intentionally so—for it's a critical sign, signifying the last and greatest number.

The rough, broken shapes and clumsy approximations he used to paint when he was young are no more. He's precise now. Methodical. He strives to make circles with smooth curves and perfectly straight lines. It takes more than just a steady hand to carve with precision through the stone's rough skin. It takes a sharp, uninterrupted stare. Discipline in the movement of the wrist. Utmost focus. And patience… most of all patience. And he must carve the stone first, for the paint alone fades after a while. A scarred impression he can always repaint with ease and much quicker. It has taken him three days to carve the sign with the kind of perfection he desired. No breaks in the curves. No stray lines.

Everywhere he looks, he sees numbers growing. Things too many to count in a lifetime. Whenever he tries to count the stars at night, he loses his sleep. The thought of how many specks of dust exist in the land brings him headaches. The overwhelming numbers of the mountain's trees. Every hair on every living creature. The vast swarm of raindrops in every storm. The world is crammed with too many things and not enough time for any mind to grasp, but just as one leads to two and then two leads to three, a trail of thought unfolds in his mind and leads to some inevitable conclusions.

Start at the lowest and count your way up. Start from a single speck of dust and let nothing escape your count until you reach Aeos. Let the one above all be the last in a trail of numbers so long no mortal mind can fathom and once there's nothing left to count in the world, behold— the number to end all numbers. A state of unbeing even gods fear, for even a god is something countable. Before this number, you can find a word, a sign, a number for anything. Beyond this number, you will find nothing. Emptiness. Absence. Loss. The number you encounter when all is revealed and everything becomes known.

What does one call the mega number? O, the sign of Aeos was the first sign I ever created. How should I name the number that rests above even the one who is above all? O, but more. Further. O, but greater. Om—

"Fos dide mega Leos," someone hollers from outside and breaks his concentration. "Fos dide," the man shouts a few more times and Leos is quick to hush him. Ra knows the voice—the first man.

How dare he raise his voice at my brother? Ra heads outside with annoyance in his pace and walks past the light without even glancing at it. He finds Leos standing at the edge of the crag, arguing with the man below whose voice keeps demanding more and more attention. Ra lays a hand on his brother's shoulder and looks down. The man is walking back and forth and waving a branch in the air, shouting so loud he gets the other men to gather around him. His son is following him around and pulling his arm back, trying to calm him down. Two of the three new men lower their heads at the sight of Ra and Leos. The other is reluctant to humble himself, seemingly agreeing with the man doing all the shouting. All three are still skinny and mumbling in the tongues of their past. Too stubborn to let the old ways go.

"Te?" says Ra.

Leos slightly raises his shoulder and looks at him with a pinched expression on his face. "Alfa aner oun pafs lale, Fos e mon, dide e ty."

Yes. Of course, he wants the light. Men always want to take from you all that you have. "Nae. Aner thele Fos. Thele hyda, thele creas. Aner thele, thele, thele." Ra walks along the edge of the cliff and back, caressing his forefinger with his thumb, watching the three men below grow in confidence.

"Pafs." Leos strikes the bottom of his spear and kicks dirt over the crag. "Pafs aner. Opiso." He instructs the man to fall back with an aggressive wave of his hand, but the man snubs him with an erratic wave of his own.

"Fos dide," the man keeps shouting, "Fos dide," and then continues with a trail of bizarre and ugly words from the old world. He just won't shut up.

Is it light you want? Ra raises a hand and gestures for the man to come up to them. "Elthe, lave Fos aner."

The man hustles across the bottom of the cliff towards the path and his son follows him. Ra scatters the giant pile of fresh branches the light has yet to devour, looking for something. "Delf," he says and beckons Leos over.

"Te peaeo?"

Ra keeps tossing sticks and branches aside. A quick snap and he turns to Leos holding a small stick cut from a thornbush. He breaks a thorn off it and throws the rest in the light. "Dide e mon, delf."

"Dide te?"

Ra points at the sickness hanging from Leos' neck.

Leos hesitates for a moment and takes a few steps back. "Aner arche omio lih," he says with a feeble, drawn-out chuckle and rapidly knocks the side of the lion's skull on his head a few times. "Esy Hierarche, emon Leondarche, aner ety Liharche. Meida, nae?"

Liharche... the one whose head is made of stones. Funny. "Meida," Ra says, but he's not laughing. *This will be this fool's name from now on.* He nods for his brother to hand over the sickness once again. This time his sharp stare leaves no room for arguments.

Leos gives Ra the sickness and withdraws to the edge of the crag just as Liharche comes forth from the path, mumbling and waving a branch at them. The boy comes dashing behind him soon after and tries to pull him back, but Liharche shoves the boy away.

Ra ignores them at first. He turns his back at them and dips the thorn in the sickness, places it in-between the roots of two of his fingers and keeps it hidden in a loose fist. He then turns and hails them. "Elthe Liharche," he says. *Come little man. Come and claim Fos.*

"Liha—te?" Liharche is slow to approach. His gaze is dashing left and right, a baffled look on his face. The boy follows in his every step, but Leos reaches out and drags him away from his father. He brings his arms over the boy's shoulders and keeps him confined in his care, with his hands crossing over the boy's chest. The boy moans and struggles to break free but his father signals him to stay put and the boy does as he's told.

Ra shows off the light to Liharche with one hand moving down from its scorched belly all the way up to the highest of its blazing tongues and encourages him to come closer. "Lave," he says and brings the same arm around Liharche's shoulder, guiding him within a grip of the light, closer than any other man of the ones below has ever come before.

Liharche tries to wipe the light's bright from his eyes and takes a few steps back, but Ra gives him a slight nudge, encouraging him to get closer.

I know, little man, it took my eyes a while to adjust too. Mother is kind to her children, but you're not a child of her, are you now? I know your kind well and so does she. Ra keeps Liharche just ahead of him, both gazing at the light in all its might. *If you stare long enough, she will bleed the darkness in you.*

Liharche reaches out to caress the light but instantly withdraws his hand and when he tries to turn around, Ra shoves him forward, takes a firm grip of his wrist and pokes him with the thorn. Liharche moans for a moment but Ra is quick to distract him and forces him to dip the branch in the light. He keeps one hand on Liharche's shoulder, squeezing, controlling him, the other never letting loose of his wrist. Once the branch goes ablaze in his hands, Liharche gasps with excitement as Ra releases his wrist and guides him towards the edge of the crag.

"Opiso delf," Ra says to Leos, who is standing in their way. "Aner thele ore."

Leos won't move. He lets the boy hurry to his father.

Ra leaves Liharche waiting and walks up to Leos. He grabs his hand, lays the blood-drenched thorn in his palm and points with a tilt of his head at Liharche. "Ore delf. Aner nekron es, aner zon exo." Ra chuckles. "Meida, nae?" He sinks his toenails in the ground to gather some dirt and kicks it at Leos. "Piso."

Leos throws the thorn at Ra's feet and makes way for them to pass. Ra waves at Liharche to leave the boy behind and come over to the edge with him, so Leos takes the boy back in his care.

Enjoy it, little man. This is how it feels to be the one above all. Ra steps aside and lets Liharche have his glory. He instructs him to lift the blazing branch high so everyone can see. The men gathered below start cheering and waving their hands in the air, ecstatic at the sight of one of their own holding Fos.

The cheers keep going strong, even as Liharche lowers the branch and staggers. The cheers fade gradually as he falls to his knees, murmuring and trembling whole, sweating and struggling to breathe. The boy screams and dashes forth trying to reach him, but Leos sinks the boy in his arms and covers his eyes. Liharche throws the branch to the side begging for air, constantly tapping his neck. The cheers end the moment he vomits. Ra looks down to catch the men's reactions before the night takes over the mountainside. Everyone stares in utter stillness. Liharche's loud, choking gasps of desperation, the only sound to challenge the boy's cries.

"Ano aner." Ra starts walking back and forth behind Liharche. "Fos lave," he shouts in condescension, picks up the fiery branch and waves it mockingly in Liharche's face. "Lave."

Liharche curls his trembling body on the ground like a wounded beast. He crawls in his vomit, heading towards the path, but Ra pulls him back by the hair and forces him to his knees. He drags him back to the edge of the crag and holds the light over his head so everyone can see.

A long moan sweeps through the men below. They stare with widened eyes and slack jaws as Liharche's mouth bursts with blood and froth. His head is shaking so fast, Ra can hear his teeth grinding against each other. The men clasp their hands over their heads and cheer in praise of the power of Fos. Liharche's eyes roll back as if trying to see the inside of his skull. He stops shaking. Arms hang like loose straps.

Ra won't let go of his hair, even when the last gasp of air chokes him dead. He pushes a knee up against Liharche's back and keeps his corpse straight. "Fos mega," he shouts, "Aner oun lave fos." He then lets the body drop like a pelt of stones, lights up a fresh branch from the pile and stands with one foot over Liharche's chest. He sweeps the branch over the men and points at each individually. Men whimpering in fear.

Pathetic. Like children.

"Aner lave fos," he says to them, "aner nekron," and kicks Liharche over the edge. Bones crack and burst through flesh as the body lands hard and splatters the men with blood and dirt and rolls further down the mountainside and stops when its back smashes against a tree trunk.

Don't worry mother. You are safe. Now they know, your light is death and despair in their hands. More men will come and if this is what it takes for them to learn, then every fresh set of eyes will stand witness to your wrath again and again for as long as it takes for me to cram my terror in every single one of their thick skulls. I shall lay before me a land of corpses for them to crawl through and a blanket of darkness over their eyes to gaze upon. A new habit in a new, better world and by the time this task is finished, there will be no doubt in their minds. No question of authority to be asked. Only the lion and the hawk can claim the love in your arms and all the rest of them be damned.

Ra instructs Leos to let go of the boy and come and join him by his side. He wants the men to see them lift the branch together, but Leos keeps holding the boy in his arms. His lips tight. Doesn't say a word. Doesn't move a finger.

"Elthe delf, aner oun thele fos," Ra says as he walks up to him."Aner oun thele, delf oun dide fos. Ama meida, apa meida." He smiles and offers the branch to him. "Aner micra, omio fis. Leonda mega. Omio ama." The boy turns and looks at him with a face drenched in tears. His eyes are glowing with awareness and at this moment, Ra realizes there are negatives in some of his ways. *I forgot the boy can understand the words I'm saying.* He takes the boy's hand, walks with him for a while down the path, then sends him away to find his father's body and morn in peace. *How fortunate you are, child, for having others to take care of you in your time of grief. I had no one.*

Ra returns to Leos. After a long stretch of awkward silence and unblinking eye contact between them, Leos half-heartedly takes a grip under his brother's grip on the fiery branch and together, they lift it high so everyone can see them. Ra pumps his fist in the air, tilts his head back and starts yelling at the men. "Ra mega. Leos mega. Fos e mon." And the men bow down and echo every word Ra says, shouting both their names in glory.

Leos stays silent. The moment the cheers fade, he takes the branch away from Ra and throws it in the light. Ra gives Leos a shoulder hug and playfully shakes the lion's skull by sticking two fingers in the holes that used to hold its eyes. "Ode es spelaon sy," he says and leads Leos back inside the cave. *Go, rest now little brother and please hold no grudge against me. Sleep peacefully. I'm watching you. Always.*

Fos sheds its light on his paintings at the cave's entrance, scars in the mountain's mouth. The newest sign stands out from the rest. No name for it yet. He had it for a moment but slipped off the tip of his tongue.

New signs on the walls. New numbers in a new world. Nothing new in the hearts of men. All rot. This evening shows more than anything, not enough lines were drawn in the dirt it seems. Men get greedier with time. Ungrateful. They need to be reminded of our undisputed rule. Sacrifice must become a habit. And even though I enjoy teaching them my words, I don't like how the child could understand everything me and my brother were saying to each other. More lines in the dirt are needed. Distinctions must be clear.

Ra takes the first shift of the night, as the light's blazing tongues beg for more food and the darkness around him flees in shame, for it cannot stop the light from spreading.

When a hawk has a word with a lion, rats should scratch their heads in ignorance.

III
II

SONG OF SONGS

AH

The lion's fur rests over Leos' broad shoulders, keeping him warm. The lion's skull, bare of all flesh, shelters his head while its teeth cast sharp shadows over his gaze. His wild mane crawls underneath, hair chasing the wind like waves of dark Fos. The seventh face of Selene breathes the morning chill in his chest. Her smile has stripped the trees naked and her gaze carries the mist. Leaves are crunching beneath his feet as he strolls down the mountain along a narrow stream, looking for snakes. Five small bones of sickness hang from his neck. One is empty.

More people keep coming, drawn by the light's shine and the dark cloud it releases to the sky. The only connection between the world of men and the world of the gods. Fos has many ways and is willing to share them all, but deceit is not one of them. It is just as honest as the thirst that drains you and the hunger that starves you. Neither beasts pretend to care for you, moments before they rip your throat apart, nor the storm holds back the rain, pretending to care if you have found yourself a shelter or not. No matter how cruel, unfair, or merciless their ways might be, everything in the world is honest.

Everything except his brother.

A young woman and an old man are sitting by the stream further ahead. She's filling a pelt with water, helping the man wash. Leos lifts the lion's fur over his shoulders and brings it up against his cold cheeks.

"Herae," he says and unintentionally startles them both.

The woman utters words full of concern he cannot understand—they all do at first—with a voice too brittle to support any threats she might be making. She helps the old man up, who seems unable to do so on his own. Her rough hair reaches her ankles and the fur she covers herself with is muddy, torn and beaten. They are both skinny and trembling—they all are when they arrive—but the old man especially appears to be sick, utterly dependent on the woman in every way. His beard is like many tiny twigs hanging from bits of cracked, wrinkled flesh; most of his hair has fallen and he lacks the authority you would expect from a man of his age.

"Elthe," says Leos and interrupts the woman as she's babbling the nonsense of the old world, urging her to come along. He points at the top of the mountainside and starts heading upstream. He takes a glance back a few moments later and sees the woman, with the man laying his weight on her shoulder, reluctantly following him.

The ascend becomes harsh over rocks and muddy soil. The man won't stop coughing. Leos offers to help by taking the man on his shoulders, but the woman rejects his help. A rare strength in her ways reminds him of his brother. Gestures sharp. Voice weak yet assertive. She cares for the man—her father, Leos presumes—as a mother cares for her child.

They leave the deep woods of the mountain behind. A stripped and raped land stretches ahead, forced into submission by the hands of men, reaching all the way up to the cave—the deadlands. The trees underneath the crag have become stiff shadows. A pale region deprived of green, as if the gods have skinned the mountain's fur from only its chest, leaving the rest untouched.

When the boy fled the morning after his father was killed, no one hardly cared, for a few days later, a woman arrived. And a few days after her, the three men who remained became five. Five became six and seven halfway through the third weather cycle, then seven were reduced to six again and not even a full moon later six became ten and then twelve and now, late in the fifth cycle, they must count the men the same way they count time—in cycles of twelve.

The others gather around them as they pass through. Mostly men in their prime, a few women and children, six cycles of the twelve numbers and a few more in a cycle to spare. It could have been eight full cycles and more if not for his brother's habit of exemplifying some of them. The naked area under the crag is the place of gathering and the small caves of the cliffside make good shelters.

They all lower their heads as he passes by with his arms wide open and they all reach out to touch his hands. "Herae mega Leos," they mutter as they humble themselves before the son of light. The one with the head of a lion and the body of a man.

Leos caresses their fingers, accepting their humility. He taps the young ones on the head and one of the boys kisses the back of his palm.

The men show him the beasts they've killed today—enough to feed everyone in the herd—and the massive pile of branches and bushes they've plucked from the woods down the mountainside, sufficient to keep the light strong for another night.

Women show him the fur they've skinned off the beasts, rinsed and left to dry hanging from the naked tree trunks. The children show him the plants, fruit and herbs they've gathered and the stones they've sharpened. They speak the words for everything they present to him, just like his brother has taught them to do.

He goes searching across the cliffside for an empty cave the woman and the old man can have for themselves, but the ones who came before them have already claimed them all. Unfortunate. He never thought space would ever be an issue, for the mountain is vast and holds shelters aplenty, but everybody wants to be as close to Fos as possible. He leaves them by a tree nearby and heads back to the cave. It's time for the great gathering now. He'll find a shelter for them later. And if there's none to be found, he'll create it.

As he walks up the path, he looks down across the deadlands at how things are and remembers how they once were. Branchless tree trunks like spears growing from the ground. No place for the birds to rest on. The deep woods further down the mountainside seem like part of a different world. Everything the light needs the mountain provides still, but Leos sometimes wonders whether the mountain has a mind of its own and any patience to lose. They seem to be destroying trees much faster than the mountain gives birth to them.

He enters the cave and finds his brother hovering a sharp stone over the roaring flames. Signs made with white dust all over his face and body stand for words only themselves can speak.

Ra has created two ways of the tongue. Only the names of the common things of the land remain the same in both. One tongue to unite the men with each other; the other to separate the men from himself and his brother. One he teaches to the herd; the other is exclusive to just them two. Only their descendants will one day be able to understand what is said between them. Hiera glyphe, he calls their tongue—the word of the hawk.

"Any new brother?" asks Ra.

"One man, one woman. Father. Daughter."

"Good." When the stone gets hot enough, Ra uses it to slash his hair and beard short, keeping them at a finger's length. "More woman come good."

The light makes a sharpened stone cut fur and hair with ease and precision. It was one of the first secrets Leos discovered back in the early days, but unlike his brother, he never cuts his hair. The lion's skull is much heavier than the hawk's skull and much larger than his head. He has a pelt placed on the inside of the skull, strapped through the holes of its eyes, but his wild mane helps fit the skull firmly on his head and keeps it steady.

"Time we go," says Leos.

Ra dips a branch in the light. They take it outside and walk up to the edge of the crag side by side. Everyone gathers underneath once Ra lifts the fiery branch and starts waving it in the air. The people raise their hands high and hail Fos and its sons, cheering and yelling like children welcoming their fathers back from the hunt.

Leos signals some men to bring the fresh pile of wood up to them and so it is done. He then instructs them to clean the circle of stones from all the dead branches and white dust. Ra keeps only a half-full pelt of dust and a small, blackened stick for his drawings. Leos scatters the rest around the cave and all over its outer walls while everyone hails the wind for carrying its unique scent over the deadlands. He then instructs the men to bring the prey: two large grass-eaters, at least ten rabbits and a small man-eater.

Ra drops the light in the middle of the circle and proceeds by placing more branches over it, making it strong enough to warm the food. Leos takes on the task of preparing the meat; he enjoys it.

One by one, the people stand in line and move up the path towards the light to collect their blessed food. The people bring fruit from the mountain's trees, mushrooms from its soil, eggs from the nests by the cliffs and daughters. They stop at the path's end, just behind a line drawn in the dirt with white dust. Ra won't allow anyone to come any closer. No one but *her.*

Regardless of who's first in line or second or third, men and women make way for her to pass. Era is her name—the one who belongs to Ra.

No one dares speak to her in any other but the humblest of tones as she passes. No man dares look at her with desire, let alone lay a hand on her, for she carries Ra's firstborn in her still young belly.

"Elthe gyne, Era e mon, lave Fos." Ra gestures for her to come close to him by the light. He caresses her belly, lays his hands on her cheeks and kisses her forehead. He drags her hair behind her ears, wet and smooth like fur soaked in the blood of trees. Her face shines like it has never touched filth and her eyes are adorned with the lightest, thinnest shades of brown.

Leos offers her shares of warm meat to spare and Ra sends her inside the cave as usual. They always rest together at night for as long as Leos guards the light. Ra is the eldest and the first to claim pleasure from the women when they arrive. Then Leos takes his turn as the second born. Most women spread their legs willingly, knowing they could never match a man's strength. Some struggle at first, for they have never felt the touch of a man, but little it matters once the fear settles.

The first woman came to the mountain with a child holding her hand and no man as guardian. A handful of men had already settled under the crag by the time she arrived. The woman sought protection for herself and the child. All she had to offer was the pleasure between her legs. Once the two brothers were finished with her, Ra passed her over to the other men, for many tensions and rivalries can be silenced between a woman's legs. It became clear to the two brothers, that no man was willing to risk a fight with another man for something they could both enjoy. The same was true for food and water.

Men vastly outnumber women. Just eight of them old enough to please the pack and a few more with breasts that have yet to grow. As long as their numbers remain uneven, all women must please all men to receive the light's favor. It keeps the men in order. Easier to control. And order is more important than the smile on a woman's face or the tears in her eyes.

Era is the one exception. Children born by all other women have a whole herd of fathers. The child Era bears only has one. When Ra chose her as his own, Leos thought of his brother's act as just another line drawn in the dirt. Nothing but another way to differentiate themselves from the rest. They had Fos. Their heads and bodies were adorned with the bones of those who rule the land and the sky. They had the ever-growing word of the hawk and through Era, women no one else could touch. So many lines, yet his brother is constantly striving to find new ones.

It didn't take long for Leos to notice the softening in his brother's voice whenever Era was listening. The calm in his stare every time he looked at her. It soon became clear that his decision was more out of care than of any other motive. Ever since Era arrived, Leos has been waiting for a woman to claim as his own, but he found nothing of interest in the few who came after her. They all bring the same pleasures. All look the same, need the same. All behave the same.

Leos scatters the crowd with his gaze searching for the new woman, but he can't find her anywhere. One after the other, people humble themselves before him and receive their share of the blessing. The ones new to the herd are apparent. Skinny. Frightened. They have yet to benefit from the light's way.

There she is. Last in line. The new woman. Without her father and hesitant in her steps. Speechless and stunned, she stands in awe of the light while Leos stares at her with growing interest and even more curiosity. There's something about her manners. A wild resilience that attracts him. The way she keeps her right hand a clenched fist while the left is loose. The straight face she keeps as she passes by men hungering for her pleasures. No fear in her tone when she utters the filthy words of the old world. As typical as her appearance is, for a woman, her behavior is just as atypical.

Ra walks up to her and speaks in the words of the hawk, so no one else understands but Leos. "New woman?"

"Yes." Leos takes the few chunks of warm meat he's holding and wraps them up in a clean pelt.

"I take her now," Ra says. "You take after." Ra shows the woman the entrance to the cave and instructs her to head inside.

"No brother." Leos lays a polite hand on Ra's shoulder, asking for his attention. "You no take woman."

"Why? You want her?"

Leos lowers his gaze and slightly tilts his head once on each side. He stays silent, for he doesn't know much of the reasons why and he's too embarrassed by the little he knows. When Ra smiles at him, his gaze drops even lower and disappears in humility under the shade of the lion's skull. Ra pats the back of his head with care and with a playful pull of his beard, he raises his chin for a direct stare.

"Her only you take, brother," Ra says.

Leos smiles back, unwraps the pelt and offers the woman two shares of meat.

Ra stops him. "Why two?"

Leos points at the bottom of the crag, now covered in the night's darkness. "Father old, brother. Weak."

Ra allows it and returns to the light. Leos lays the meat in her hands and opens his mouth to speak, but as soon as the woman takes her share, she rushes back down the path without ever looking back, leaving Leos open-mouthed without ever uttering a single word. Leos hears his brother giggling first and moments later, the other men harassing her as she passes through the deadlands. He worries the night will be harsh for her, so he grabs a fiery branch, walks up to the edge of the crag and yells to get everyone's attention.

"Fos e mon," he shouts with authority and presents the light, for it belongs to him. "Gyne," he says and points at the woman first, then at himself. "Gyne e mon."

The men standing in her way step aside. Their filthy tongues go mute. She moves further down the mountainside where the bright of Fos can't reach, beyond the naked trees and into the thick blackness of a moonless night. The lion's word is the law of the land; his will looms over the deadlands the way a tree looms over grass.

As the light belongs to me, so does she. And my will be done.

H

Water is running down the side of the cliff, like a stream falling from the sky. She washes the blood off her father's fur and the mud stuck to her hair. Filth flows off her body like black sweat. The morning is hazy and frigid. She's shivering, sneezing and wiping her running nose. The cold is intense, unexpected and so much different than what she's used to. The mountain hasn't been kind to her so far; it has made the sickness in her father worse. The gods have moved the light back inside their cave at dawn, but the spear of dark cloud in the sky is still strong.

She can feel their looks. Eyes as snakes slithering all over her body and even though she doesn't understand any of the words they speak, she can tell they speak of her. Men keep staring at her like drooling beasts as they get ready for the hunt, but no one dares get close to her; the young god forbids it.

Only the young woman, the one bearing the child of the old god, comes over to greet her. The woman offers her a clean fur, thick and warm, then helps her gather her overly long hair with straps.

"Era," says the woman while gently tapping her own chest, then repeats the word a few more times.

Era must be the word that belongs to her, she assumes.

"Sy?" Era points at her, with a face glowing with kindness.

Me? A word for me? She doesn't know what to say. Never had a name. There was never a need for her father to name her. There was never any other daughter, nor any other woman but her.

"Habat," she says hesitantly. This is how her father calls for her from afar. It means *daughter* in her father's tongue.

"Habat esy," acknowledges Era and smiles at her. "Herae Habat." She then takes her hand, encouraging her to go along with her. "Elthe."

Era takes Habat to her own resting place on the other side of the cliff. A short—Habat must mind her head while standing inside—yet deep shelter, with more than enough space for three, or even four people to sleep with comfort without having to gather themselves in awkward positions. Habat sees no one else inside. While many pieces of fur are gathered in a pile near the wall, only one is laid out on the ground. A pile of sharpened stones rests near the cave's mouth and a huge chunk of a tree's trunk is placed in the corner with all sorts of pelts hanging from its broken branches and flowers and other things she can't recognize. Era kneels by the trunk in the corner and comes back after a short while, holding some colorful plants and herbs wrapped inside another large piece of fur and a pelt of water. She then takes Habat through the deadlands and after a while they reach the tree where Habat's father is resting. He's coughing and shivering under a filthy, thin fur, barely long enough to cover his chest and the top side of his skinny arms.

Habat covers her father with clean fur. Era offers to treat his wounds, but Habat knows there's nothing anyone can do for him, for besides some minor cuts and bruises, wounds are not the cause of his sufferings. The sickness eating her father is severe and comes from within. Some moles on his skin have grown bigger and darker and red like stains of blood. She has tried cutting them off, but they keep growing back, every time getting worse.

"Elthe gyne," a man shouts. All eyes fall on her as if she was the one doing the shouting. Habat turns and sees the young god standing at the edge of the crag, the dark cloud of light rising behind his back.

"Leos, ode," says Era and shows Habat she must go to him, willing to care for her father until she comes back.

Habat wants to stay with her father, but she does as she's told. Ever since her father got sick, she has learned well not to disobey men. If she talks back, she will get beaten. If she resists, she will be forced and shamed and her struggles won't matter. The man always gets what he wants of you. The man always walks away pleased, having reaped pleasure and food and water and a descendant he won't need to take care of. Disobey a man and you're left with blood running between your legs and a smashed face and his stench creeping all over you. A father, beaten down to the last breath of his life, too humiliated to look you in the eyes anymore. In the end, they always get what they want. In the end, it's best not to struggle. When the time comes to birth the shame, you can have your vengeance. You can leave your crying burden in the open fields for the beasts to devour and you move on. You must move on.

As she walks through the deadlands, Leos shouts again, this time to the children. They gather around Habat and join her on the way to the cave. One of the children, a little girl, comes along and grabs her hand. She welcomes the little girl with a tight-lipped smile and walks with her while the rest of the children rush up the path excited, leaving them behind.

"Poena," says the little girl and points at herself. "Sy?"

"Habat."

The little girl chuckles and starts dragging Habat's hand playfully back and forth. "Herae Habat," she says and starts repeating both of their names as they walk up the path, the smile of the land and the sky drawn across her face. "Poena e mon, Habat e sy. Poena e mon, Habat e sy…"

When they reach the cave, the other children have already sat with legs crossed by the remains of the great light, whose dark cloud has almost faded, losing its argument with a frigid wind the children seem accustomed to, but she is not. The young god is there, tossing some fruit high and then catching them in the air, making the children laugh. He looks at her and she finds warmth and care in his stare instead of mindless lust and his eyes hide deep thoughts behind them, rather than the one single thought all other men cannot hide from her.

The young god shows her a spot amongst the children to sit and the children welcome her. They smile and chuckle while Poena starts playing with her long hair, which she enjoys, quickly forgetting the awkwardness of being the only adult in a group of children. The young god offers her a green fruit, the size of her palm. When she reaches out to take it, he takes her hand in both of his own as he lays the fruit in her shaky palm. He caresses the back of her hands until they get warm. She looks away, feeling her cheeks getting warm too, her belly fluttering, his gaze snatching every breath from her chest.

The young god leaves her with the fruit, speaks strange words to the children and goes back inside the cave. He turns into a walking shadow as he enters the cave's deep, dark bowels, where she sees the glorious light shining strong in the blackness as if the god of the day has found a way to invade the night and steal the moon's place. Another shadowy figure is standing by the light—the old god—holding something. The young god walks up to him. Words are spoken, barely reaching her ears like soft echoes full of secrecy. The young god takes the old god's place by the light. A shadow for a shadow. A god for a god.

The old god steps out of the cave dragging a dead beast along with him. The children abruptly stop laughing and rush back to their spots. The air thickens. Some of the children lower their heads as he approaches and tuck their hands between their legs; others stay completely still as if holding their breaths, staring at the old god with widened eyes.

"Herae Ra," they all say in unity, and the old god nods.

He looks straight at her. Her breathing quickens. She bites her lips to stop them from shivering, for the skull over his head is also staring at her with hollow, black eyes. She lowers her head, unable to match the will in his gaze. Everything around her comes together in one clear end—if there is only one thing in the world to fear, it is him.

Ra drops the dead beast in front of them and starts teaching them words. A word for every part of its body, starting from top to bottom: horns, head, neck, back, belly, legs, tail. Every word he says, he demands it be spoken back to him by everyone individually.

Habat listens in total absorption to Ra's teachings. These words are different than the ones she knows. She repeats every word she hears and just like the children, some she remembers with ease; some she forgets soon after. Whenever someone mispronounces a word, Ra is forgiving and simply repeats the lesson. At some point he speaks a word and takes a hold of the beast's leg, but one of the boys says a different, unfamiliar word instead— probably the word for leg in the boy's old tongue. Ra jumps up at the sound of this strange word, smacks the boy hard on the mouth and shouts at him. The boy starts crying and Ra hushes him, threatening to hit him again. The boy swallows his sobs and with trembling red lips, the lesson continues.

Ra repeats the same lesson from head to toe-—a word for every main part of the beast's body. And then he repeats it again. Then again. Whenever Habat's turn comes, her father's words jump ahead in her mind first, as if they're jealous of the new ones, trying to push them over the edge of her thoughts. She tries hard not to let her tongue slip. Finally, after too many lessons to count, she begins to feel a lot more comfortable with the words, even able to repeat them in random order when Ra instructs her to do so. Some of the children still struggle with some of the longer words, but he seems pleased with them regardless.

The morning slips away fast and as the day approaches its peak, Ra returns to the cave and comes back moments later, holding two pelts full of water and some fruit. He hands them over to the children and instructs them to pass them down to everyone. He then kneels over the dead beast, takes a sharp stone from the pelt on his side and starts slicing it open.

The children eat and drink and pass everything down to each other. When it's Poena's turn, she has her share and reaches out to Habat.

"Hyda Habat," she says and tries to give Habat the pelt of water.

"Te?" says Ra and startles them both, just as Poena is about to hand over the pelt to Habat. They turn their heads towards him, neither letting go of the pelt. Habat hesitates to take the pelt from her. The way her hand is shivering, Habat senses Poena is too scared to pull it back. Ra's face has gone pale at the sound of Habat's name. He stares at her, still as a rock, stopping halfway through ripping the beast's belly wide open. He rises to his feet.

"Te Poena?" he says again with a harsher tone. Habat feels Poena's grip on the pelt getting tighter. He walks up to them. "Te," he shouts at Poena, who's gasping and looking at the old god with eyes about to jump out of her head and with trembling lips, unable to utter a single word.

Habat worries Ra will punish Poena for speaking her name, a new and strange word to his ears. "Habat," she utters with a broken voice and keeps repeating her name while anxiously tapping her chest. *It's just my name, great god, it's only a name. Change it if you hate it, I'll never speak of it again.*

Ra doesn't do anything. He doesn't say anything. His eyes are oozing with disbelief and upset while Habat brings Poena in her arms and starts caressing her face, trying to calm her down. Then, with one sudden move, Ra reaches out and snatches the pelt from Poena's hands. Poena starts crying. Habat sinks the little girl deeper into her arms while all the other children drag themselves away from them, each child trying to hide behind another.

Ra pours some water in his palm, shows it to Habat and speaks words she doesn't understand.

"Hyda," whispers Poena in her ear.

"Hyda," she says, but Ra shouts at her. She covers her head and closes her eyes, thinking the old god is about to strike her. He pulls her hand away, forcing her to uncover her face and spills some more water to the ground. He points at it, demanding of her to speak. She doesn't understand what's wrong. Perhaps the old god has misheard her, or maybe in her confusion, she has misspoken. "Hyda," she says one more time and the moment she utters the word, Ra slaps her.

He grabs her hair and drags her through the dirt as she screams for help and forces her gaze to the distant fields. Leos comes rushing out of the cave but when he tries to calm Ra down, Ra shoves him back, yells at him and commands him to return to the cave. He then forces Habat on her knees and starts throwing water to her face, constantly yelling her name. Habat shakes her head in confusion, screaming and crying as the old god keeps yelling and slapping her, splashing water all over her, persisting, demanding of her to say something. Lost in her dread, the only other word she knows for water slips through her bleeding lips.

"Ma—maim," she cries out in despair. "Maim!"

The pelt falls to the ground. Water spills and runs through the dirt till it hugs her sore knees. The old god lets go of her and takes a few steps back. She lowers her head and gathers her body like when her belly hurts, her chest rushing to catch every breath as if they know the reason why the old god is so cruel to her. Silence grows between them. She looks up at Ra, her eyes drowning in tears. Why does he care so much for the words me and father speak? His stare emanates vile astonishment, as if she had three eyes and two heads with roots to the same neck, snakes instead of hair, or some other trait just as revolting and anomalous.

"Maim..." he mutters. The astonishment fades away from his stare. Now there's only calm, but the most dangerous kind. Like the calm during the most silent and darkest of all silent dark nights, when you sleep peacefully, unaware of the ruthless beast lurking in the bushes just a step away from you. "Maim..."

He calls for Poena and she goes to him, dragging her feet, one hand over the other and both covering her mouth, as if death had just summoned her. He speaks to her and Poena answers back with a nervous point of her finger over the crag. He takes her hand and instructs her to lead him, leaving Habat behind as they head down the path.

Habat hobbles back to her feet. Her head aches while everything that shouldn't be moving can't seem to hold still. She rushes after them, leaning on the cave's wall as she stumbles down the path, with only one thought finding balance in her unsteady mind—father.

Poena takes Ra through the deadlands. Habat follows them, struggling to keep up. Everyone around them makes way. Poena stops and points at a naked tree further ahead where Era is taking care of Habat's father, washing his face with a wet pelt, feeding him as he coughs and chokes with every bite. Ra caresses Poena's hair and gestures for her to stay where she is.

Habat catches up with Poena. She hugs her, makes sure she's well, then starts walking behind Ra, mindful not to make any sudden moves or say anything that might upset him even further.

Ra approaches the tree. Era humbles herself before him. She is but a face of concern. Ra gestures for her to leave and as she walks by him holding her belly, he doesn't even look at her. His stare stays fixated on Habat's father, sitting under the tree.

Habat tries to get to her father's side, but Era stops her from getting any closer. More women gather around her.

Ra crouches in front of her father. He raises her father's head by lifting his chin. Father is coughing, unable to focus his gaze. His eyes are dark hordes of old wounds and broken flesh. Ra grabs him by the neck, drags him up to his feet and pushes his back against the tree.

"Va," moans Habat, calling for father, while the women struggle to hold her back and keep her calm.

Too weak to stand properly, father resists. His legs, thin as sticks children play with, jiggling as if even a soft breeze could break them. Ra tightens his grip around his neck and forces him to stand straight and face him. He wipes his chest clean of all drawn signs and tracks a scar stretching across his chest with his finger.

Habat twists and turns and bites one of the women's hands and breaks free from their hold. She rushes to her father's side. "Va amats, V—"

With an incoherent cry of rage, Ra pulls a sharp stone from his side and stabs her father in the neck.

"Va!" Echoes of Habat's screams take the deadlands. She charges at Ra and the women rush to grab her. They pull her back before she gets the chance to lay a hand on him.

Ra twists the stone and blood squirts all over his face. He covers her father's mouth, choking him with his own blood and slices his throat from edge to edge. Father's body leans forth and rests on Ra's shoulder. He doesn't step aside to let it fall. He keeps staring at the tree as the body gradually slides off him and hard onto the ground, leaving a trail of blood on his shoulder.

Habat screams her chest barren. The women cannot hold her anymore. She claws and bites her way out of their hands and runs to her father lying face down in the dirt. She turns him over and pushes her hands against his neck, desperately trying to gather the spewing blood back inside him. "Va," she cries out to him, "Va azan. Va ahhor." She keeps shaking him, tapping his chest and she lifts his arms only to see them instantly crash down again. His face. A desolate land. Skin broken and dry. Eyes as black stars on a white night. Lifeless.

Her forehead meets his forehead as she weeps for him. Her tears trickle down all over his face, so she wipes them away. Drops of blood fall on her hand. She looks up. The blood is dripping from the wings hanging on the side of Ra's splattered face, standing right above them. The hawk's skull on his forehead painted red. He shoves her aside, lifts her father on his shoulder like dead prey and heads back to the cave.

Habat jumps up and rushes to stop him, but when she tries to snatch her father away, Ra turns and punches her in the face so hard she collapses in agony. The dark clouds above her start spinning and twisting. The tall, naked trees bend as if to hug each other. She wipes her nose. Blood. She hears Ra shouting, nervous steps pounding the ground all around her. Many shadows gather over her. Everything goes dark.

Bright light. She feels hands under her shoulders, carrying her. Her feet are hovering over the land, the tips of her toes caressing the soil. Her head is spinning. She looks around with half-lidded eyes, too heavy to open wide, mumbling her father's name and searching for him, but soon the burden of keeping her eyes open becomes excruciating; the ache passing through her head, unbearable. And the darkness welcomes her back.

A violent splash of cold water soaks her face. She wakes up lying on the floor. Clouds are still spinning, but after a few moments, they settle down. Everything is blurry and slow-moving. She hears children speaking, taking turns repeating the same word. "Cardia." She lifts her head and finds herself back at the cave, with all the children around her.

The children help her sit. Poena comes and sits by her side with a face covered in dried tears. A hand reaches out to her. A bloody hand, holding something shrouded by gore. She wipes her eyes. The blur fades away gently while everything comes back to focus. The hand reaching out to her is Ra's.

"Cardia," he speaks and shows her what's in his hand—a piece of meat in the shape of a closed fist.

She moves her anxious gaze around and finds her father's body on the floor where the dead beast used to be, lying over a pool of blood, ripped wide open, sliced from his neck all the way down to his manhood. She then brings her gaze back at Ra's dripping hand and stares at the piece of meat, speechless. Motionless. "Cardia gyne," says Ra once more and this time he kneels over her father's body and shoves his hand in his open chest and moves it around for a bit as if stirring water, pointing out that it is now hollow. Cardia—this is the word for *heart*.

Habat remains as still as her father. She can't cry anymore. There are no more tears inside her. She can only cry from within and she does so as hard as she can, without even shedding a single tear. She screams inside to bring down the heavens, but no one hears a thing.

Ra demands that she speaks the word. He returns to her and points at the heart with a sharp stone soaked in blood, chunks of flesh stuck all over it. He taps at the heart and squeezes it, imitating its beating sound, repeats the word and waits on her to react.

"Ca—cardia," says Habat, unable to utter anything above a faint whisper.

Ra gives her an affirmative nod, returns to her father's body, rips his liver out and shows it to the children first. "Epar," he speaks. This is the word for *liver.*

"Epar," all the children say in one voice. With a circular wave of his hand, Ra instructs them to repeat the word once more and the children do as they are told.

He then turns to Habat and lays her father's liver in her hands with much care and attention, as if it were an infant. Too weak to keep her hands up, she brings the liver down to her belly and stares at it.

"Epar, gyne. Sy pes. Epar." Ra's voice is intense. Demanding.

Habat mutters a crumbled version of the word just before she faints.

And so, the lesson continues.

ΑΦΗ

"Why?" Leos asks.

Ra is by the pond, washing all the blood off his face. "You no remember?"

"Remember what?"

Ra looks at him and after a brief pause, he splashes some more water on his face. "You young." He turns and shows Leos the long scar across his chest, one he's been carrying since as far back as Leos can see his brother in his mind.

Leos still holds memories of that day, for it was a special one. The first time he ever came across others of his kind. Though everything is blurry and scattered in his mind like fragments of broken rock, pale images of what happened flicker before his eyes. A man and a girl. He can't see their faces, only dark figures dressed in blank expressions. He remembers horror taking over his whole being, watching his brother suffer. The despair of not being able to do anything about it. The sound of a spear tapping, constant, nerve-racking. A girl's long hair following the wind. Wounds. Sweat. Heat under the skin. Blood-red paintings on the walls.

This doesn't answer Leos' question. Too many scars of too long ago, proof of too many struggles on both of their bodies. *Even if it is them, it shouldn't matter in the slightest now. What happened that day is in the past and the old man was no longer a threat to us.*

"Why brother?" Leos persists, with demands gathering in his rising tone. "Man old now, sick. No hurt us."

"You small child back in drylands," Ra yells at him, welcoming the fight. "You no remember, mind dark. Man cruel." He points outside at the cave's entrance. "Man like lion you kill, beast. No like me, you. No like our father, good."

"Girl good."

"Girl like her father. Beast makes beast."

"No like beast. Like you. Like me."

"No." Ra goes berserk and kicks a pile of branches, scattering them all over the ground. "You me like father. You no remember father. Father bright, like Fos." He starts walking around the light, unrest in his steps, hovering his hand over its blazing tongues. "Mother like Fos. Fos makes Fos. No man like father. No woman like mother."

"Me no remember father, no mother," Leos says with a ragged voice. "Me, remember you." He steps up to Ra and raises his forefinger right between Ra's eyes and once he has Ra's full attention, he points up to the hawk's skull over his brother's head. "You change."

Ra slaps his hand away. "Change how?"

Leos takes a few steps back near the edge of the pond. "You back home, like fur, warm. Now cold like rock."

"Like rock brother?"

"Yes, rock."

"Rock?" Ra picks up a rock the size of his fist from the ground and throws it with all his strength at Leos' feet. The stone bounces off the ground between his legs before plummeting into the pond. "Me cold? No. Men cold."

"No. They want food, home, they want Fos. Like you, me."

"Yes, they want. They want eat. They want drink, women, they want piss, they want, want, want… what they give? We give Fos. We give warm meat. We give words. What they give? This?" He points at the scar on his chest. "This?" He points at another scar of a stab wound on his belly. Then at another stretching from the side of his forehead, all the way down to his cheek. "This they give, brother?"

Leos listens to his brother's rant. For a while, he stands in thought, hands on his waist, silent. He knows what his brother has been through to keep them safe. He understands that for every man he has ever come across himself, there are ten others his brother has had to deal with on his own. No words can express his gratitude. No sign can stand in place of his love for him. He could keep their fight going all day and night if he wanted to. He believes his brother is wrong in his cruel ways and he knows how to stand by his beliefs, but he chooses not to. He shuts his eyes. The sound of water falling in the pond clears the muddled thoughts in his mind. He never answers back to his brother's rant, for even when his brother is wrong, he owes it to him. He owes him the silence.

"Your scars from beasts, brother," says Ra with a deep, low voice, gasping, now calm as the land is calm after a violent storm has ended. "My scars. Few from beasts. Many from men." He picks up a branch and lights it up as the time of the great gathering approaches. "Scars from men hurt more."

Ra leaves the cave. Leos stands there in silence with arms crossed, lost in his thoughts, watching the light… or is it the light that is watching him?

The gathering starts with Leos still in the cave. Determined to let his brother do all the work this time, he only comes out when he hears Era's voice, the next in line to take her share.

Once Ra sees him, he takes Era's hand. When he tries to lead her into the cave, Era shakes her head and imitates coughing.

"Te?" Ra says. Era lowers her head and hesitates to answer. She keeps coughing and behaving like she's not feeling well, but despite her efforts, when she tries to free her hand from Ra's grasp and step away, Ra tightens his grip on her, refusing to let go. He drags her back to him with force and when he asks her again, Era gives up on her unwell pretences, too scared to deny him anymore.

"Habat," she says, her eyebrows like wrinkles above her imploring glance.

Ra glowers at her. "Oun," he says and drags her towards the cave's entrance against her will.

"Nae," says Leos and comes between them, breaking them apart. He takes a few more extra pieces of warm meat, gives them to Era and sends her away in a hurry. Ra frowns at him, so Leos sets a branch alight and heads back inside the cave, knowing his brother would never fight him in front of the others, nor he would ever abandon the light to go after Era. He waits in the cave for the great gathering to end and for his brother's return.

After everyone leaves, Ra storms inside the cave and Leos gets up to face him. Ra pushes him back a few steps, his feet barely escaping the light's grasp. Leos shoves Ra back, something that instantly feels wrong and awkward, for he has never done this before with cruel intentions; it has always been for fun, a tease, or to play as brothers play.

They start yelling harsh words at one another. Leos keeps walking up and down the length of the cave while Ra stays near the entrance, taking frequent, nervous glances at the light outside, roaring all by itself, with neither of them guarding it. Even though it's still within sight and with no one else near it, this marks the first time the light has ever been left unguarded.

"Shush," says Leos and brings a finger over his mouth, for he thought he heard something lurking in the brief gaps between their shouts; something odd, coming from outside. Ra ignores him and keeps shouting at him. "Pafs," Leos insists, demanding of Ra to shut up for a moment and listen.

Another voice is fighting the light's roar for attention. They stare at each other in silence for a moment. Ra seems he can hear it too. They head outside and Ra starts throwing branches in the neglected light while Leos follows the voice to the edge of the crag.

Coming from the far-left side of the cliff below, neither a scream nor someone talking; something else. A woman's voice that flows in the air as waves flow in water, outwardly calm but full of despair within, looking for a shore to smash into. The voice rises and falls with grace and fades away in the dark of night, as the waves would fade away in the emptiness of a world without a shore to meet. So gentle to the ear like a mother's whisper, but loud and full of ache, like the wails of a mother birthing a stubborn child clawing its way back inside her, determined to never leave her womb.

Leos heads to the deadlands.

"Where you go, brother?" Ra shouts at him, "your turn watch light. Brother?" He gathers more bushes and branches to throw in the starving light. "Brother."

Leos ignores him, never looks back.

As he walks down the path, he hears none of the people's usual chattering and snoring and moving around. Everyone is dead silent. He passes by them, tracking the voice across to the other side of the cliff. Everybody's sitting in their shelters, or leaning on trees, utterly still and mesmerized. Someone starts tapping something on a rock, a piece of wood or a spear, joining the natural flow of her voice. A tap repeating at the silent count of four. Tap, two, three, four. Tap, two, three, four. Tap...

More join in. Some by banging rocks together, others by clapping their hands. Their paired, well-timed knocks become the soil this wounded voice sheds its blood upon. The bleeding flows straight through Leos' heart like a river, his heartbeat rising, battling against its violent current.

The voice is getting louder. He sees a dark figure at first, standing ahead in the open. Once he gets closer, he realizes it's Era standing outside her own shelter looking in. Era is with one hand resting on her belly, the other over her mouth. The voice is coming from inside her shelter. When Leos walks up to her, she turns her head ever so slightly to greet him and Leos sees her face shining with dry tears.

"Ha—Habat," she mutters.

Leos reckons he should have known, for such great sorrow could only have come from her on this day. But the voice sounds nothing like her. Depths and heights in her sound, as new to his ears as she was the moment he met her. Such elegance in the drift of her wails. The passion she holds captive when she inhales right before each pause and the heartache she unleashes when she exhales is so ethereal and unsettling, it makes you question whether it's actually real or mere voices inside your head. His heart knows, but his mind needs to see to believe this voice is of a woman and not of a divine being, like the ones his brother paints.

He lowers his head and enters the shelter. The cave's roof, too low for him to stand straight. Habat is sitting in the corner. Her eyes wide shut, shaking her head back and forth, matching the claps and the knocks coming from outside in perfect synchrony. Her hands are gathered between her legs. He stands so close to her, yet she shows no reaction to his presence. It's as if he's not even there. The tremor in her voice makes every hair on his body stand. Her torment, god's tears, drowning the cave in melancholy.

He wants to get closer to her but chooses not to, afraid his presence might frighten her. He stays close to the cave's mouth instead, watching her, listening to her. She seems to be in another world now, a world far beyond anyone else's reach. Having never felt loss like she has—or like his brother has— he doesn't know what it's like to lose the only ones you love, but her voice pulls him in. He shuts his eyes and her voice carries him away to a terrifying place of loss and hopelessness. He embraces the darkness and for a moment, he finds himself in the land of death, shattered by loneliness, while everyone he loves is still alive. He opens his eyes just moments later, frightened, trying to escape from his thoughts, but what he finds through her voice is a feeling much worse.

The beauty in her voice attracts you. It lures you in, to face the strength underneath the beauty that forces you to feel as she feels. And what she feels is unbearable.

He returns to the land of the living with a burden in his chest. He leaves the shelter quietly, trying not to disturb her, with her scars on his flesh. The crushing guilt of being the only one alive, while everyone you love is dead.

He returns to the cave and finds his brother sitting at the edge of the crag, listening, utterly focused on Habat's voice. He walks to his side and sees warmth in his focused stare, the eyes of a troubled mind. He's not sure if it's guilt, remorse, or the grief of the past coming back with a vengeance. All he knows is that their argument is over.

"Go brother, rest," Leos says. He puts his hand on Ra's shoulder. "I stay."

Ra caresses his hand and avoids meeting his eyes as he heads back inside the cave. He wipes his face and tries to hide it, but Leos can tell—the grief in her voice has touched him too.

Leos starts nurturing the light. Habat's wails grow more intense and more elegant throughout the night. When some people stop clapping, others pick up and follow along. No one sleeps on this night. Never has he ever heard anguish, or any other emotion, expressed in such a profound way. The sound of pain to shatter all pains, so ugly and overwhelming in its true nature, blooming through someone's voice like the most vibrant flower. A gorgeous grieving.

Late into the night, her voice fades away. The claps keep going for a while at the same pace, eager for her return. He longs for her too. A sense of guilt inside him tries to make peace with the desire to hear her voice again. He wishes no more pain for her, but her grieving signifies she remains safe in the cave.

Her voice never returns. The claps soon fade away as well, making way for murmurs and overlapping chats, awkward, like the buzzing of flies over your head while trying to sleep.

Leos looks down, trying to make out shapes and movements through the thick darkness of a moonless night. He hears Era shouting Habat's name. He tracks crying and moaning, a shadow moving through the deadlands. The rattling and shuffling of stones and sticks, unsettled by feet pounding the soil, running wild and heading towards the deep woods down the mountainside with no care, provoking the night to unleash its rage. So far away from Fos, the rules of the old world remain unscathed. Silence must never be broken.

He takes his spear, lights a thick branch and hurries after her. He tries to run as fast as he can, but the light won't allow it. The wind of his run weakens it, so he slows down enough to find a balance. He follows Habat's sobs into the deep woods, where the old ways still rule, more unforgiving than ever. He picks up more sticks and branches along the way to keep the light strong, his only real weapon out here.

The night heightens every minute sound. The crackling of leaves under his feet. The hissing and squeaking of things slithering in the bushes. The trees whispering the cries of those who feel the mountain's teeth digging through their throats, stealing their last breath. Habat's sobs are getting louder and just when he thinks he's about to catch up to her, every sound of her goes mute, as if the earth has opened its mouth and swallowed her whole.

"Habat," he says, hesitant to raise his voice too high, Hab—"

She screams and he almost drops the light, barely managing to hold his grip on the branch. He storms by the trees, dashing through bushes and over broken trunks until he sees a large man-eater, roaring, trying to claw itself up a tree. Habat is sitting on one of its branches screaming, holding on by whatever she can.

Leos jumps at the beast, waving the flaming branch, forcing it away from the tree. A beast like a lion but with no mane and black fur shining, gathering the moisture in the air. Its yellow eyes match the light's shine as it starts creeping around the tree. Leos throws his back against the tree and keeps waving the light from side to side as far as he can stretch his arms. Unwilling to wait for the beast to strike, he charges at it and smacks it hard on the head with the light. The beast flees through the bushes moaning, with sparks of light flying off its head and dying just before they hit the ground.

Deep breaths take the edge off. He smears the sweat from his cheeks, then lays a hand on the tree's trunk. He looks up at Habat. No longer screaming but not quiet either, moaning and struggling, cracking sticks and forcing the branch to shed its leaves as she can't seem to hold still. She drags herself close to the tree's trunk and puts her arms around it.

"Elthe," he says, urging her to come down.

She hugs the tree's trunk tight, refusing to let go. He can barely reach her feet, but when he tries to pull her down, she kicks his hand away and lifts her feet further up the branch like he's just another beast she needs to be wary of.

Leos tracks the area around the tree. Sly shadows dare of him to show ignorance; dashing sounds await for a moment of negligence. The loners he can deal with, but out here in the open, even the light can't save them from packs of man-eaters. He can't be patient with her. They must head back now.

"Here, take." He lifts the light high and offers it to her. Habat can't understand a word he's saying, so he might as well speak in the tongue he's most comfortable with. "Take Fos."

Habat eases her grip on the tree's trunk. Leos clears all the grass and the leaves from a small area by the tree, creating a patch of nothing but dirt, then carefully lays Fos on the ground. He moves back, urging Habat to come down from the tree and take it. She speaks words unknown and waves him further away. Leos takes a few more backward steps, his hands at chest level, palms out.

Habat slips down the tree, but the instant her feet touch dirt, she picks up the light in a heartbeat. Her arms are shaking. With every spark that leaps off the branch, Leos' heart jumps to his throat and crashes back in his chest. *Be careful, woman, for you know nothing of the terror you hold in your hands.* He waves for her to stay calm and takes a few steps forward. She shouts and thrusts the light at him; Leos halts, begging her to be still and quiet. There is no time for this. He needs her trust and he needs it now.

The lion's skull rattles the grass as he tosses it aside. He takes a pelt from his side and ties it around his head, covering his eyes. He starts walking towards her blind, with soft steps as if trying to walk through a land of snakes, hands gathered behind his back. He follows the light's roar through the blackness, the only sound in the world that matters right now besides Habat's nervous panting. She can kill him if she chooses to. She can scorch the whole mountain to ease her grief if she wants to. His breathing quickens with every step he takes. Palms getting clammy.

He feels the light's warmth, so he stops. The heat starts moving across his face. She's hovering Fos so close to his flesh, it dries his sweat. He can hear her panting, slowing down to a normal breath. The warmth leaves his face and crawls down to his chest as it gradually fades away. When he can no longer feel its touch, he unties the pelt. When he opens his eyes, the relief in his stare meets the storm in hers.

They look at each other in the flickering glow of the fading light. Her lips are quivering. A comforting silence between them, as if the air they breathe carries a truth no words can explain and they're sharing this truth with every breath they take. They stare at each other for what seems an eternity trapped in a moment unfettered by time. Habat daring him to enter the storm and Leos brave enough to last through it, earning the first glimmer of hope in eyes red-blooded by sorrow.

Leos doesn't want to leave her eyes, but he has to. He points at the light. She's holding the branch at her side with a steady hand, but its shine is fading away. Leos shows her how to make it strong again but never tries to take it back. She seems calm as she gathers sticks in a bunch. Leos takes her other hand and they walk side by side as they head back to the deadlands through the deep woods. He doesn't want to let go of her, gently caressing her fingers all the way back. She walks at a slow, hesitant pace, never taking her eyes off the light.

They reach the deadlands just as the early dawn spills her dim shine over a night like no other, leaving behind a day of wounds destined to never heal. A day full of reasons to never forget. Habat's pace has grown in confidence.

People gather around them. Every mouth is in the shape of Aeos. Habat keeps the light in front of her at a waist's height, with her arm stretched to keep its influence off her. Leos brings his arm around her as people bow before them without lowering their heads, unable to take their eyes off Habat. Sounds of gasps and murmurs, in the lowest of tones, yet so many uttered concurrently, manage to reach every ear. A woman is holding Fos in her hand. Fos, held by a mortal.

Era is the only one who dares to come close. She walks up to them just to caress Habat's face, heaving sighs of relief. Habat takes herself away from Leos' arms and stops Era before her knees meet the ground when she tries to bow down. Habat gives her a one-arm hug, keeping her safe from the light's reach.

"Fos brother, bring."

Leos sees his brother standing at the edge of the crag, calling for him. His voice draws everyone's attention, not just his own. When Habat sees Ra, her hands start shaking again. Her eyes bulge. Lips tighten. Leos takes her hand and gently pulls her back. Strength gathers in her, enough for him to feel the pressure of her nails against his flesh. He gestures for her to give him back the light and she does so without ever taking her eyes off Ra.

"Lave Habat, ode spelaon," Leos says to Era and she takes Habat's hand from him, urging Habat to follow her back to her shelter. He wants his brother to see Era treating Habat with care.

Leos heads back to the cave to confront his brother. *Habat is safe,* he thinks. *The people have seen she can carry the light. No one can hurt her now. Not even my brother.* He walks up the path, visualizing different outcomes of their imminent confrontation in his mind. None of them end well.

A giant stack of flaming branches in front of the cave. Fos, as strong as ever, stealing the dawn's glory. Ra is standing at the edge of the crag, still looking down. Leos has already thought of what to say when his brother asks for explanations. No matter what comes out of his brother's mouth, he's determined to retaliate.

Ra won't turn to face him. He just stands there, looking over the crag.

Leos takes the lion's skull off his head and tosses the branch over the stack, not caring where or how it lands. "Brother, I—"

Ra comes at him with a fierce stride, slaps him first with the back of his hand, then slaps him again with the front; the first hit takes Leos aback as he drops the lion's skull to the ground; the second sends him crashing next to it. His back meets dirt. He shuts his eyes, lost in a daze. Pain spreads all over his face, before it settles at the corners of his mouth and jaw. He opens his eyes. Ra has a forefinger all up in his face, leaning over him with one knee pushing down on his chest.

"Never," Ra says before a brief pause. He pulls his finger away ever so slightly, but then dashes it right back in Leos' face with force, stopping just a hair away from between his eyes. "Never take mother. Never take father from me again." His stare is all rage, but the glow that gathers at the inner edges of his wet eyes betrays his sadness. "You leave—"

Ra pulls his knee away, freeing Leos before turning his back at him. He picks up an armful of branches from the nearby pile.

"—You leave me," Ra continues and carefully places some branches in the heart of the hungry light. His voice is now low yet strained, like a storm hiding in the calm of distant clouds. "You leave me for her."

Leos pulls himself up. He opens his mouth to reply, but then closes it right away. No words dare come out. The taste of blood from a split lip gathers at the edge of his tongue instead, for his thoughts are children ascending a mountain's slope made from the skulls of their dead parents. It's true. He left him for her.

Deep silence spreads between them, filling the space where there should be an argument. When Ra finally turns and walks up to him, he looks him in the eyes and taps the back of his neck with care, then lowers his gaze and heads back inside the cave without uttering a single word.

Leos had so many things to say, but now he finds himself ready for a fight that has already come and gone. He stares into the heart of Fos like a hunter stares at a ruthless beast from afar while planning his attack. A flash blinds him. His eyes can stand no more of its surging glare. Lost in a daze, he suddenly finds himself outside his own body. He looks down. His feet aethereal, hovering over the ground like mist. The beast of light is already ripping his mortal body to shreds. His spirit ready for the fight of a lifetime. A fight the body has already lost.

ΥΦΗ

With the dusk fading into the night, people gather around her shelter still. Murmuring shadows, peeking inside. She ignores them for the most part. They bring no harm and lots of fruit and even though she hasn't eaten any of it, she appreciates the gesture. Strange thing it is, when grief finds a way to make a home of your soul. Your body seeks food no more, for it feeds on sorrow as maggots feed on soil. Every voice you hear is a bitter reminder of the voice you have forever lost. Whole gulps of water still leave your mouth dry, for all you wish to drink is memories. When you stare unseeingly into your past and find the brightest, clearest images of the ones you lost, the absence empties you; it removes you from the world. Every cheerful memory sickens you. No act of kindness can bring your mind to rest. And rage… rage unending turns the brightest days blackened.

She hasn't left Era's cave all day. The whole floor is adorned with fur and the walls have a wet skin that gathers the dimming light from outside.

Commotion rises. The sound of feet hustling and voices crossing paths. Habat is lying curled up, facing the cave's wall, when Era comes and gives her a slight nudge, urging her to get up. Era has been taking good care of her and she has been kind enough to do it in silence. She keeps bringing her water even though she has yet to drink any;

keeps bringing her food even though she made it clear she has no craving for it.

"Fos oda Habat," Era says to her, "Ra Leos kreas emon dide."

Habat understood three of the words Era just spoke and it was enough for her to comprehend the message. She pats Era's hand in acknowledgement but makes no effort to get up. She instead gives her a faint smile of gratitude and shakes her head sideways, letting her know she has no intention of participating in their gathering. She caresses her belly and imitates feeding the child with her hand. Era responds with a nod and a faint smile of her own. Habat turns around to her other side, now facing the cave's entrance, as Era exits the cave.

Outside people are passing by with haste and along with them Habat's thoughts get entangled in the moment's urgency. On her first night here, while Habat was standing in line to get meat, she saw Ra kissing Era. No wonder no one else sleeps in this shelter. The child she bears must be his.

She feels sorry for her, for she knows well of the burden of carrying the offspring of vicious men. The first time she was raped, her breasts had barely grown. A man found her hiding in the bushes while father was away on the hunt. She tried to fight back. Father never warned her not to fight back. The man left her bleeding from between her legs and with a belly that kept growing, gradually revealing to her a secret she had hidden in her own body. When the time came to give birth to her child, father smashed its head with a rock as soon as he pulled it out of her, instantly ridding them of its shame. He never asked for permission. Not once, during the months leading up to her labor, did he hint at his intentions. She didn't even get the chance to see it, but she cried for it. She screamed and mourned for it. And for a long time, she hated him for it.

The second time was more recent. Father had gotten sick and already was a shadow of the man he once was. Three men came to them while they were scavenging the barren fields in a group that looked like a father with his two sons. They stripped father and beat him half to death and took turns with her. Took turns for days. She never fought back. They left when they ran out of water; left her and father behind, for in a land of drought, two more mouths to feed were two too many. With father so sick and beaten, the men probably thought they wouldn't last long anyway. But she did. They did.

When it was time to give birth, father was too weak to help her. He was drifting in and out of this world, as if he was lost in his own body. She had to pull the child out of herself, by herself. Father urged her to kill it immediately, but she couldn't do it. Left it in the fields to die only to rush back to it moments after, shattered by guilt. No matter how much she wanted, she couldn't love it less than father or herself; in her life, she had loved no one else. That first day, when the child cried, she felt warmth. And when the child reached out for her, she felt joy. But at nightfall something happened. During that first night together, mother and son, something changed. Whenever the child would cry, all she could hear was laughter—their laughter. She couldn't rest, couldn't sleep. When the child touched her breasts, it was their hands all over her. Its mouth on her nipples was them licking her, spitting and drooling all over her. Its breath left their stench slithering on her neck still. Even though they were gone, this child was their way of staying with her. Still pleasing themselves with her.

She took the child out into the fields in the middle of the night and left it there. Turned around. Never looked back. Sometimes she thinks about her dead children and gets overwhelmed with sorrow. Sometimes not. Sometimes she feels half a woman. Sometimes more than just a woman. Love and hate, forgiveness and retribution, she's not sure of the order of things in the world. One thing she knows with absolute certainty—pride is stronger than shame.

Era enters the cave and Habat pretends to be asleep. Lost in her thoughts, time went by without her realizing it. She hears Era moving around, arranging things. She can tell Era is gentle with her ways, trying not to disturb her sleep. Silence comes after a while and Habat waits patiently. She waits for Era to fall asleep. She opens her eyes and whispers Era's name to check if she's still awake. No response. She gets up, mindful of the noise she makes, grabs a sharp stone from the pile of stones near the entrance of the cave and stands over Era.

I feel sorry for you. You carry in you a burden I know well. A child as evil as he is, as brutal as he is. A child unworthy of even the least of all mercies.

Era is lying on her back, her head leaning slightly to the side. Hands are resting just under her chest. Her belly is exposed.

Father taught me to be wary of the snake, for that is the founder of all our sufferings. You took the snake inside you. You have its venom, crawling in you. One day it will talk like him, smell like him, move and think like him and you... you will be blind to its wickedness, for even the devil's mother is still a mother, and her love for the devil is still love.

Habat is holding the stone with both hands, sharp edge looking down.

One strike. One strike to rid me of the shame he brought upon me; one strike to cleanse me of the pain he caused me.

She leans her body forth, ready to let her weight rest on the stone. She gathers her strength in her arms and aims for Era's belly.

One strike to avenge you, father. One strike to avenge all who suffer as we have.

She looks at Era's face. She hesitates. Loosens her grip on the stone and takes it in one hand. She looks at Era's belly. Determined, she brings the stone again in both hands.

One strike. One strike and vengeance will be mine.

Her eyes get drawn to Era's face again. Brief glances back to her belly do nothing to change the fact that she somehow wants to focus on her face instead, on the peace lingering behind her closed eyelids.

What you carry inside you is my shame… but not yours. You have only been kind to me and my father. You don't deserve this. It was never your fault. Never our fault.

Many long breaths and even longer stares later, she quietly moves away from Era and steps outside the cave.

Just as my father waited patiently for me to birth my shame before he had his revenge, so will I. One day I will strike down upon your child and your man and your god and whatever else he might be, but not you. I know you will hate me for it. I would too. And if you choose to avenge them, I will understand. But I won't hate you.

She hears noise coming from above her. Rocks tumbling and cracking. She looks up at Fos and sees a shadow moving, spilling over the edge of the crag. At first, she wonders which one of the two gods is on guard, but moments later she hears a voice—the voice of the young god. He's uttering words in short bursts, as if urging himself, or debating with himself.

Twice he came to visit her today and twice she ignored him, pretending to be asleep. Now she goes to him in need of company and not just anyone's company—his company.

Last night, when she held the fiery branch in her hands, he surrendered his life to her. He just closed his eyes and laid every chance bare before her. She had every opportunity to hurt him, leave him, kill him. Every right to hold the light, drop the light, steal the light… no other man has ever given her a choice. No other man's will has ever been so considerate of her own.

She finds him standing behind a line drawn in the dirt, about to throw a stone at another pile of stones. Some sort of a game, it seems. The moment he sees her, he smiles and gestures for her to come close to him. He gives her a stone and shows her how to play the game.

A fun game, she admits to herself after a few tosses, but not as fun as Kugelach, the game she and father used to play together. She brings together another pile of carefully selected stones—five stones small enough for all to fit in a single palm—and she teaches him the rules of the game. You throw all five of them on the ground. Pick one up and toss it in the air and using the same hand, you must pick up as many stones as you can and catch the same one you threw. If you fail to catch the one you threw, you lose. The one who catches the most stones, wins.

They play a few turns of each game and then switch. He's neither swift nor graceful enough to be good at her game. Herself, not accurate enough to be any good at his. They laugh and tease each other about it. Long into the night, they're still enjoying each other. He shows her how to nurture the light; offers her food and water and the safety of his warm embrace as they sit by the circle of stones. His kindness has cleansed her mind from sorrow, even for a little while. She welcomes his heavy breath on her neck and gathers his hands on her breasts.

No words are spoken between them. There is no need of them.

III
III

GNOSIS

ᛏᚹᛏ

A new painting on the wall. Lines astray and incomplete. Ra hears their whispers throughout the night, begging for his care, tormenting his ears. A constant murmur wriggling in his mind and starving him of sleep. The three faces of god, all three with eyes painted open wide. *Maybe that's why I can't sleep,* he thinks. *If I paint their eyes shut, they might let me sleep tonight.*

The first face is what the people see, painted with the white of light's dust—the face he wears because he wants to. The image of a god who never bleeds, almighty and all-knowing. He is the white light whose touch is a blessing all men yearn for. The creator whose word is righteous and constant. His law everlasting. Definite. He has given their lives a deeper meaning, a grand purpose far beyond survival.

The second face is black. Hidden from strangers. He and his brother, the only ones who can see it. The face of a vengeful god, meticulous and cunning. A god that only sees men as a collection of useful numbers. He is the black cloud, whose wrath falls upon whoever violates the law. A destroyer full of gripe, unable to forget, unwilling to forgive. A god that will never trust men with the light, for they have proven themselves unworthy. They will burn the whole mountain down if he lets them hold such divine strength in their weak, mortal grasps. No man as worthy as father. No one. No woman can match the spark of mother. A face painted with the black of scorched wood, dedicated to preserving authority. Only caring about the numbers. The face he wears because he must.

The last face is just an outline still. Empty lines carved on the wall with a stone, awaiting fulfillment.

"Herae mega Ra," speaks a man's voice from outside, "yvris."

Ra takes Fos outside while the evening is still young, sooner than it is custom. They have all gathered under the crag at his command. The many old faces know what this means and the few newcomers are about to find out. His brother is missing, again, and so is Habat.

Two men, with faces painted with white dust, are holding another man captive at the path's end, forcing him down to his knees. A man from the woods, where most of them live now. Too many people have made a home of the mountain, with not enough time in a day anymore to have a great gathering for everyone. There's not enough time for Ra to teach the common words to the new and still teach new words to the old. So, he has allowed others to spread his words for him. Men with white-painted faces were assigned the task of teaching everything they knew to the people of the woods. By force, if they must, for nothing is more important than uniformity in the way of the tongue. It is that simple—the words of the old world must die.

More of them come every day. Their numbers double with every full moon. Some find shelter in the deep woods, others by the rocky lands further down the mountain's roots. The newcomers need to learn quickly that whoever speaks the lost tongues of the old world suffers great punishment, so examples like today are necessary. The light is what brings them here, but it's Ra's words that keep the herd united in understanding and at such great numbers. No beast can taste man's flesh anymore unless man himself is negligent. The people seem to believe Fos is the one keeping them safe.

If only they knew...

Ra starts hovering a sharp stone over the light, often turning it around, so the light can crawl on all sides. When the stone gets warm, he shoves it in the charring branches at the bottom and waits for its hard skin to darken. He pulls the blazing stone out with a stick and uses a wet pelt to lift it. He walks up to the men, feet pounding strong over dirt and white dust.

Once the captive sees the sharp stone, he starts shouting, struggling to free himself. Ra neither knows nor cares who this man is. It's getting progressively harder to remember any specific face or a voice. To his eyes, they all look the same. The same voice speaks through everyone's mouth. All he cares about is that the words they speak are of his own creation and he was told this man still speaks in old tongues and refuses to learn the words of the herd. Yvris, Ra calls it—this is the word for *sin*.

Ra takes a wooden cup. One of the women made it for him. It's a remarkable creation, yet so simple; it makes you wonder how it never crossed anyone's mind to create one before. He places the cup right between the sinner's knees, then pulls his head back as the other two men stretch his arms wide. The man shakes and grumbles and spits out words no one understands, which infuriates Ra even more.

He pushes the scorching stone up against the man's cheek. Screams of agony send the birds flying upwards, off the cave's roof and straight into the arms of Aeos. He then shoves the stone in the man's mouth and starts slicing as if trying to rip out his thoughts, smashing his teeth and choking his screams in blood. He makes him suffer for as long as the stone stays hot.

White dust leaps off the ground and follows the wind's path when Ra drops the blood-drenched stone, leaving the sinner with a swollen, carved face and a mouthful of blood and broken teeth. He grabs him by the back of the neck and forces him to spit the blood in the cup, then instructs the other men to let him go. The sinner falls hard, crying like a woman. Ra allows him to keep his tongue—he never takes their tongue.

He pulls another sharp stone from his side and repeats the heating process. This time he calls for the two men to come closer and they do so with a glow in their eyes, like the morning shine. He allows them to feel the light's warmth, then leads them to the edge of the crag while all the others below keep cheering them on. He takes the stone and carves a sign on the side of their foreheads— the sign of the light's chosen. They welcome the pain, embrace it as joy. Ra gathers their blood in the cup as well. The people's cheers, subtle at first, become noise. The two men raise their fists in the air and yell of victory over the storm of voices.

Most men living in the deadlands carry this sign. Men that do as they're told and speak as they should. They wear the light's mark with pride, proof of their devotion and willingness to serve him. But some of them have grown in confidence a little too much for his liking. He can tell by the hesitancy with which they bow before him lately. He can see it in their eyes when they come to collect their share during the gathering. Not much fear in their gaze anymore. Eyes full of ambition.

This is all her fault—Habat's fault. Not only do the people know she can carry Fos at will, but she can speak the word of the hawk too. He recognizes his words in the trail of her voice every night when her singing spreads as the light would spread if he tossed a fiery branch down the mountainside. She paints the air with invisible colors and drowns the deadlands in a mournful yet attractive cadence people can't have enough of. His brother seems to be teaching her more words every day, careless as always. It's as if she has turned the blood under his skin into water and guides the stream of his manners as she desires. Like a beautiful flower, Leos treats her; too blind to see, even the most charming flowers have deadly thorns.

Habat never comes to the great gathering for her share. She has yet to speak a single word to Ra since that day. She stays as far away from him as possible. The rare times Ra comes down from the cave, she shows him her back while everyone else bows before him. A vile breed of a vile man she is.

He has chosen not to punish her, even though it would bring him great pleasure to cut off her tongue, dip it in white dust and shove it down her throat. But as much distraught as she brings to him, she brings equal joy to his brother. He has also noticed her belly growing.

He sends the sinner crawling back down the path to his people. A few men and women are waiting for him. The people of the deadlands start kicking and shoving them, spitting and throwing rocks at them as they carry the man away.

A natural hierarchy has developed in the shape of the mountain; one Ra had no intention of creating but grew out of necessity instead. The people of the woods stay in the woods, whether they like it or not. And the people of the deadlands keep them there, for there's no more space for newcomers in the deadlands. They force them to carry the piles of branches that Fos demands every day. Only the ones who bring the piles get to taste warm meat. He allows it, for it keeps the men occupied with each other. He doesn't mind the hierarchy's shape, just as long as he and his brother remain safe at the top.

A gust of wind throws sparks of light against his face and he slits his eyes against them. The two men bow before him in gratitude before they leave. He waves his hand at them without ever looking.

If only they knew...

He takes the blood-filled cup and goes back inside. He stands facing the wall, gazing at the painting, teasing the blood in the cup by making circles with the tip of his finger. The soothing feeling of blood crawling under his long nail helps him think. The last face of god. The one only he alone can see. A face he's too embarrassed to reveal, even to his beloved brother.

He will never admit it, but deep inside, he envies them. They all come here in search of gods and gods they find. Gods they can touch, feel, listen to. He is to them a father who cannot die and not a day passes without wishing father back to life.

The face of a jealous god he paints, bitter and sensitive. He is the red light, the one who bleeds for eternity. All the envy inside hurts like sickness in his blood, and the blood never stops flowing. The face of a god wishing he was just a man. A child again, under his father's care. A face painted with the red of man's blood.

ΑΛΦΑ

The night mates with the day and together they birth the brilliant moment of dawn, reminding Leos of how the light is still a force beyond his understanding. What makes Fos? At this most glorious moment of exchange between light and darkness, what makes a spark burst into life through the womb of total blackness? What does this phasma of divine menace want from such inferior soils? How can something so powerful and ruthless need so much care and attention from lesser beings? There's a secret hidden in the sky's cunning ways. A secret the night and day keep for themselves, too complex for any mortal mind to grasp.

A loud yawn ends his inner contemplation as Ra comes out of the cave to take his place watching the light. Instead of heading back into the cave, Leos takes the path to the deadlands.

"Where you go?" Ra asks. "No sleep?"

"Sleep later." He keeps walking down the path and waves his hand at Ra without turning around. "I come soon."

Every morning, he takes Habat for a walk beyond the deadlands to the green slopes at the mountain's shoulder, where waterfalls are aplenty and the ground is full of flowers and friendly to her gentle feet. He likes to get away from the others and so does she.

But not this morning. Today, he leaves early and goes about his way through the woods alone, hoping he can get this done before she wakes up.

Ever since her belly grew apparent with a child, he has been wanting to make something for her. He's not sure what. Something unusual and creative; something only she can have that only speaks of him. It would have been much easier if he could ask his brother for help. Ra is so good at creating things from his mind alone. If only time could heal her wounds and calm his rage, but time alone can't stop a bleeding wound when the cut runs to the bone… time can't soothe the rage in men whose minds have never known peace.

His gaze strips the ground, moves up the trees and beyond, to the blue of the sky sliding through the branches, looking for something an idea can flourish from. It's the most beautiful time in the weather's cycle, with flowers blooming everywhere, giving his eyes the pleasure of seeing the stunning colors only the flowers possess and only during this time.

I could gather flowers for her, he thinks while wandering around. *But then again, she does that by herself, for herself, all the time. No, everyone can pick up flowers for anyone. It has to be something only she can have, that only I can give.* He keeps looking while constantly tapping the side of the lion's skull over his head with a sharpened stone.

Why not give her the lion's skull? She will be the only one to possess such a rare thing, and I, the only one who can provide it for her. He stops by a tree and starts carving random, tilted lines intermingling with each other on its trunk. He reviews his thoughts for a moment. *No, that's a fool's act. A beast's skull speaks of the way of the hunt. Such an act has nothing to show of my feelings for her. Think. Something else…*

He halts his inner reasoning and just as he's about to start wandering again, he looks at the tree's trunk. He has been spontaneously carving the mountain's sign all this time, over and over again. And the same sign again as many times, but upside down.

Coming out of deep concentration, the mind can sometimes do better work than the hand. He visualizes the two shapes coming together. Two opposite mountains, attracting each other like lovers. When their peaks meet, it's as if one mountain is standing upside down, laying all its weight over the other mountain's peak.

X

He tilts his head slightly on one side. His eyes narrow. Focusing. Challenging his mind to see further, to create motion where there is none. He tilts his head over to the other side. *It's the exact same shape any which way you look at it.* He keeps staring at the tree's trunk as the shape in his mind comes to life right before his eyes. All that truly exists on the tree's trunk is a messy gathering of many random, slanted lines. That's all it is. Chaos. Casualness. Accidents. But his mind finds hidden order where his eyes cannot.

It feels odd but enthralling. As if looking is one thing and seeing is another. The two lovers keep moving towards each other, as each peak gradually passes through the other.

What he sees forming in the gap between the two peaks is the most charming shape, of four sides, made with four lines equal in length, whose four edges come together in harmony, making it seem like a mountain is standing over its perfect reflection in the water.

What a beautiful, perfect thing, he ponders. *No stone is like this. No tree or shrub, no leaf, fruit, or cloud. This shape is not innate to the world I know. Such strict excellence must come to life in the mind first. A perfect shape in an imperfect world.* Using his finger, he follows the lines forming the shape, barely touching the tree's skin. Not even Habat has felt such gentle touch coming from him. *The flawless love of a flawed man. She will love this.*

He remembers the wooden cup a woman gave him. An awkward-looking shape, round at some points and with steep corners at others. The woman was focused on creating the hole in the middle—serving its main function as a holder of water—rather than crafting something friendly to the eye. Nevertheless, the cup is proper in its intentional use and now he wants to create something using the exact opposite mentality. A wooden piece of no actual purpose. An object which exists only to please the eye.

He needs a piece of wood he can manipulate, thick and heavy, so it doesn't bend or break by the grinding of stone. His gaze moves around the tree's branches. A branch is at its strongest at the point it meets the tree's trunk. He soon finds one he can use. Sturdy, unbothered by the wind's flow and thick as a man's leg.

It takes him a long while to cut down such a strong branch. By the time it finally snaps and tumbles to the ground, he's already sweating all over, hands aching. He hasn't even begun grinding for the shape he wants yet.

He holds the branch steady with one hand and starts cutting through it with the sharpened stone, trying to get rid of the useless part, which is most of it. He only wants to keep the strongest, thickest piece. The length of a forearm should do. He grinds as fast and as hard as he can until his hands can grind no more. He takes a moment to catch his breath. Cutting through such wood is a grueling task, so much harder than just breaking it off the tree. He can't push, pull, or use his weight in any way. He can't even cut using both hands. He wipes the sweat dripping down his face and looks to find Aeos' position in the sky. The time he usually meets with Habat is long gone. He resumes grinding again, faster this time; with malice even, groaning and hating at the wood's stubbornness.

Halfway through completion, he stops. *Fool,* he thinks, *useless, with a head full of flies.* Seeing a shape in your mind is one thing; getting it done in the real world is another. He leaves the stone jammed in the wood, punches it with the bottom of his fist once, then starts whacking the side of the lion's skull repeatedly, furious with himself. He has been cutting the piece at the wrong length. Its length should be the same as its thickness for it to be a perfect shape.

Head full of flies. Flies, flies, flies. He draws the stone out of the wood with a sharp move and sits back. He rests his arms on his knees, holding the stone with both hands and squeezes its tip as if it was at fault. *God of the flies. I can't b—*

He squints and pulls his hand away in pain. The stone's warmth just hurt his palm.

That's what...you are...

The warmth the stone emanates, a force of harm he knows well.

God of...

Intense heat, as if it came from…

"…Fos."

He rubs the stone's tip with his thumb. The warmth is fading but still a force to be wary of. He pulls himself forward, sits on his knees and sinks his finger through the lips of the wound on the branch. The cut is barely wide enough for his smallest finger to fit in. He shuts his eyes and focuses on his touch. The wood is warm inside, hot even. He hears a voice in his head. A young boy's voice and the clatter of stone striking against stone, remnants of times long gone.

The warmth you feel is nothing new. Must I remind you? There is warmth in all things and you have known this your whole life. Sometimes the truths of life are hidden in plain sight, old man, but your sight can only get you so far. Sometimes, all you need is a strike of lightning in your mind. And as you have followed the line's path on the tree to create the perfect shape, I now dare you to follow the warmth's path. Pay attention, old man. I'm just the boy in you and even I know where it leads. I have always known where it leads, but sometimes… sometimes you need to wait for the day fortune strikes.

His eyes widen. His breathing quickens. The more you grind things, the warmer they get. If the grind never stops and the warmth keeps growing, where does it end?

He takes the edge of the branch and snaps it off. The edge is not as thick as the rest of it, much easier to handle. He brings his knees together and fits the branch in the gap between his knees. Now he can hold the stone with both hands. He starts grinding down the length of the wood, scraping through its rough skin with fierce determination. He unleashes all the strength he has in his arms, all the speed he can muster in his hands. He keeps grinding, refusing to stop, no matter how much his arms hurt or how much sweat he spatters.

The branch snaps in two pieces and startles him.

Shit.

The stone has ripped straight through it, cracked it in half.

His breaths are heavy. With every inhale, it feels like he's swallowing water. *What am I doing wrong?* He looks at the stone. It's much harder than wood. Fit for cutting through things with force, but not for what he's trying to accomplish—sustained friction.

At this moment, he realizes he has never used wood to grind anything. Ever. The stone has always been the obvious grinding tool of choice and for a good reason. Why use wood when it's so much easier with stone?

He takes the smallest of the two pieces of wood and uses the stone to break it into an even smaller one. A wooden grinding tool, the length of his forearm, as thick as a thumb. *Using my strength in long, dragged-out moves is for cutting,* he assesses, *and that's not what I need. I must balance power with speed. The warmth fades away quickly. I need to keep it persistent, constantly growing.*

All that matters is conflict. One piece of wood moves and attacks; the other stands still and pushes back. He grinds wood against wood using short and rapid thrusts and pulls. His hands keep sliding with a back-and-forth motion over the length of the branch. He chips away at its surface as it gradually curves inwards, creating a shallow, thin groove down the center.

After grinding for a while, he stops, with his hands trembling in complaint. The wood hasn't snapped in two like before, but not much else has happened either. When he pushes his palm against the groove, he feels intense warmth. It's as if he's back in the cave hovering his hand over Fos, but there is no source of light here. There's a barrier he can't see and everything he's been doing so far is not enough to push through. He lays on his back to rest for a while. He needs to think.

The conflict has created a slightly hollow area in the middle of the branch. Again, the image of the cup comes to mind. Its primary function is to hold water, but if you were to take it—or any other small and hollow artifact—and fill it up with light, what would you use to feed the light in such a confined space?

The tiniest, most fragile shreds of wood. The wooden dust that gathers around the area I grind. I have been blowing them off the shallow area, keeping it clean. Perhaps I should let the dust pile on and see what happens.

Once the strength returns to his arms, he starts grinding. He grinds while Aeos moves past his highest point and the shadows gradually begin to move sideways. No matter how much his arms hurt, he doesn't stop. No matter how much he wants to wipe his sweat away, to scratch off the itch crawling under his beard, he keeps going.

The tiniest, faintest wisp of smoke comes rising through the wood's dust. A pain grows in his chest as if his heart missed a beat. He grinds faster, blinking more often than he needs to, convinced his eyes are lying to him. Soon many delicate wisps of tiny clouds appear. A truth as pure as clean water, feeding off the wood's dust at the edge of the hollow area. He keeps grinding faster and harder.

Curls of grey clouds, becoming thicker and whiter, rise and fill his nose with the scent of scorched wood, soaking his eyes with the sourness only the light's dust can excrete. He groans, feeling like someone is ripping his arms off his shoulder joints. His tortured wrists refuse to bend anymore. But he never stops.

An ember forms in the wood's dust. His eyes narrow. *Am I really seeing what I'm seeing, or have I killed myself from exhaustion?* He leans his head forward to take a closer look. A spark jumps out of the ember and lands on his forehead.

He drops everything, jumps back and crawls away. His arms can no longer hold a stick, let alone carry his weight around, so he falls hard on his back, dazed and drenched in sweat but trembling like a naked man freezing to death in the heart of the mountain's cold. A few moments pass when he can do nothing but breathe and take shy looks through heavy-lidded eyes, incapable of lifting a finger or even turning his head. He tries to get up but falls back down. He lifts his chest and manages to steady himself on his elbows. He sees the wisps of white clouds spreading over the branch like mist before dissipating into the air. The ember turns into black, scorched wood. The tiniest sparks in the ember, jumping in and out of existence still.

The impossibility of what just happened soon gives him the strength he needs to crawl back to the piece of wood and sit on his knees before it. He wipes his aching eyes.

What have I done?

ΦΩΣ

Ra hurries through the deadlands just as the early evening sets. All eyes are on him, for he holds the light in his hand. Fos should never leave the cave, but this time he has no choice. Leos left at dawn and has yet to return.

Era's agonies have unsettled him, her screams sweeping over the deadlands like a fierce wind. He shouldn't worry—her pain is of a woman in labor—but he needs to see with his own eyes that she's well taken care of.

The people make way for Ra to pass. Most bow down in humility, making supplicating gestures, while some others simply lower their heads. A few don't even bother, pretending to look elsewhere and doing other things, but he can sense their side-looks stealing the light's flare. The last time he passed through the deadlands was the day he killed Habat's father. The people were faces painted in fear back then; every reaction to his actions was a sign of respect. Now, they seem so unaffected by his presence that it sickens him to be walking amongst them.

He lowers his head and moves a few steps inside Era's shelter. He sees one of the older women reaching between her legs and Habat by her side, holding her hand and comforting her. Poena has Era resting in her arms and that is all the cave can fit inside.

The light draws everyone's attention; everyone except Habat's. She turns and looks straight at him, skipping the light with her gaze as if it was air.

"Leos, where?" she says with worry in her tone. Ra is taken aback for a moment. So long it's been since she last spoke to him.

"Leos, leave early. No sleep," he says, unable to hide the irritation in his voice. His brother teaching her the words of the hawk is a lump in the throat he can't swallow.

"Why? Where go?"

Ra shrugs. "Leos know. Me no." He moves another step further inside the cave, enough for his eyes to meet Era's eyes as she moans through growing pains.

"Ra, paes oda," Era says to him, taking one long, heavy breath after another. He nods at her and a shadow of a smile appears at the corners of her mouth. He reaches out for her and Era reaches out for him too. Her smile grows bright and clear as their palms meet. Ra caresses her fingers with care and then draws his hand back.

"When child come?" he asks Habat. He waits a while for her to answer, but Habat never replies. She won't even turn to meet his eyes. So he looks to Poena for answers and asks her the same. "Pote paes oda?"

"Ra Fos oda, paes oda," says Poena.

A little me, mother once said, he thinks as he leaves Era's cave. He heads back, eager to get all the preparations for the great gathering out of his way, expecting the birth of his firstborn to come around the same time.

Further up ahead, a woman is feeding her infant child. A child wrapped in fur, its tiny hands all over her breast. He only gives them a passive glance, nothing worthy of notice for him at first. But as he passes right by them, he slows down and takes another look at the hungry child emptying its mother's breast, longing for warmth and care. His eyes see skin and hair and a dull evening glare on the woman's face. His mind drifts further, piercing through the surface of things, spreading the world's chest wide open to expose its naked heart.

He stops and faces them, caressing his forefinger with his thumb. His eyes see a woman holding a child; his mind sees a woman holding herself—her new self.

Once the child is full, the woman drags her breasts back behind the fur she's wearing and hugs the child, resting its head on the side of her neck. *What a selfish thing to do,* he ponders, *to hug yourself. To love yourself. Would she have fed the child if it had not been her own?*

He walks away.

His gaze moves around the deadlands as he walks up the path to the cave. A man is drinking water from a pelt, pouring it all over his face.

Predictable.

Another man sitting by a tree is eating something, some fruit maybe, he can't be sure of what exactly.

Dull.

Children playing in the dirt, laughing, running after each other in circles. Two boys start to brawl, rolling on the floor like young man-eaters fighting over a bone. A woman comes in and stops the fight. She picks up one of the boys and checks to see if he's hurt. She doesn't even look at the other boy, whose knees are bleeding. She doesn't check to see if he's well. She only cares for her own. All that matters is herself. The well-being of her new self.

Ungodly.

He starts the preparations for the great gathering, still contemplating, building structure with the visuals pouring in his mind. *It's all about preserving the self. Man eats, man drinks, man protects his own. All man does is for himself. Man breeds children not because he wants to, but because he needs to.* He takes as many branches as he can carry in an armful and places them carefully within the circle of stones. *A woman holding her child. A mortal, holding tight the only way she can outlast death. The only means she has to save herself. The natural law of the desperate. A fool's way to fool immortality.* He realizes he has forgotten to clean the circle from the white dust left over from the last gathering. He needs to do this before placing the fresh branches. He's trying to focus on the task, but his mind is a cluster of blazing thoughts smashing into each other in frantic speed.

A way to bring the fear back. The last line in the dirt I will ever need.

He cleans the circle of all the white dust. He doesn't even use pelts to do it. He just drags it out with his bare hands. Era's screams become more intense. *To make a home of fear in people's hearts. A cave that, once you enter, you can never escape.* He lays a massive stack of branches in the middle of the circle and spreads the stones further away from each other to enlarge it. *A barrier at the cave's mouth, so high, no man will ever break.* He sets the stack of branches alight. He wants Fos to rise higher today, the highest it has ever been and stronger than ever. This will be a day to remember.

The barrier of death. All mortals, forever trapped inside the cave of fear. Only the gods outside, roaming the fields free. Real gods are immortal. They do not fear death. Real gods don't need—

The cries of a newborn break his trail of thought. "Mega Ra, paes," he hears Poena shouting. He looks down over the crag and sees her gasping with joy, holding his firstborn in a pelt while others around rejoice. "Elthe mega Ra," she says and lifts the child high, "paes aner."

Ra waves for her to bring the infant boy up to the cave. He stands straight, still holding a fiery branch in one hand, feet touching each other, arms stretching outwards at shoulders height. The sign of the hawk.

"Fos," he shouts, pushing his voice to its limits, stretching the word to last as long as it would take to utter it ten or twelve times. The hawk demands everyone's attention and the people rush to gather at his command.

He turns and throws the branch in the light. Crazed by a strong wind, the flaming tongues make voices out of crackles and crisp snaps, words of pure ruin and havoc, yet always confined within the circle of stones. The scorched heart of the heavens beating against the contrived restraints of the land.

Poena comes up from his side, bows and offers him the boy. He takes the pelt and unwraps it, revealing his firstborn son, who has been washed, cleaned and dried, not a single spot of blood on him. *How things have changed.* His brother's early moments come to mind. Mother's blood all over his hands, blending with filth and sweat and dust like red mud stuck all over his dark flesh.

With a flick of his wrist, he instructs Poena to leave.

"Paes Ra?" she says and reaches out to take back the boy, but Ra denies her. The boy stays.

"Sy ode Era."

"Nae Ra, nae. Emon ode Era." She keeps her head low, constantly nodding as she retreats and off she goes back to help Era.

Ra pulls the pelt from under the boy and lays the newborn barren in his stretched palm, throwing away the pelt. He stands at the edge of the crag and the moment he lifts his son high over his head with both hands, people start throwing fists in the air, cheering and praising and clapping and knocking spear against spear, stone against stone. The noise of their celebration is so loud and constant, Ra can barely hear his son crying.

Listen... they cheer for you, son. They cheer because you give them hope. For them, you are all the breaths in the world to share; you are the beat of all their hearts pounding as one. You stand for life beyond death and they will pretend to love you for it, but their love for you is a lie, son. Love impure as they are, for they only love themselves. If I had told them your blood could wash away the stain of death forever, they would argue and rip the eyes off one another, push and drag and step all over each other, scrambling all over you like rats on who will be the first to taste your blood. And they would drain you, son. They would smash your head and rip your chest and wash themselves with your insides… they wouldn't waste a single drop of you.

Ra lowers his son and lays him in the palm of his hand, resting its fragile little head on the tips of his fingers. He points with his other hand at the faint shine of Aeos descending beyond the line at the edge of the world. "Herae Fos," he says and the people rejoice. He sees Habat helping Era as they make their way through the crowd and Poena comes along moments later.

"Brother, I—I show—I show you." Leos is coming up the path running wild, his words stumbling over ragged gasps as he's trying to run, breathe and shout at the same time.

Where has he been all day? He needs to see this too. More than anyone else. Ra turns around and stands facing the light. *My love for you is pure, son. Forgive their lies, they are mere mortals living in fear. Embrace the truth of your divine bloodline, for real gods don't fear death.*

The moment Leos steps his foot on the clearing, he leans forward and rests his hands on his trembling knees, struggling to bring words together. "Listen brother—Fos I, I show—I show you… child brother? Child you—no!"

Real gods don't need children.

Ra throws his son in the light and the roaring flames swallow the boy's cries in an instant. Cheers turn to startled gasps; gasps fade to eerie whispers; whispers recede to nothing just as Era's shrieking wails shatter the momentary silence.

"No." Leos rushes and dips both of his hands in the flames. "No, n—no, brother why?" He almost jumps in the light himself, trying to snatch the boy, but Ra pulls him back.

"Calm, brother," Ra says and shoves his brother all the way back to the cave's entrance. "My child safe. Child, mother, father, together. Child Fos together one."

Leos keeps trying to reach the light, but Ra won't allow it. One push, harder than Ra intended it to be, sends Leos to the ground. Ra moves with authority towards him, pretending the strength in his push was intentional. Leos doesn't try to get back up. He just sits there and buries his face in his hands.

Ra searches the light with his gaze. A tiny, blackened head is moving, sinking through the cracks of dying branches and twigs, as if his son is still gasping for air somehow. The head soon drowns in bright violence, slipping and tumbling further down the blazing cluster until Ra can no longer tell the difference between smoldering flesh and scorched wood. If not for the smell, no other sign remains of his son.

He returns to the edge and faces a crowd of shadows. For a moment, there's a nervous exchange of murmurs amongst them, then silence returns once Era stops wailing and loses her senses. Habat and Poena rush to grab her before she falls. They lay her down and disappear in the crowd's shade.

A skin of horror has covered the land. He sees the faces of so many reduced to only one. There are no more men or women amongst them. Neither young nor old. The same look of awe and dread is painted on all of them. One common stare. His finest, most gorgeous creation. If only he could rip this image from his eyes and place it on the wall next to his other paintings, for it truly belongs there amongst his greats. A lifeless, still moment of a glorious memory hanging on a wall, so all mortals can know how it feels to see through the eyes of a god.

Feet come together at the ankles. Arms stretching outwards at shoulders height. He lowers his head, hiding his face behind the hawk's skull.

Behold, children of the dirt. Rats, looking to the heavens as if they were another hole you could crawl through. Let my son's sacrifice be the flesh that forever holds you bound to your mortal bones. Love him for all the hope that he may be and fear me... fear me, for all the thunder that I am.

"Herae Ra," someone says from the crowd. A trembling voice, afraid to speak out. A breath later, another voice shouts the same, louder, with more confidence. Then a trail of voices rises to praise, voices balancing themselves between wonder and dread. The cheers spread faster than the light spreads over fresh, dry shrubs. Only one shadow rises through the crowd and stands still and silent, surrounded by a mess of raucous hails and frenzied gestures. Ra takes a closer look. Only she stays calm—only Habat.

Ra waves at the frenzied crowd, urging them to revel in his divine ways. "Peaeo paes," he shouts, "aner lave gyne." There's no reason the people shouldn't find pleasure in their horror; no reason not to savor their servitude. *Have sons and daughters and have many, for you are no gods and you never will be. Might as well enjoy the flesh, for you can never become more. Only less.*

Men begin to take their pleasure from women as Ra turns his back at them and walks up to his brother. Leos is still sitting on the ground, with his hands covering his face up to his nose as if struggling to keep himself silent. The light's bright is dashing through his wide-open eyes.

"Children for weak men," Ra says while staring down at Leos. "We gods, strong like Fos. We no need children, brother you no—"

Even though he's not finished, he restrains his words, expecting his brother to jump in and say something, but Leos holds his tongue. Never moves a muscle. All Ra can see is the lion's skull and glowing eyes hiding in shadows behind jittery hands.

"—Habat birth soon… yes?" Ra finishes.

The moment Leos hears these last words, he jumps back to his feet and brings his face so close to Ra's they almost share the same breath. The lion rises against the hawk, as Leos pulls a sharp stone from his side; Ra welcomes the menace in his brother's eyes and stares right back, accepting the challenge and refusing to back down.

"Show me what?" Ra says, changing the subject. He got the reaction he was looking for.

"What?" Leos mutters. Since he got up, he has yet to blink. He looks like his body is in one place while his mind is elsewhere. After a long, silent moment of them staring at each other, Leos moves his gaze away from Ra and takes a swift glance over the crag, so swift that Ra could have missed it with just an ill-timed blink of his eyes.

He's thinking of her. He worries for her. Even now, with my firstborn's scorched stench still lingering in our breaths, she's clouding his vision more than ever.

"You say before," Ra reminds him, "you want show me." He shakes his head ever so slightly but never breaks eye contact. "Show me what?"

Leos' lips move, but just as the words are about to slip from his tongue, he hesitates. He turns his back at Ra and takes the path to the deadlands, tapping the sharp stone against the side of his leg.

"Nothing," Leos says.

He never looks back.

ΑΛΗΘ

Leos looks for Habat through a feverish crowd of terrified women running away from men who have lost all sense of composure and restraint. Everywhere Leos looks, he sees his brother's touch caressing everyone's hair. He hears his voice whispering in every ear. A madness turning to habit right before his eyes.

Some of the older women give in quietly, as men carrying the light's mark take their pleasure in turns. The younger ones, girls with breastless chests, rattle the land with the sobs of their martyred youth, for they struggle and bite and claw and refuse to give in, but too many men are demanding too much flesh and the women are not enough to please them all at once.

He hurries through the chaos with relentless purpose. A hand grabs him by the ankle and stops him in his tracks. A girl lying on the ground, screaming under the weight of a man trying to force her still. Leos pushes him off the girl and she wastes no time in running away. The man's first look at him is a reactive one, full of aggression; with the second look the man realizes who Leos is and flees.

Just ahead, two more men are holding a girl down by the wrists while another man thrusts his way inside her. And a few others are by the cliff, violating a woman who is either dead or unconscious. Her legs lay flat while she takes a man's force, not moving or reacting at all to his rage.

Further down, another man is slamming a woman's back against a tree, with one hand squeezing her throat, the other reaching up to her womanhood. Then the same man appears—the same he shoved just moments ago— passing behind the tree, dragging another unwilling girl through the dirt and slapping her to tears.

"Leos."

Habat's voice rises over the sickening howls of the crowd like a blossom grows through the cracks of skin-slicing rocks. He follows her voice, pushing people left and right to clear his way and finds her standing by a tree, searching for him through the crowd in utter despair. Era is sitting under the tree with Poena at her side, both still as if they're a jagged piece of wood extending off the tree's trunk.

Habat rushes to him and hugs him tight. Her whole body is shivering. The warmth of three of her breaths overwhelms the side of his neck in the time it takes for him to breathe just once.

"Calm," Leos whispers in her ear, "I here now."

She starts breathing even faster. Leos feels her hand creeping nervously up the back of his neck and through his mane, looking for the man hiding under the lion's skull.

"They—they no move," she mutters, "Er—Era like stone."

Leos hunkers down opposite Era and Poena. Era's face hides under the shadows of disheveled hair as Poena caresses her; she is murmuring words too faint for Leos to understand.

"Oun dakry, gyne," he says and tries to drag Era's hair away from her face to wipe her tears, but she grabs his wrist and stops him. She pushes his hand away and raises her voice just enough for Leos to make out some of her words. Nonsensical words. *The child is alive in death.* Delusional. *The child is waiting.* Dangerous.

Leos reaches out to take Era's hand. "Elthe gyne, e mon e sy. Poena, Habat, meida evre ."

She slaps his hand away. A vague expression takes over her grief-stricken face. She looks at him like she can't even recognize him. She drags her eyes, opening and closing them halfway as if constantly falling in and out of shallow sleep.

The realization comes to Leos as sudden as waking up from a nightmare and finding yourself lying at the edge of the mountain's highest ridge, one slight nudge away from falling over. His weary eyes struggle to focus, jumping from one heartless act of hysteria to the other. All around him, a violent storm of manic delusion spreads, determined to drown the world in his brother's ways. It doesn't matter if he sets a branch alight right now. He won't be turning one god into a mortal; he'll be turning many mortals into gods, eager to storm the mountain's foothills and beyond with their new-found power. For the light is many things, a tool yes, but a weapon also. More than anything… Fos is confidence. Fos is influence.

Era gets up and stumbles past Leos and ignores Habat completely. Poena goes after her as they disappear into the crowd, heading towards Era's shelter. Era starts shouting praise for the light; her muffled moans blend despair with sickening delight. It disturbs Leos so much that he loses his footing while getting back to his feet and has to lay a hand on the tree for a while to keep his balance.

A burden sinks in his stomach. A cough stops in his throat. He lowers his head and closes his eyes, losing himself in a world of just sound. The madness in the men's roars, the terror in the children's cries. Countless feet pounding against the dirt, the wailing and screaming of bleeding girls passed around from one ravenous man to the other like warm slices of tender meat. His mind fills with thoughts that ache.

I am the reason for all this disarray. My brother only ever longed for us to be left alone, to make the mountain our home. I was the first drop of rain and out of me came this tempest and I just went with the flow as the soothing ripples grew into puddles and the puddles grew into violent rivers. And I washed away all ethos in my path, leaving behind a mud of despair as my testament. I set in motion the beginning of a new oppression, standing on the wretched shoulders of the old. A new delusion flooding the parched fields of a heartless land. Nothing I can do now. No way to stop the flood. Unless...

He turns to Habat. She's holding her belly as if expecting the child to come any moment now, even though it has only been a few full moons since her bearing became noticeable.

Unless...

"We go now," he says to her.

"Go? Where?"

"Far."

"Era? Poena?" She tilts her head, trying to catch a glance at Era and Poena through the crowd. "They come?"

"No. You, me." He caresses her belly. "Child. We go."

"No." Habat says, "Era like me, Era come with—"

"Era lost. All lost. My brother wants you in light. My brother wants our child. We go now."

Leos grabs her hand firmly from the wrist, forcing her to stay by his side as they make haste through the crowd. They move down the descending line of the cliff across the far side, staying close to the rocks. Habat sinks her feet in the dirt and pulls Leos back when they walk past the rocks that form the start of the cave's path.

"Fos Leos," she says and points at the path. "We need Fos."

"No need. We have Fos."

Habat gives him a confused look full of questions but doesn't defy his ways. They keep heading further away from the deadlands and deeper into the woods, just as Aeos reaches his resting place, shedding his pale orange skin on the world.

A burst of screams coming from the deadlands startles Leos, forcing him to stop for a brief moment as Habat squeezes his hand even harder. The screams rise above everything else and last for a while, turning all other noises coming from the crowd into faint murmurs. Then the screaming ends as if sliced in half by a sharp stone that could cut through agony.

Leos gently pulls Habat's hand a few times, signaling to her they need to keep moving. They must go deeper in the woods, where no eyes from the deadlands can see them, no matter how hard they try. He keeps looking over his shoulder as they heave themselves over a small ledge. After sliding further down through thick bushes, he takes another glance back. He can no longer see the light's bright through the dense trees.

"We stop here," he whispers and shows Habat a tree only a few steps ahead. Habat rests her back on its trunk while Leos clears the area around their feet from anything that isn't dirt or rock. He takes his sharpened stone, slices a long piece of wood from the tree's trunk, then climbs up and snaps a small branch. The noise from the snap makes Habat gasp.

"Leos," she mutters, "what you do? Noise. Beasts come."

He gathers everything he needs and lays it all on the ground in front of Habat. "I show you now. You watch me. You watch close."

He places everything as it ought to be and starts grinding while making all sorts of noise. The dense trees all around him block the already weakened evening light, creating night before nighttime, forcing the eyes to focus on the dimmest shades of grey they can find.

"Leos, I—I no understand," Habat mutters. "Noise you make, why?"

"Fos."

"What?"

"Soon… you see." He keeps grinding and when he feels his arms getting tired, he knows it's almost time, so he grinds even harder. All he needs is a spark. One spark and everything else will fall into place.

"Leos, I smell—" Habat whispers with the faintest of voices as the scent of burning wood spreads.

"—light. I smell cloud of light," she concludes, raising her tone to an anxious level, the astonishment in her voice evident for Leos to hear.

The smell of smoke makes him grind wood against wood harder and faster and when the first spark leaps and lands in the wood shavings, Habat releases a long gasp and jumps back against the tree. Leos keeps going, as Habat's first gasp leads to a trail of many. One moment there is one spark, the next moment countless. Wood shavings dissipate into scorched wood, while Leos nurtures the faint light by puffing air into its heart. He feeds it the tiniest of sticks and soon the newborn light grows strong enough to shine over Habat's face, watching with both hands pushing against her mouth, eyes wide and brows raised as far as they can go.

"Fos from nothing," Leos says, but Habat stays unreactive, speechless and motionless for a good while. Leos gives her some time to come to terms with what lies before her eyes. When she starts mumbling the "hows" and the "whys," he shows her again the way. This time he keeps the light to his side, so she can see his every move. After he sets another branch alight, he lays back, exhausted. "Now, you make."

Fos is confidence. Fos is influence. Even a swine in control of the light can rule over a den of lions. Unless…

control of the light, is the only thing a swine and a lion have in common.

They walk deep into the infant night, safe under the light's shine. Leos is leading the way with the fiery branch and Habat follows his every move, stepping wherever he steps, reaching wherever he reaches. He has chosen to take the rough paths that lead to the other side of the mountain. Narrow gaps of loose rock, cutting through the slope like open wounds to the mountain's chest, ascending over its shoulder and around its back. Dangerous paths to take during the night, but still the fastest way around the mountain and it keeps the deadlands out of sight.

He never tells her the truth. The path to the other side they walk together; the path of guilt, for deceiving her, he walks alone.

The ascend becomes descent. The cold in every breath is less harsh as the path grows wide and fades below into a lake of mist, with drowning treetops gasping for air. They are high enough to gaze above the mist, into the blur of the night sky, cloudless and almost starless. Selene is close to its full glory and Horaste, the mountain star, shines brighter than ever.

Leos stops and signals Habat to do the same. They have passed over the mountain's shoulders. He doesn't have to worry anymore about anyone from the deadlands seeing the light. Now the path down the other side of the mountain is a straightforward descent. Habat doesn't know the mountain as well as he does. Habat doesn't know how to move and keep the light out of sight as he does—this is the only reason he has come thus far. The only reason he has yet to send her away.

"Take," he says and offers her the light.

Habat looks at him with concern as she reluctantly takes the light from him.

"Why?"

Leos moves behind her. "You go now," he says. He brings one arm around her waist and caresses her belly. He lifts his other arm over her shoulder, points to the sky and guides Habat's eyes to Horaste. "Follow him. Follow Horaste. Never stop."

"No." Habat nearly burns his hand by accident when she turns to face him. Leos takes a step to the side. "You come with me, Leos. You no leave me." She tries to get close to him, but Leos moves further back. "Why no come?"

"I want go back."

"Why?" A tone of complaint overwhelms Habat's voice. "Why go back? Me here. Child here. Fos here. Why?" Her words clash with rising sobs while her eyes struggle to hold back tears. "Why Leos?"

Leos removes the lion's skull from his head. He turns and looks away, avoiding Habat's eyes, but his gaze moves beyond the rocks and the bare twigs and the dirt. It's like he can see through time, going back to their home in the fields. He remembers his brother, a blur of a father to his blameless, childish eyes, coming back from the hunt. He remembers the shelter he found in his brother's arms during nights of pure dread out in the barren fields. He remembers looking around and only seeing darkness covering the world whole. He can feel once more the rising menace the blackness carries in its stride.

"Why you come here?" he asks Habat, finding the courage to face the bitterness in her eyes. "You, your father, out there. Why you come to mountain?"

"I… I see light," she says, holding back tears. "My father old, sick. We die alone. Fields empty, people cruel. Days only pain. Nights only fear. One night, I see light high on mountain… hope. We follow light. We follow hope." She brings the light closer to her face. "We point nowhere. Light comes. We point mountain."

"Why no leave father? He slow. You young, he old. You strong, he sick."

She frowns at him. "I never leave father. Father my life."

"Yes. Like you and father. My brother, my life." Leos takes the lion's fur off his shoulders and brings it over hers. He straps the fur around her neck and waist while Habat just stands there, still in her grief. "I start all." He caresses her cheeks, wiping the dust away. "I am why people here. I am why you see light one night. I no leave my brother. I start all… now I end."

"But you leave me?" Habat's lips begin to shiver. She can no longer hold the light steady in her hand. She takes Leos' hand and brings it over her belly. "You leave child?"

"No." Leos caresses her belly. "I never leave you. Never leave child." He points to the light. "I am Fos. I keep you safe. Always. I keep you warm." He kisses her forehead. He looks at her straight in the eyes. Eyes he will never see again. Eyes he will never stop missing.

Habat looks away. All the tears burst out from the corners of her eyes. Leos takes from his side a pelt full of water and straps it to her side. Then he unties the leash of bones full of sickness hanging from his neck and ties it around her own. Another pelt he straps to her waist, with a couple of sharpened stones inside.

"Follow Horaste," he says, "never stop. Follow him to edge of world, like you follow light to mountain. Never stop emon Habat. Never stop."

"I never—I never stop," she says in a whisper, almost a moan. A dazed expression on her face when Leos takes her hands in both of his own. She shakes them off. He feels a powerful urge to tell her to forget everything he just said and to ask for her forgiveness. He opens his mouth to speak. Nothing comes out but a tired breath.

He turns and walks away from her and only then he allows his watery eyes to run free. Just before he's about to move beyond a wall of rocks and forever lose sight of her, he takes a look back, hoping to see her one last time, but all he sees is the light's blurry shine moving down the mountainside, fading away at first, then vanishing in a land of mist.

So, this is how it feels... to lose someone you love.

A hidden bleeding, killing you from within. People you love disappear and your love becomes suffering; your most cherished memories of them, enemies for life.

ΙCΑΦΘΟ

Late in the night, after the madness has settled under a blanket of snores and groans, Leos returns to the deadlands. His ears catch a girl's failed attempts to muffle her cries, wailing through fur, or through her own hands, or something else pressing against her mouth.

He walks past sleeping men and women and follows the cries until he finds the girl sitting on a rock about half her size, trembling, one hand pressing a pelt against her mouth, the other deep between her legs.

"Poena?" Leos says, "elthe e mon." He raises his hand and gestures for her to come to him. Poena neither moves nor says a word. Leos looks around as if it's daytime for any signs of Era, forgetting for a moment that it's too dark to see much, even with a strong moon shining over their heads. "Era? Te?"

Poena keeps wailing through the pelt, swinging her whole upper body back and forth, too shaken to answer. Leos crouches before her. When he tries to calm her down by laying his hands on her knees, she drops the pelt and sinks both hands between her legs. The fur she's wearing is covered in dirt, torn, hanging down from her right shoulder, exposing her entire left side.

He caresses the sides of her arms as she leans forward and lays her head on the side of his neck, asking for his care. He feels her tears running down his shoulder and when he hugs her tight, her trembling goes away. He picks her up and holds her until she calms down. The warmth of her ragged breathing dries the tears on his neck. He notices blood running from between her legs. *Not even half a woman... how could they have done this to you child.*

He draws a clean hide from over a sleeping man nearby. The man wakes up ready for a fight but doesn't dare to make another move, once he sees Leos is the one who took his warmth away. Leos brings the hide around Poena's shoulders. "Era?" he whispers in her ear.

Poena pulls her head away from his neck and with a trembling hand so weak she would struggle to rip a flower from its roots, she points towards the direction of Era's shelter. "Era ano fos," she mutters, "omio paes."

They reach the shelter. Leos calls for Era at the entrance. Silence welcomes him, as thick as darkness. Poena starts crying again, biting his shoulder. Her nails dig through his flesh and the tremors of her lips make it clear— a horror hides in the cave of which she knows of. Leos leaves her outside by the entrance and instructs her to wait for him there. Poena pulls the hide up to her nose and nods behind it.

He walks in. His eyes take a moment to adjust, enough to make figures out of the shadows of shadows. A few steps inside and the muddy warmth of blood gathers around his feet. He finds Era at the far end. Her back against the wall. He calls her name in a whisper but gets no answer. He moves closer. Her belly slit. A sharp stone in her hand. A bright star in each of her eyes. Still. Cold. Unrepentant.

I should have forced you to come with us. You knew there was no escape from him. Even if you had run away, you could never un-feel your child. Could never un-grow its youth inside you. You knew he would make you birth more sons and daughters and Fos would devour them time and time again and you couldn't take the pain. Couldn't stand the loss. I should have forced you to run away. He caresses her hair. Forces her eyelids shut. *Forgive me Era. Wherever you are… forgive me.*

He leaves the shelter, gathering heavy breaths of guilt in his aching chest. He hides Poena in the bushes further down the cliff, brings the hide over her head and she pulls her knees up close to her chest so he can cover her whole. He gestures for her to stay still and silent and wait for his return.

I have a few words to say to my brother.

Fos slays the night trapped in its reach as the darkness around it flees. Leos finds his brother sitting by it, tossing twigs in its blazing guts. Its tongues rise in the air like hair made of claws, reaching as high as two grown men standing over each other. The circle of stones around it, wider than ever, could easily fit ten or twelve men standing inside.

"You come," Ra says. His face lit by the red glow of fierce light. Doesn't even raise a chin to greet him. "Where you go all night?" He yawns.

Leos approaches the light. The dirt under his feet, warm as day. Like a lion made of flames, the light's roar rises over the crackling and snapping of tortured wood in its belly, releasing the familiar stench of white dust. "I take Habat away." Leos moves closer but keeps the distance of his height between himself and the light, for the wind is strong and careless and the light's sway unpredictable.

"Good," Ra says and keeps throwing sticks in the light. "You, like Fos brother. Women like wood, but no Habat. Habat like water. She make you weak. Mountain full wood. You take another."

"You brother? You take another woman now?"

"No, Era well soon. Era knows our child safe, up with Aeos. More children soon we m—"

"Era nekron."

The next twig Ra was about to throw stays in his hand. He turns to Leos with a vague expression on his face that seems forced as if putting great effort not to look surprised. After a long pause, he resumes throwing twigs in the already well-fed light. "How? Beast? Man?" he says appearing calm, but there is no way to miss the tension in his voice.

"How? With stone." Leos points to his belly. "Guts out."

"Man kill her." Ra flares up to his feet and grabs his spear.

"No man. A god."

Ra, who was ready to head to the deadlands, turns around instead and stands facing Leos. "Choose your words with care, brother."

"Why angry? Women like wood you say. You find another, yes?"

Ra turns his spear on Leos. "Hold…your words."

"More women birth more dead sons, more wood for Fos."

"My son no dead." Ra thrusts his spear and holds its tip a finger's length away from Leos' throat.

Leos doesn't flinch. "At Aeos side, you say. Where mother and father rest?"

"Yes."

"Why you no go?"

"What?" Ra pulls his spear back.

"Mother. Father. They wait for you. Your son wait for you. You can go now. Sit next to them." Leos saunters close to the light and shows it to Ra as if a path lies before them. "So go."

"Yes…" Ra starts hovering his hand over the flames. "One day, I go. We all go. No gods in dirt, rot like men. No rats eat our eyes, our insides. Gods go in light. White cloud takes us to Aeos. We rest next to our father, our sons. Men… men go in dirt. Rest next to their fathers. Rot. Shit. Like father. Like son.”

“Then go, brother. Rest in light.”

“Yes… my rest.” Ra keeps waving his fingers and tilting his wrist, caressing erratic, flaming tongues. “Me tired, brother.” The flames leap out and grasp his hand, but he doesn’t pull it back. He keeps sinking his hand deeper in the flames, even taking a slight step forward. He drops his spear and brings his other hand in the light to join in the hurt. “I wait long time, see mother and father.” His eyes, red and chock-full of pain, gather tears but remain wide and focused as if carving a path through the blazing violence with an unblinking, fixated stare. He allows the light to reach his wrists. “Maybe you right. Maybe now is time.”

Ra leans forward. The tears burst out from the corners of his eyes and just as he’s about to take the one step to end it all, Leos rushes and pulls him back at the very last moment before the flames take hold of the fur he’s wearing.

“You kill yourself, fool,” Leos yells. He whacks Ra’s fur to get rid of the light skidding at the edges, sparks leaping off it and creating smoke. He grabs his brother’s forearms and holds them up at chest level to see the damage to his hands. White blisters already forming over swollen, broken skin. Not a single hair left from his fingers up to his wrists.

“No brother, no death,” Ra says, forcing words out through a clenched jaw, “Fos life brings.” His eyes are bursting with ache when his burned hand meets Leos’ scruffy beard, but he seems to welcome the anguish just to caress Leos’ face. “This no first time I go in light. The night you born, I crawl in light. For you.”

Leos can’t tell if his brother is describing an actual event or one of his many visions, but he finds a hint of a smile on his face. “Was there pain? Like this now?”

“No. More.”

Leos has always found his brother's ways of promoting the light to be full of deceit, aimed only for the ignorant eyes of strangers. But now he sees Ra is not afraid to jump in the light himself. And he genuinely seems to believe he has already done it before. There's sincerity in his tone, his touch steeped in a brother's warm care. He uncovers a layer of calm under the sorrow of his voice, like roots hiding under rough soil. A grief that has grown over time into a thriving tree, with sturdy and unyielding branches carrying the bitter fruit of loss. It doesn't matter whether his brother's words are children of reality or his twisted imagination; what matters is that he's willing to act upon them.

"Go brother, sleep," Leos says. "My turn watch light." He takes off the lion's skull and sits by the circle of stones.

Ra has been watching the light all by himself for a full day and night and it shows in his bleary eyes. "Yes," he says, "I—I rest now." He wipes his eyes and lets out another long yawn that makes him stagger a bit as he heads back inside the cave, leaving Leos alone with the light, like so many other nights.

All alone with the light, like no other night.

It's astonishing how much Fos demands of you. The strength required to gather and carry its food. The time it takes to clean and nurture its space. Fos is the one thing everyone wants, but no one can touch, always acting like a needy infant. Its roar is a constant cry for attention that can steal all your sleep if you care enough for its well-being. And it knows how much you care. It knows what its warmth means to you, what its slithering tongues can entice you into.

So much strength it takes and so much time. Hungrier than any starving beast, its belly is always empty. More treacherous than the steepest of slopes leading into the deepest, blackest crevices. So vicious and merciless and menacing like no other creature, thing or happening in the world and yet…

All it takes is for me to do nothing, Leos thinks as the light gradually settles, begging for more of his care. *So much horror lives in your blaze, but there's no need for me to fight you; no need to run away or hide from you. The most dangerous being of all and I can kill you just by doing nothing.*

If it had been daytime, he could have a look over at the wastelands from this high vantage. And even though the choking darkness of the night won't allow it, he can still see the myriad choices, luck and chances that have led them to this place—at this moment. He waits for his brother to fall into a deep sleep, signaled by his snoring. Calm like a stone, he waits for the light to fade. He remains unmoved by its desperate pleads for care and attention. Soon enough, the starving flames retreat, rushing back to the scorched depths of ash and death like scared children running back to their mother's arms. He sets a single branch alight and puts it aside, takes the pelt of water from his side and pours it over the charred remains of wood, drowning the last of its searing breaths. Dying snakes of flame are hissing for mercy as they suffocate. Clouds of smoke thicken and choke the shine in utter blackness. The last drop of water meets no resistance. He leaves nothing but dead wood and ash in the circle of stones.

Fos has now been reduced to a single fiery branch in his hand, bound to his will. Some of the people notice the brightness as he moves through the deadlands. Murmurs gather around him like flies over rot; he pays no attention to them. He takes Poena and together they make their way down the mountainside.

Poena walks by his side at first, holding his hand, but she loses all the strength from her torment-stricken body just as they reach the woods. Leos kneels before her and taps the back of his shoulder. She crawls on his back, bringing her arms around his neck and he carries her the rest of the way, one hand holding the back of her knees, the other holding the light.

It doesn't take long for them to get noticed. The light's shine draws out of the shadows two men holding spears, standing guards through the night. They humble themselves before Leos. Men who don't carry the light's mark, still trapped in the struggles of the old ways, simply because they arrived at the mountain too late.

Leos instructs the men to lead him and Poena to their shelters if they have any. The men take them to a group of families resting under a ridge not too far down the mountainside. Everyone rushes to greet them, gasping at the sight of Fos. Some old women and a younger girl holding an infant. Two beardless boys and a child Leos can't tell whether a boy or girl. A few weather cycles younger than Poena, he shines the light near the child's face and he still can't tell.

The instant Leos lets Poena down, she reaches out to take his hand. Leos shuffles her hair. A young man appears from over the ridge, his shelter probably not too far away. The light's bright draws more eyes from afar. Soon another man shows up, coming from further down the mountainside. A girl by his side holding his hand.

Leos signals everyone to gather in a circle around him, even the young ones. He lays Fos on the ground and allows them to marvel at its shine for a moment, then drags dirt with his feet over it, covers it, stomps it. Everyone jumps back. Clear gasps of fright make way to confusing waves of overlapping murmurs. The light tries to slither away from the sides, but Leos drowns every single spark in the dirt, then proceeds to assemble everything he needs from the nearby trees, leaving everyone baffled by his ways.

He grinds wood against wood, with Poena never leaving his side, watching closely at his every move as he shows everyone the way of the light. Their startled voices come together as one when the infant sparks leap into the air and they stare in awe as light comes to life before their eyes. Light birthed from seemingly nothing.

The woman holding the infant bows before him and the newborn light. She speaks incomprehensible words to him, but her face is shining with gratitude. Leos instructs Poena to join the woman at her side and brings both their hands together.

"Poena lave gyne," he says to Poena and covers their joined hands with both of his own. He then turns his gaze towards the woman. "Gyne lave Poena."

"Sy?" Poena asks Leos. Her eyes absorb the light's shine, getting watery. The woman allows her to hold the infant for a while.

Leos rises, leaving Poena under the woman's care and both under the light's protection. "Un, emon horos," he says and makes a shelter with his hands over Fos, then spreads his hands apart, imitating light growing and spreading all over the mountain. "Horos lave Fos e mon." He then shows the men they must take the light and descend back to the drylands they came from.

He sets a fresh branch alight and leaves Poena with her new family as he makes his way across the mountainside, searching for the next shelter of men. With every step he takes, his pace grows quicker. The night struggles to stay alive against the early signs of a new day, though it's not the red in the sky the night should fear.

Tremble at my will, darkness, for I bring the dawn before dawn. Stay blind and silent and limbless as I steal the light from the heavens and claim it for the earth. Men have spent lifetimes gazing upon hopeless nights adorned with stars. Not anymore. From now on, the gods shall gaze down with grudge at stars of our own. I shall bring forth a new world and burn down the old and if any god wants to challenge me, be warned, for tonight I stand proud upon the shoulders of no one.

    I am Alpha.

ΑΩ

Ra wakes up to the sound of frantic shouts. People are interspersing his name over pleading cries for help. His eyes open straight to a wide state, as wide as they can get.

"Leos?" he shouts. No reply from his brother.

He gets to his feet at once. A pounding heart chokes any lethargy left from his long sleep. As he rushes outside, the fierce morning bright blurs his vision. *There's so much light. I overslept. Why didn't he wake me up at dawn for my turn?* People keep screaming his name along with words like *light* and *death* and *lost* all muddled in turmoil.

The moment he takes his first step out of the cave, he halts in his tracks. A wave of loss smites him. Nothing but a cluster of dead branches and charred bones in the middle of the circle of stones, with no hint of living light in them, not even the tiniest wisp of smoke rising from its blackened bowels; his brother nowhere in sight.

No.

His eyes discard the cave's dark colors and slowly adjust to the only light around him, that of a bright day. The morning blur clears as the wind fills the air with the scent of white dust. When he moves his gaze over the crag, a rush of fright takes over his whole body. Sudden. Violent. Unable to move or speak, all the shouts from the deadlands become nothing more than incoherent muffled voices as if people are talking underwater. Only a voice inside him screams so loud and clear it cracks his chest with shivers.

No. It can't be…

Long clouds far in the distance are rising from the ground like giant trees of dark smoke, scars to the sky's blue skin. Countless. Dominant. Their roots are deep in the woods down at the mountain's waist. Broad areas of treetops separate one cloud from another, stretching across and beyond as far left and right as the eye can see. Fos is everywhere.

He closes his eyes in disbelief. His thoughts are lightning strikes blazing through black clouds. No way his brother would ever do this to him. No way this is real. He must be still in the cave, sleeping. This is just another vision, that's all. This is father and mother, reaching out to him before it's too late, a warning of what may come if he gets too complacent.

"Leos Fos lave," a brittle voice speaks from below.

He opens his eyes. His hands become clenched fists. His chest aches like it's about to spit his heart out. *Brother, what have you done?*

The night he lost them… he couldn't see much. It was all shadows moving in the darkness, the howls of beasts taking turns ripping them apart. Mother was screaming at him to keep going and all he could see was rock and shades of black and grey and outlines of his hands, clinging from any ragged corner they could find.

Now the slaughter becomes clear. Now he sees father's severed limbs scattered across the mountain. His eyes and ears tossed away and spit out like a game amongst predators. Mother's body cut to pieces. Her womanhood raped and passed around and her breasts sliced off her chest and a gathering of hands touching her and the tongues of a dozen times a dozen filthy mouths licking the scent off her bright flesh.

Rage gathers well up to his throat and blocks his breathing like a patch of fur and out of his mouth comes a scream so loud and fierce it slaps all children to tears in one strike; one word that sends all women hiding behind trees and stomps all men down to their knees with foreheads touching the ground. The violent echoes which follow carry the word far, a warning that spreads over the mountainside like a soar of shrieking hawks.

"Yvris!"

He heads back in the cave and returns moments later, with the hawk's skull over his head, a pelt of water and a spear. He washes his face, sinks his hands in the heart of the circle of stones as the hawk sinks its talons in flesh and keeps scratching the blackened skin off the scorched wood until his palms are full. He brings his trembling hands over his wet face, sneaks the tips of his fingers under the hawk's skull, reaches the line of his hair and without blinking the slightest, he drags his hands down, pressing against his skin until his fingers meet his beard, painting his face black.

Run, sons of mud and grime. Hide, crawl, for I am the one whose cry can shatter mountains. Wherever you are, I will strike you down where you stand with heaven's wrath. If your children are with you, I will burn their eyes and cut off their tongues and if you rush to hide under a tree, I will strike down the tree till it turns to ash and if you crawl in the mountain's caves, I will strike down the mountain till it breaks in half.

He raises his spear and with a cry of war, he calls for all the men to gather. He slams the spear's bottom to the ground demanding absolute silence and focuses on the rising clouds down in the woods. He waits. The first spark matters not. His piercing gaze, sizzling with rage, moves frenetically back and forth from left to right, looking for the only spark that matters—the next one. The one that will betray its master's position.

Before the men have a chance to gather, he catches with the corner of his right eye the birth of a new cloud of smoke, rising deep in the mountain's bowels. The moment he sees it, he storms down the cave's path and with ten times ten the strength of men following him and shouting his name in glory, he charges to the woods with the frenzy of a starving hawk descending upon the last rat left in the world.

Beyond the treetops ahead, he follows the cloud of smoke until he walks into a clearing stripped of grass and leaves, only dirt and nothing else. He slows down his pace and signals the men to hush. He finds the light's scorched remains further ahead, its dark cloud fading. The dominant scent of white dust in every breath.

He drops his spear and rushes to save the light. He drags aside the dead branches looking for a spark, a piece of wood that might be burning still, no matter how tiny. One spark is all he needs. He feels moistness on his fingers as he digs through the blackened stack. The dead branches are wet. No light remains.

Ahead of the stack, he finds the foot tracks of many, heading straight down the mountainside. Moving away from the stack to his right, he finds the trail of just one, breaking away from the rest. The many are descending; the loner is on a side path, going around the mountain.

He follows the loner's tracks, which lead him sideways across the mountainside and over a small ridge, deeper in the hostile woods where the old ways still rule supreme. Not long after, he sees a newborn cloud rising just ahead and beyond the gaps between the trees, the light shining strong and bright. He hears voices. The cheers and gasps of many. When he moves past the trees, he finds his brother in the clear, crouching before the light with his back turned at him. The lion's skull is on the ground, lying by the side of his right foot. Twelve or more people are gathered around the light. People of the woods, mostly men, but some women and children too. They're all overjoyed, cheering and honoring his brother. Leos is nurturing the light, idle to their praise.

"Leos," Ra shouts. His voice snaps the cheers off like the wind snaps a rotten branch off the arms of a dead tree.

Leos slightly raises his head at the sound of his voice. At first, he makes a move to turn around and face him, but then stops halfway. His focus returns to the light.

As Ra and his men step up into the clear, their presence drains the excitement from the air, leaving just the bitter scent of Fos. The men of the woods reach for their spears in panic while the women drag their children back and rush to hide behind the men. Leos gets to his feet and instructs the women to take the children and leave. One of the women reaches out to take a branch from the light before she goes, but Leos forbids it.

Some of Ra's men dash forward, eager to hunt down the fleeing women and children, but since they're not running away with the light, Ra raises his hand and orders the men to hold back.

"You want Fos back, brother?" Leos says and finally turns around to face him. He tilts his body slightly and takes a few steps to the side as if trying to make way for Ra. He points at the light. "Come, take it."

"Yes… Fos," Ra says. "I take back Fos. I take their heads—"

He points at the men of the woods gathered around Leos, dragging his hand in the air from the first man at the far left to the last man at the far right. He then brings his hand back to the middle and lands a sharp finger-point on Leos.

"—you. I take you," Ra finishes.

All the men on both sides give each other baffled, tense looks. Their grips on their spears tighten, for no one understands the words being spoken.

Leos lets out a long sigh. He turns his gaze to the men by his side. "Let them live. I give them Fos, you take Fos back. All like old. All well."

"Nothing same. Nothing well. You take Fos from me. Fos now everywhere. You take mother, take father from me. You no brother. You thief." Ra moves a few steps ahead. The men around him extend their spears, taking a few steps forward. Reflexively, the men on either side of Leos take a few steps backward.

Leos doesn't move. "Fos no for you brother. Fos for all take."

"Fos mine alone."

"Fos comes from thunder, you no—"

"I am thunder!" Ra slams the bottom of his spear to the ground.

"You, my brother. We together always. Thunder in sky alone."

"No. Sky my home. My breath like wind. Thunder my voice. Hawk never alone. I have light. I have rain." He picks up a handful of dirt and throws it at Leos. "You, lion. Ground your home. You have shit. You have dirt." His condescending glare meets resistance in Leos' eyes. The dark clouds of a rising storm fight to take charge over the clear blue sky. Leos looks to his side and picks up the lion's skull from the ground.

"Yes, dirt," Leos says as he places the skull firmly on his head. His wild mane crawls from the sides and falls behind his shoulders. His saddened gaze turns sharp just before it disappears under the shadow of the lion's upper jaw. "Mountain my home. Dirt my flesh." He points at the men to his side. "Their blood, my blood. Their voice my roar." He leans forward, sinks his feet in the dirt and gathers his body to a fighting stance. "Light in sky you keep, brother. Light on land I give to all."

Ra can't stand his brother's defiance. A traitor, who has spat on everything he believes in. He wants him dead, to make him suffer as no other man has ever suffered. But in his mind, he still sees an infant lying in a pelt strapped around his chest. A child crawling in his arms during the night, longing for care and safety. A young man caring for him at times he couldn't care for himself. How could he ever make shut, the eyes of the one who has mother's eyes?

With a forward wave of his hand, Ra signals his men to attack. He stays where he is as the men behind him dash into view, eager to do the deed he cannot do himself. Creeping under the shade of the hawk's skull, a gaze of thorns lies on his brother and wishes death upon him. Behind that gaze, a restless mind drowns in sorrow, hoping it could leap back in time and change something, anything. To form a different path, leading somewhere else, anywhere else. Anywhere but here.

Ra's men flood the area around the light shouting *yvris*. Leos tries to fight, but no one dares to attack him. They all move past him like water moves past a rock rising just above the surface of a shallow stream.

The fight ends in moments. The men of the woods can't stand their ground against such great numbers. For every thrust of their spears, Ra's men punish them with ten of their own. Blood runs wild from throats sliced from edge to edge. Spears rip through chests looking for naked hearts. Every breath carries agony as rocks crack skulls open.

Leos now stands alone, surrounded, over a ground adorned with dead bodies and spilled guts. No one dares to challenge him at first, but then one of the men—young, with just a hint of a beard on his face—lunges his spear at him. Kill the lion. What better way for a young hunter to impress his elders. The man's strike is weak. Leos gets a grip on the spear just below the tip and pulls him within arm's reach. He grabs him by the neck with a swift move and before the man has any chance to react, he thrusts his head and headbutts him in the face with the lion's jaw. The man drops his spear in agony. Blood squirts from his thrashed nose all over Leos' face. Leos takes a firm grip of the fur covering the man's chest and headbutts him again, crashing the lion's jaw into his forehead. The man falls to his knees while all the men step back as their gasps fill the air with dread.

"Never send man to kill god, brother," Leos says. He pulls a sharp stone from the pelt hanging from his side and as he turns towards Ra, the men scatter, clearing the way for their stares to meet. Blood drips from the lion's nose and teeth onto Leos' cheeks and runs down to meet his already blood-sodden beard.

"Come, fight me," Ra says and taunts Leos. He snaps his spear at the edge and takes the sharp stone from its tip, tossing the rest aside.

Leos snubs Ra and walks to the light instead. He takes a fiery branch and returns to the man, who is on his knees holding his nose, quivering whole and crying.

"No," Ra says. "What you do?"

Leos stands before the man. "Lave Fos," he says, urging him to take it.

"No. Stop." Ra signals the men to stop him, but no one dares to. The ones in front stand their ground. More faces creep up from behind their shoulders. Curious. Nervous.

"Lave aner. Lave mega Fos." Leos takes the man's wrist and forces the branch in his grip.

"No, you fool."

Ra charges at Leos shouting and they both end up with tight grips on each other's wrists. Ra wills Leos down, bringing his brother's head at chest level, but Leos suddenly stops pushing back and yanks him forward instead, using Ra's momentum against him. Ra staggers and falls onto his brother. They roll over each other in the dirt. Ra, stuck in a daze, loses the stone and his grip on Leos as the world keeps turning upside down in a loop. As the dust clears and everything comes back into place, Ra finds himself with his back against the dirt. His head still spinning. Warmth crawls over the left side of his face. He catches a bright blur with the corner of his left eye. His head is just a few steps away from the light. Ragged breaths fill his chest with warm air. He tries to move, but he can't. Leos is all over him, pushing his knees against the inside of his elbows. Leos raises his hand, holding the sharp stone. Ra's eyes widen. He breathes all the air out of his chest. Leos' hand comes down with force.

Ra screams his eyes shut as the stone tears through his right shoulder. His shoulder goes numb and cold first, then turns burning hot in a single heartbeat. He opens his eyes. Darkness still thickens for a brief moment before it clears. The searing pain lingers around his wound and once Leos plucks out the stone—its sharpened edge three fingers deep in blood—the burning floods his neck, spreads to his chest and creeps all over his back. His whole body drowns in cold sweat and shivers. After so many scars, which tell of so many struggles; right now, as he feels the hard skin of a stone pressing against his neck, he knows—this is the one. This is the strike that will end it all. The lion's skull looming over him is the last thing he will ever see. The light's roar is the only sound that matters now, for only its dark cloud can take him where he wants to be. He gives Leos a pleading stare.

Don't leave me here to rot in the dirt, brother. Please, throw my dead body in the light. Let me go to them. I miss them so much. Do what you must and I promise you, I will wait for you by Aeos' side with no grudge. I will cheer for you from above and take pride in all that you have become. But, please, I beg of you, let me ride the cloud to the sky.

His arms loosen. He shuts his eyes, ready to accept his fate. Many anxious breaths come and go and nothing happens. He feels the stone's sharp tip leaving his neck, the weight crushing his arms withdrawn. He opens his eyes and sees Leos still; the sky shedding its bright blue skin through the gaps between the trees. "Why?"

Leos says nothing. He rubs the bloody stone in both his palms, puts it away in the pelt hanging from his side and upraises his hands, palms facing outwards, showing everyone the blood on his palms.

An awkward moment for Ra, for he's not sure what to do, while his brother seems confident in his choices, with great poise in his every movement.

"Speak. Why?" Ra shouts in demand of an answer, but his brother remains silent. The calmness Leos flaunts infuriates him and with all his strength gathered in a pair of clenched fists, he pulls Leos down and throws him on his back. "Why?" He grabs Leos by the lion's skull and strikes the back of his head on the ground. He pulls the skull off Leos' head, hits him with it first, then tosses it aside. He punches him once. Leos doesn't fight back. He punches him twice, with all the rage in the world gathered in his fists, but Leos doesn't even try to fend for himself. "Why you no fight?" Ra keeps shouting at him, landing one fierce punch after the other.

Leos spreads his arms wide, showing no resistance. Palms open, facing outwards. A glow in his red-blooded eyes welcomes every punch. His calmness soon fades behind a face covered in cuts and bruises.

Ra keeps beating him till he runs out of breath. He lets his arms hang loose in the air and stares down at Leos, who's a punch or two away from losing his senses.

"Brother, speak." Ra can only squeeze a whisper out of his wearied voice. His fast breathing makes fragments of words as they struggle to come out. "Please t-tell, tell me. Show me. Why."

Leos lifts and tilts his head slightly to the left and coughs out blood all over the side of his face. He rests his head on the ground before turning his half-fainted gaze back at Ra. "I love you, brother." He coughs out more blood without turning his head. Most of the blood lands on his beard, some of it crawls back into his mouth. "You have more darkness than night inside you. I love your darkness, more than night loves darkness. The men, they fear you. They hate you. And now—"

Leos pauses for a moment and points with a quivering hand at the oozing bloodstreams running down Ra's shoulder.

"—they know you bleed. Now they know, you man like them," he finishes as his hand falls to the side of his hip.

Ra looks around at all the men. Fos is changing hands, being passed around like a tool, or a weapon, or like a fruit. He sees beyond the pale paint of white dust on their faces; beyond the light's scars and the frowning brows sheltering fever-lit eyes and recognizes a rise in confidence. Ambition. Vigor. At this moment, he knows, just as he has once brought the end to the old ways, today they bring the end of him too, for he has become the old ways to a new world. He is to them a nightmare and darkness persevering and now they can turn the night into day at will; they can wake themselves up from the nightmare. Everybody wants to rule the world. Everybody wants to be a god and a god-killer.

Leos gently taps the side of Ra's leg, asking for his attention. They look at each other for a long, silent moment. Leos then takes the stone from his pelt with the bit of strength he has left. He lays it over his chest. Points to his heart.

Ra shakes his head.

Leos nods.

"No," Ra says, barely any strength left in his voice.

"Look. Our light, everywhere. Hear. Our words they—they all speak. We live forever, brother. We together. Always." Leos takes the stone and slides it into Ra's hand, its sharp edge pointing at his chest. "This day... a good day. One more good day. Together." He closes his eyes. His hand falls to the side.

Ra brings the stone over his head with both hands. His throat clogs with sobs. His chest fills with air. *They will make us suffer for everything I've done. I deserve it, brother, but not you. You deserve peace.* Memories of a lifetime come together in a single moment of determination. Bittersweet thoughts. Feeding him, washing him, teaching him, loving him.

His hands come down.

Killing him.

Dust leaps off the ground where he drops the blood-drenched stone. He tries to lift his brother's dead body, but the weight is too much for his wounded shoulder to withstand. He looks to the men for help. Some remain silent. Others laugh. Some stay as they are, while others begin to move around him. Murmurs turn to curses.

He drags his brother like a dead prey too heavy to carry and brings the body close to the light. One of the men spits at him. When the rest converge around him, he waves them off, pleading for time. He sits on his knees, with his brother's body between him and the light, face to face with all its glory. He looks beyond the flaming tongues to the sky over the treelines. Spears of dark clouds rise from the lower layers of the mountain, wavering high and fading. So many of them. Fos rising in all directions. It's as if his brother has found a way to paint the sky.

It's beautiful, brother. Creative. Authentic. Bold. The sound of your voice is now and forever bound in flames and for as long as men set the night ablaze, darkness shall tremble at the sound of your roar.

A storm of footsteps of men behind him blends with the clatter of numerous spears bumping onto each other.

I have crawled through life with bleeding knees, ashamed of the blood that flows in me, hating on the skin and sweat of me. Forgive me, father, for I have misled the weak, pretending to be as strong as you are. Forgive me, mother, for I have loathed and stolen the smiles of many in a dire need to replace your own. All my life, I thought of the gods as the only way to reach you. But now I see… I see the great divide between the immortal and the eternal, imagination and reality. False gods demand of others sacrifice; real gods become the sacrifice.

He rolls Leos over into the raging flames. The stench of flesh burning comes fast and strong and soon nothing remains but a blackened figure sinking in light, dissolving before his eyes.

Real gods like you, my beloved brother.

Words are spoken. Chatters and arguments behind his back. On who will have the first strike; on whether to carve the light's mark on his face or not, before or after they cut off his head; on slicing the tongue, the ears and fingers first, as he has done to so many of them. Words of spite and loathe, cruel and vengeful, yet full of clarity and splendor. So many words, all his conception, like newborns growing and learning and playing in a vast land with no known boundaries.

Brother, listen…I can hear my voice in their voice.

A smile gathers at the corners of his mouth. He drags himself closer to the light. The warmth spreads to his knees.

False gods hide their wounds, for they see themselves as indestructible. Real gods slice their wrists wide open and let their blood rain upon barren lands, so the hopeless can quench their thirst and wash their bodies clean. Blood becomes puddles and streams and then ponds into lakes. Sounds become syllables and grow into words. Nouns, pronouns, verbs and adjectives; violent rivers progressing and expanding, crashing and smashing on periods and dashes, forming sentences destined to give birth to more sentences. All cognate and articulate, elegant and eager to flood the world, inspired by their ancestors to defend their descendants; to never let the land go dry again.

And the bleeding never ends, for the thirst of the world is too grand.

He senses spears rising in the air, looming over his back. He brings his knees together. Body straight, arms stretching outwards at shoulder height.

My flesh shall burn like all flesh burns. And whenever men speak, listen carefully. Pay attention. Every word is my thunder. It doesn't matter which word. Focus…and you will hear the screaming of the hawk.

A spear tears through his back. He gasps. Another spear rips through his side. The breaths in his chest fill with blood, choking him. His eyes widen. One of the men tries to cut off his ear but he shakes his head, stares into the flames and throws himself forward. Naked tongues of light grasp his being and drown him in pain.

You and me, brother. You are to me what dawn is to dusk and we are to the blackness, what day is to night. You are the beginning and I am the end, together as one. One spark. One voice. And for as long as men refuse to give in silently into the night, you will have the first light and I will have the final say.

The flames grow into pure light. The light takes the pain away. It takes everything away. Finally, all are accounted for. Only one word remains. The greatest word of the greatest sign. What lies beyond the end of all numbers is the single last thought that leaps through his mind. A final spark in a scorched world, facing the end of all sense of time and space and meaning, with nothing else left to burn.

I am Omega.

||||
|||

APOKALYPSIS

NICHOLAS NIKITA

♀

Her steps falter over harsh soil. Swollen ankles and a large belly; everything else is skin and bones. The pain is getting stronger. Neither stabs nor beatings could ever make her feel this horrid urge she feels now, as if all her insides are hating on her body and pushing outwards against her skin, trying to burst her open and spill the burden out like yolk running from a cracked egg.

Habat can only carry her weight for a few steps at a time, then collapses to the ground and moans herself to tears. A fiery branch in her hand. A heavy load of sticks and branches strapped around her back—wrapped in the lion's fur—only makes her struggles worse as she roams up a hill in dire need of shelter. Any shelter. Any kind of roof over her head.

The skies roar with gathering clouds, dark as filth over skin. Distant thunder warns the dry land of a fight. The hill is a barren land of rocks and thornbushes, pale and thirsty, begging the clouds to cry.

Fos dies in the rain. If the branches she's carrying get wet, she has neither the time nor the strength to gather more. She must find shelter before the storm comes.

She moves her gaze over the slope to the other nearby hills, all overwhelmed with colors just as pale, except a small hill she couldn't see from the fields below. Scattered patches of green shades surround its peak. *Could*

I have done any better over there? She wonders, but before she can finish her thought, a burst of agony in her belly brings her down to her knees, screaming. She drops the fiery branch to keep herself from falling face down in the dirt. *No, no, please. Not yet, child. Not here, please.*

The pile of branches plummets to her side, too heavy a burden for her weak legs to carry anymore. The agony spreads with her every heartbeat like a violent stream of flames flowing inside her, burning her entire being. Mind and body, smoke and ash. She sinks her nails in the dirt and screams at the ground as if she has a gripe with the land itself. She crosses her legs, gathers the strength in her waist and pushes back the gore that demands out of her.

She lays on her back, in battle with her own body, hoping the pain will wear off. Short breaths rush to catch the smell of rain in the air. Sweat all over her makes the dirt stick to her skin. She shuts her weary eyes in need of rest but finds no calm in the darkness.

A thunder startles her. There's no time to rest. She must keep going.

She looks to the branch. The light is fading. Its humble flames are bending to the force of the wind. She brings together a few sticks and branches and makes it strong again. She can't lose the light now. The strength and speed and time it takes to create it, she no longer has.

As she struggles to pull herself up, she catches a passive glimpse of the mountain. It sits at the edge where the sky meets the land, so far away yet still a beast amongst insects, looming over the hills like a cruel father refusing to get sick and die. Gray lines of hazy clouds still rise over its peak, barely visible, though she can tell they arise from many different areas at once, most of them coming from the small hills around the mountain. At night you can see tiny bright spots all over it, massive gatherings of light she imagines them being, looking like mere sparks from this far away.

Whatever you did my lover, I hope it was worth leaving us.

In a world where men take whatever they want whenever they want, he was the only one that never forced himself on her. The only one whose child she carries willingly, with the intention of keeping it.

After she left the mountain, she came across a few men in the fields. Some families too. Everyone ignored her. A woman bearing a child is a risk no one is willing to take. And a woman dressed in the fur of the land's fiercest beast would make any man think twice before going anywhere near her. So they all treated her like a rotten corpse they had to skip by. All heading towards the mountain, following the dark clouds.

She kept her knowledge of the light hidden from them, only using it during the night to keep the beasts away, for she didn't trust anyone. It felt like she was the only one in the world turning her back on the mountain, going towards places everyone had already abandoned. And as her belly grew, so did her loneliness.

She crawls and stumbles her way up the hill, dragging the branches from the straps, unable to carry them on her back anymore. She wants to reach the top where giant rocks lay broken over each other like a pile of dead bodies, as if a fierce wind blew long ago, strong enough to rip apart a whole mountain, making small hills out of its scattered ribs.

Long breaths keep her calm, so she tries to focus on her breathing and nothing else. Her waist is bones grinding against each other. The ache of their friction sends streams of violent shivers up and down her backline.

Her eyes widen when the first drop of rain falls over her hand as she crawls through the dirt. Another drop hits the side of her face, washing away any sense of calm. Long breaths help with nothing now and a new rush of urgency forces her back to her feet. Her pace grows as her pain grows. Her breathing quickens. Nothing scarier than giving birth out in the open, under heavy rain. No other thought more dreadful than the thought of having no light to keep her safe and warm. Not when she's so exposed, at her most vulnerable time.

She reaches the top just as the few scattered drops of rain become many and the sound of them clashing with the stone overcomes that of the wind's howl. She sees an opening. A large hole in the rocks, tall and wide enough to walk through. Hope eases her growing pain for a moment, but there's no time to rejoice. She feels wet between her legs. Her body floods with spasms.

The opening becomes the mouth of a long, narrow cave. Darkness thickens the further she looks inside, the cave seeming endless, as the light on its rough walls fades away into pure black. She drags her feet and the pile of branches inside, moaning endlessly, and drops everything but the light and covers her nose when a horrid smell, unfamiliar and vomit-inducing, comes charging out from the cave's dark bowels.

She leans on the wall, barely keeping her grip on the light and screams herself to tears. A wave of fragmented pains flows from her belly to her womanhood, as if the child is scratching its way out of her with sharp claws. The pain reaches new heights before it wears off. It soon becomes bearable again but keeps lurking inside her.

Long breaths now hurt her chest. Tears and sweat burn her eyes. She wants to drop the light and lay her burden down, but the awful smell worries her. Not knowing what dangers lie ahead in the dark fills her mind with dreadful images of massive beasts waiting inside, vicious creatures born of darkness. Her nose might have caught the warning of their stinking breaths.

The light reveals more and more of the cave the further she moves inside. The roof rests twice her height from the ground; the cave's width is about three times her height but keeps getting narrower. The sound of rain outside intensifies. Drops of water splash all over from the thinnest of cracks on the roof.

A thunder makes her heart jump. Its roar so loud it might have left a scar in the sky forever.

No tracks on the ground ahead. None. No markings on the walls. Nothing signifying anyone ever stepping foot in here, neither man nor beast. Just the footmarks she leaves behind and the waves she creates in the dirt by dragging the lion's fur and the branches.

She reaches the far end of the cave. Like standing right at the tip inside a hollow claw, there's not enough space to stretch her arms wide without touching its opposite walls. The stench grows stronger, filling her chest with acrid breaths. *There's nothing here. Just a long, narrow, stinking hole in the rock. It must be the smell... the smell has kept everyone away. But where does it come from? Is it the rocks?*

Her legs are trembling, begging her to lie down. She notices a black layer of moisture on the wall's skin and on the roof as well. The rock is gleaming, absorbing the shine of Fos, but the dirt under her feet is dry. She touches the wall. The black skin sticks to her fingers. She brings her fingers under her nose, takes a whiff and pulls her head back instantly—the smell. It's as if the whole cave is bleeding and its black blood stinks of nightmares.

She turns around and heads back as anxiety overshadows her initial relief of discovering the cave is empty. *This place reeks of all the wrongs in the world. Best to stay near the cave's mouth. More light, more space and the smell is—*

Violence bursts inside her. She collapses onto her knees. It's not just the pain this time. She can sense her insides moving, ripping through her. Her heart starts pounding as fast as pouring rain, spreading cold shivers all over her body. She tries to scream, but the pain chokes her. Some force inside her, one she cannot control, blocks her only way of release from agony like a chunk of thorns shoved down her throat. One deep breath unblocks her throat, fills her chest with warm air and as the force loosens its grip on her neck, she lets out a scream so loud and fierce it puts the roars of distant thunders to shame.

She tries to get back to her feet, but her legs have given up. She tries to crawl further away from the cave's end; brutal spasms hold her captive, punishing every feeble move she makes. No way to cheat the body anymore. The pain is incapacitating her, refusing to wear off.

It's time.

She turns around, facing the cave's end, unties the pile of branches and pulls the lion's fur from under, scattering them all over. She doesn't want Fos blocking her way out, for she can't stand the thought of getting trapped inside this bleeding cave.

Echoes of her wails make their way back and forth the cave's narrow passage. The countless jagged edges on its blackened walls caress her agony like the scorched hands of dead children. She lays Fos on the ground and swiftly gathers some sticks and branches to strengthen its flames. No need to create a circle of stones since the floor is made of dirt. She pushes herself away from the light's reach and drags the lion's fur between her legs.

She tries to pull the lion's fur under her bottom and feels blood flowing from her womanhood, drenching her thighs. An uncontrollable urge overwhelms her to rid herself of this suffering. She screams her throat dry and barren and pushes hard through mounting pains. A wet burning sensation between her legs, blood made of flames and the wrath of a new life, rushing to join the living and stretching her, killing her, tearing her apart. *Keep pushing.*

She gasps and takes in all the air she can find. *Don't stop. Push it out.*

The child comes with rage, feeling like a rock the size of her hands is stretching her gash. She screams and pushes and cries and screams and pushes again, sensing the child is crammed. She takes a trail of long breaths and gathers her strength for another push.

A short burst of a hissing sound takes her breath away. Her gaze runs amok around the cave's floor, looking for snakes. She hears the hissing again, coming from beyond her legs, so she lifts her head, moaning, and looks over her belly. Her eyes widen. Her tear-ridden face shines with the light's bright.

No... please no.

Raging flames have slithered to the scattered branches as if something in the dirt can sustain them. The cave's blood dripping from the roof strengthens the light. Hissing, blazing tongues creep up the walls, feeding off the cave's black blood, flare high on either side and converge at the roof over Habat's head in the time it takes for her to blink a few times in disbelief. As her eyes struggle to make sense of what's happening, the light spreads both inwards and outwards, faster than she ever thought was possible.

The cave's far end becomes a monster of brightness, slaughtering the fleeing darkness, charging, expanding towards her. The walls around her; the roof over her head; a mouth of roaring flames, eager to swallow her whole.

For a moment of pure terror, she forgets in what state she's in and when she tries to drag herself away from the charging flames, her aching body reminds her. She keeps screaming and pushing hard while still struggling to crawl away with her elbows and one last push eases the swelling between her legs as the burden slides out of her.

An instance of relief. A newborn cry. Ferocious teeth of flames gather all around her legs. The ground pushes back against the mounting light while everything else around her burns. Not a moment to spare. She pulls herself forward, takes the newborn into her arms and brings the lion's fur over her head. The fur is burning at the edges, but the rest remains unscathed.

She tries to stand, but her legs can't hold her. She crawls with bleeding knees, getting closer to the cave's mouth, with one hand pushing the child against her chest, the other dragging herself through the dirt.

Flames leap from the walls onto the lion's fur on her back as the monster's mouth swallows her, spreading outwards faster than she can crawl. The cave breathes out insufferable heat.

The little girl inside her screams for her father. She weeps, reaching out, seeking his hand, to grab her, to pull her out of the monster's fiery jaw. But father isn't here anymore. And the monster's breath chokes the little girl in smoke.

The woman inside her has nothing to say. No tears to shed. She loses her sight, her voice, her will. In a world where everyone has abandoned her, she lies still, refusing to struggle any longer, for the time has come to abandon herself. And the monster drowns the woman in its spit of pure light.

Then the mother inside her speaks:

Whether the pain or the flames kill you, I couldn't care less. All I care about is the boy. Stand up. Run. If it's your time to die, let it be because you ran till your heart burst and if the boy's first breaths are meant to be his last, let it be because you had no more flesh and bones to sacrifice. Let my voice be the push that makes you walk through flames. Let my words guide you through a world ablaze. Run. Run right now. And stop either when the boy is safe or when your scorched soul turns to ash.

She gets to her feet and runs, stumbling like a beast wounded on both legs. The light has stopped at the cave's mouth ahead of her, tamed by the pouring rain outside. All drown in flames except the floor, like a path leading to a calm, dark pupil in the center of a burning iris of pure hate.

Every step she takes, more painful than the last. Countless small pieces of charred rock falling from the roof set the lion's fur ablaze. She falters up the cave's throat screaming, feeling the light's touch all over her. It rips through the lion's thick skin and glides on her back. The path to the cave's mouth seems endless. Flaming tongues rush from the walls, licking the outside of her arms, closing in on her, burning her. When they reach out to take her boy, a sudden push sends her dashing out of the cave and into the pouring rain.

Barely outside and not a step further, she plummets to her knees and skins the hillside with cries of anger and despair. She clutches the lion's fur and tosses it aside. Not a single hair remains on what was once a thick mane, while smoke rises from what's left of its scorched, hole-riddled skin. The violent rain starves the flames with ease.

She looks to the boy, in bounds with her still and sees its hands moving and the rain slowly washing away the blood and gore from its brittle body. She closes her eyes and lets the rain wash away her panic.

Every raindrop that strikes the burns on her skin overwhelms her body with agonizing shivers. At first, the pain is worse than the light's touch itself, but after a while, the darkness behind her eyelids calms her down; the sound of her boy crying safe in her arms slows down her rapid breathing and the cold of the storm becomes soothing, tender like Leos' hug.

She loses herself in her thoughts.

What will it take, my love? You have sent me away, on a path to the edge of the world. And here I am, following the brightest star in the night sky, always following your word. But the struggles seem unending. The land I roam, bleak and heartless. How much blood must I shed? How much pain will it take to get there? And when and if I ever reach the edge, will I be greeted with kindness by whoever lives there? Or will I find myself staring down an endless cliff with no one else in sight? For even the gods have abandoned this cursed land many lifetimes ago and went to live on the mountain.

Her mind drifts to a place of pure loneliness and as if the boy knows, he starts moving lively in her arms, crying and demanding attention.

She opens her eyes and looks at the boy. A smile struggles to show its virtues at the corners of her lips but never gets the chance to shine, for she hears voices mingling with the rain's rant and her smile goes hiding again behind a face of worry.

People are walking up the hillside, coming straight towards her. Two men in their prime and a younger one leading the way, while a woman follows right behind them, with a little girl holding her hand.

They get close enough for Habat to hear them speak to each other. One of the men signals the others to stop. Long gasps lead to an exchange of murmurs among the men, words unknown to her. They stare at her with faces just as drenched in awe as much as rain.

Habat is oblivious to their reaction at first. She knows this look well. It's the same look she had—the look everyone has—when she first saw the light. As she tries to get up, she notices the people slightly lifting their heads and their eyes following her. She stands on her feet and realizes the people aren't just staring at the light—they're staring at her too.

She takes a few steps forward. The people take a few steps back. The little girl hides behind her mother and the younger man drops his spear by accident. The two grown men seem lost in a daze and in a moment of revelation, Habat finds herself outside of her own body. For a single heartbeat of hers that feels it could belong to any one of them, she can see that she's no longer a woman to their eyes. The cave's mouth behind her is no longer just a hole in the side of some random rock.

Now they stand in wonderment before the mother of all mothers, engulfed in the halo of a fallen god. A newborn in her arms, born of a woman's union with the might of pure light.

The people bow before her in the pouring rain. Humble. Submissive. Petrified. She never had to say a word. Never asked them to; never forced them to. And at this moment, she knows she will never walk alone again. They will follow her to the end of the world if she wishes to. They will protect her and the boy with their very lives if they need to.

She looks down at her boy and with the return of a smile long forgotten, she uses the rain to wipe his tiny face clean of blood.

Don't worry, my boy. They will learn our words and tales of us they will carve in stone long after we're gone. Stories of great wars between the earth and the sky. The eternal grudge between night and day, darkness and light. They will worship symbols of lions and hawks, monsters and gods, abstractions and fallacies of all the blood we shed and the loved ones we lost. No one will know how, when, or where the first spark came to be. The Alpha that set their stale world in motion. Some will search for answers in the rocks. Some will guess. Others will lie, but it will matter not. In the end, all it takes is a spark.

One spark… and you can set the world on fire.

Limited editions of Logos are available exclusively at
www.nicholasnikita.com

LOGOS

www.ingramcontent.com/pod-product-compliance
Lightning Source LLC
Chambersburg PA
CBHW020334180726
47991CB00020B/1619